TH

LIAF

HOUSE

BOOKS BY CARLA KOVACH

The Next Girl
Her Final Hour
Her Pretty Bones

THE LIAR'S HOUSE

CARLA KOVACH

Bookouture

Published by Bookouture in 2019

An imprint of StoryFire Ltd.

Carmelite House
50 Victoria Embankment
London EC4Y 0DZ

www.bookouture.com

ISBN: 978-1-78681-881-2
eBook ISBN: 978-1-78681-880-5

This book is dedicated to friends. New friends, old friends, wacky friends, fun friends and our more serious friends. Amongst all this, there is a really special category of friends to whom I'd like to give a big mention to, those we class as family.

PROLOGUE

Saturday, 5 May 2012

'I've had it, you've left me sitting in the corner while you mess about with your bloody camera all night. How stupid of me to think we could come out and have a good time.' She shrugged as she continued shouting in his ear. 'You know something, your photos aren't even good.' His wife certainly knew how to ruin a good night. The DJ started playing Katy Perry's 'Firework' and several people began shaking their bodies on the dance floor.

Frowning, he tapped the last photo on the camera display screen. Two dancers beamed a smile back at him – a moment in time captured forever. He was sure he had the settings right but his wife had a point. The photo was overexposed. As far as he was concerned, he didn't care that they weren't perfect – he wouldn't tell her that though.

People writhed against each other, dancing closely, kissing and laughing. There was something about the whole scene that made him squirm and fidget. He wanted to scratch the annoying itch that irritated his sweaty armpits. All the revellers were in a public place and acted as though they'd just entered an orgy. A few drinks and a bit of music, and anyone was anybody's.

Even his wife's expectations had increased since they'd joined the stupid club a couple of months ago. The idea sounded so innocent, a local social club, a bi-monthly disco, the odd quiz, skittles and pool, and the odd covers band. Idea and reality were so different. So far, all he'd seen were couples mingling with those they shouldn't have been mingling with, just like the last time they'd come. He'd seen husbands flirting with bar staff, girlfriends dancing and screaming raucously on the dance floor, arms like spaghetti around other men's necks and waists.

No longer was his own wife content with their cosy nights in, she wanted more and it was nights like this that were giving her these silly expectations. He didn't want to get drunk and gyrate with strangers, and he didn't appreciate the effect this new environment was having on her.

He held the camera to his eye and squinted as he looked through. Coming to the club had been the worst thing ever for them, especially when he'd seen that Samantha had been a regular.

'You're not even listening to me, are you? You stand there, experiencing the world through your amateur-level camera, but you don't join in.'

'What do you expect me to do? This isn't my thing.'

'I expect you to make an effort but that's too much to hope for.' She snatched her coat from the back of a chair, red-faced as she stormed out of the function room.

A flutter filled his stomach. Just as he'd hoped, she'd gone and left him alone. He knew exactly which buttons to push. It wasn't the first time she'd left him standing alone and it wouldn't be the last. Why she stuck with him, he'd never know. Maybe they were in a classic rut, neither wanting to leave but neither being happy in the relationship. Whatever – he really didn't care.

He adjusted his flash and stared through the lens, directly at Samantha, the very person this was all for. *Life and soul of the party. Samantha knows how to have fun.* She liked being called Sam but he'd never call her that. It's a man's name. He'd always refer to her as Samantha. He zoomed in on her nails, long and pink, as richly painted as her full lips. The automatic focus adjusted, blurring her image for a few seconds. As she came back into view, he zoomed in on her lips again then slowly pulled out, revealing her full head and shoulder portrait. Long blonde hair cascaded over her elegant neck and shoulders, framing her stunning cheekbones. All the men loved her full lips and beautiful bone structure. They'd all be jealous if only they knew what he and Samantha had been up to.

Disco lights began to flash in his direction. Squinting, he watched Samantha calling a passing man before dragging him along, his pint sloshing over the side of the glass as he placed it on a nearby table before being pulled into the centre of the dance floor. The man wasn't familiar – maybe he was a new member – but he was classically handsome and well sculptured. He swallowed. Samantha was certainly enjoying the feel of the man's hands on her body.

'Do You Love Me', the song from *Dirty Dancing*, blasted out. Samantha let out an excited yell and pulled the staggering man closer, grinding against him in time to the music.

This is what he was looking for. He gripped the camera and swallowed as she caught his eye, biting her bottom lip and performing for the camera. She knew exactly who he was and this show was just for him. He was under the illusion that she was punishing him for bringing his wife along.

He caught her perfectly as she pointed into the camera while sticking her tongue out. Damn it! The photo was overexposed – his wife was right. Fiddling with the dials and settings, he tried to fix the problem. Aperture or ISO? He couldn't remember what to adjust. He couldn't even remember what those functions were. His hands started to jitter. He'd forgotten what to do. Sweat beads slipped down the side of his face. Flash. He adjusted the flash settings and exhaled. That had to be the solution.

Glancing back at the corridor, he spotted his wife sitting on a window ledge, clamping an unlit cigarette between her lips. She must have come back. A tear ran down her face as she stared at him. She knew he'd been watching Samantha and she was hurt. He'd make it up with her as soon as he returned home and hopefully she'd end their nights out at this hideous club. She stuck two fingers up at him and stumbled to a stand before leaving the building. He wouldn't chase her. He'd continue taking his photos until he got what he came for. Everything was going to plan now she'd really left and gone home.

As he sipped his one and only warm pint, he spotted another woman sitting on a bench at the back of the room.

She stroked her glass as she watched the man dancing with Samantha. Vodka and Coke, he guessed. She looked like a vodka drinker. As the red and blue lights flashed past her, he caught a moment, one he wished he'd managed to capture in a photo but as usual he'd been too slow. He held the camera to his eye, not wanting to miss out on the perfect opportunity again. A long necklace dangled in her cleavage. The silver J hung on a chain. J for Joanna. J for Jenny. J for… There was no use guessing. The only thing he knew was that J was distraught at her partner's behaviour. He'd hurt her and it probably hadn't been the first time. J twisted her wedding band like she wanted to rip it off her finger and fling it across the room but J had dignity. She wouldn't cause a scene. He's her husband, not partner.

J's husband was now sticking his tongue in Samantha's ear. The distraught woman almost toppled the table as she stood and slammed her drink down. Storming out of the room, she glanced back as she reached the door. He could see the expectancy in her eyes. One moment caught on camera forever. One moment that told him a story, one he'd explore for a long time to come. Her cheating husband hadn't even noticed. He'd been too drunk and enchanted by Samantha, the seductress.

He thought of his own wife who'd be almost home by now. His wife probably wanted to be more like Samantha; she'd certainly been trying, especially on the clothes front. He didn't like what she was becoming. She had envy written all over her face. Samantha was leggier, Samantha was firmer; Samantha was perfect – too perfect. The marriage destroyer. The hedonist. The slut. His wife hated that word, but that's what Samantha was and he wasn't going to hold back. The thought police would never censor him and neither would his wife. He thought it as he saw it. Samantha was a slut, he knew that all too well. She'd been an easy lay for him and her reputation was based on truth, as half the men in Cleevesford knew.

He reviewed his last photo, staring at J's image. That photo was perfectly exposed, just like the thoughts running through J's mind, spelled out across her face. He knew her story. Just before she had left the room, this is what she'd been thinking. *Please run after me. Tell me you're sorry. Hold me like you love me and you didn't mean what you did. I'll forgive you because I always do. You're just drunk and you'll regret everything tomorrow morning.* But J's husband didn't run after her and he didn't look apologetic.

As the song ended, Samantha loosened her grip, headed over to the bar and gulped down her drink. The man glanced over to see his partner's empty chair. The realisation sobered him quickly. He grabbed his jacket and ran out of the door. The music faded and the house lights went on. The party was over and party girl needed her beauty sleep.

He watched as Samantha searched for her bag and coat and began the rounds of hugging and kissing everyone goodnight. It was time for him to leave before people took any real notice of his presence. Samantha would linger to the end, she always did. Maybe she'd pull, maybe she wouldn't. He hoped she wouldn't tonight as her time had come. She needed to be taught a lesson, a firm one.

He checked his watch. At ten to one in the morning, he wondered how it could take someone so long to leave a party. He knew this was the route she took home, which is why he'd parked the car in the quiet alleyway earlier that day. He'd even walked to the club with his wife, telling her that he'd walked home from work, leaving the car there.

Maybe Samantha had left with someone and wasn't coming home. Maybe she'd taken a different route. No, she was a creature of habit. This was the route she always took if she was walking home. She didn't always go home though. Maybe she'd gone down a back alley with J's husband. His mind flitted back to poor bedraggled J. 'This is for you, J.' He respected J. She didn't prance around the dance floor, flaunting it all. She had self-respect. After tonight, he doubted he'd ever see J again but deep down, he knew J would be thankful for what he was about to do. 'Come on,' he whispered as he slipped behind a hedge and waited.

A familiar clipping noise filled the still night air. As it got louder, he knew she was close. The clipping became more irregular before it stopped. Had she suspected his presence? A heaving sound came from nowhere as she threw up against a fence. *That's for drinking so much.* She cleared her throat and began walking once again, not suspecting a thing. He stood poised for her passing, then brought the tool down on her head before she could respond. Nice and fast, just the way he'd hoped it would be. No screaming, no struggling, nothing but a quiet whimper as she tried to focus on him.

His heart raced as he watched her jerk and shake on the concrete path. He needed to get her to the car. Within a few moments, she was still. He bent over and felt for her pulse. She was still alive, just as he'd planned. He was going to teach her a lesson and he'd need her to be alert while he delivered it. He carried the slight woman down the path, pressed the boot release button and flung the dead weight into the plastic-lined space. Let the lesson commence.

CHAPTER ONE

Monday, 6 May 2019

A tear slipped down Jade's cheek. She couldn't understand Noah or where his obsession had come from. They had the perfect life, so she'd thought. Married with a beautiful four-year-old daughter whom they both doted on. All she wanted to do was find Noah, go home and cuddle Lilly.

She wiped her eyes with the sleeve of her coat, shivering as she headed down the dark path. Her bare legs were tickled by the gentle breeze as she turned onto the path leading behind a row of long gardens, backing onto a small dividing row of thick bushes.

Fun way to spend a bank holiday, Noah had said. Not for her. It was far from fun, as far away from fun as it could ever be. She'd never want anyone to know what they'd done. Noah had pressured her for months until she'd caved. *You never do anything I want to do,* he'd spat as she'd cried. He was right, their relationship had gone stale. Sex was only on his terms and not that often; in fact, she couldn't remember the last time they'd been intimate. Every time she tried to make a move, he'd say he had work to do before retreating to his office. Whatever she was doing, it just wasn't doing anything for him. She'd have done anything not to lose him. Have being the operative word. Not any more. From now on, she was putting herself first. Some things couldn't be saved and that evening had shown her that her marriage was one of those things.

She gasped and leaned against one of the garden fences, shaking as she broke down. The evening hadn't been pleasurable. In her mind she had been screaming *no*, but that tiny little word had failed to escape her lips. 'No', it sounds so easy, but she'd let Noah down. She wanted so badly to keep him, but this was not happening again, ever. She'd happily let him go now. The evening had spelled their end. She wiped her tears away and continued walking down the path, not knowing which route to take. All the backs of the houses looked the same and she rarely ventured out onto their estate for a walk.

Home, that's where she should have stayed, but she needed to find Noah. What she had to say couldn't wait. If she slept on it, she'd never tell him.

A hot flush speckled her face and neck as she recalled everything that had happened. Her stomach turned as she passed an alleyway.

As she continued to walk along the quiet path, she heard footsteps approaching. Heavy thudding steps. As she clip-clopped ahead, the footsteps got louder and faster. Her heart began to thud against her aching chest. Stepping out of her heels, she bent to lift them and jogged barefooted.

The other pedestrian was probably walking with innocent intentions, maybe leaving a friend's house to go home. She held her breath as she scurried along the path, aiming for the bright yellow street lamp that shone in the distance.

Her mind kept telling her to glance back and say good evening, breaking the silence between the two strangers in the night. Then she might realise how silly she was being.

'Ouch,' she yelled as a piece of jagged stone wedged itself in her fleshy heel. She hopped towards the fence and leaned on it. The footsteps continued until the stranger stopped behind her. His warm breath tickled her hot neck and she felt a tremble start at her knees before spreading through her whole body. He was no innocent stranger just leaving a friend's house. His presence felt menacing. He hadn't spoken a word even though she whimpered in pain. As she held her breath, she could hear him breathing, calmly in and out.

Adrenaline fired up from within. She gasped as she darted for the orange light but it was too late. He swiftly caught her, gripping her around the waist as he dropped his bag to the floor. She went to scream but he placed his large hand over her mouth and nose as he dragged her back into the darkness, the skin on her feet peeling off as flesh scraped along pavement. She glanced back. He placed his finger on his lips and moved his hand slowly away from her mouth.

'You?' she asked with a quivering voice. Gasping for breath, she opened her mouth to yell again. He brought a gloved hand swiftly back over her lips, suppressing her scream.

Fight, she needed to get him off her. She opened her mouth and tried to sink her teeth into his glove but he was wise to what she was trying to do. He beat her around the side of the head, knocking her slightly senseless as he pulled a strip of plastic sheeting from the bag. Speckles filled her vision as she tried to refocus on the moon, honing in on the only light she could see. With his free arm, he pinned her to the floor using his heavy body to keep her fixed in place.

As she tried to release her hands and grab at his clothing, her thoughts flashed to her daughter. All she wanted to do was go home, forget that night and be with Lilly in her jungle-themed bedroom, just mother and daughter. She wanted to breathe in her daughter's smell, stroke her soft wavy hair and read her a story. She just wanted them all to be exactly as they were a few weeks ago. Okay, things hadn't been perfect, but perfect doesn't really exist, she knew that.

Freeing a hand, she wriggled underneath him, grabbing the bottom of a garden gate to pull her body from under his. He leaned up, poised to attack. 'Stop moving, I don't want to have to hurt you, but you're coming with me,' he spat.

She wasn't going anywhere with him. She knew he'd kill her. As she opened her mouth to scream, he brought the mallet swiftly down onto her head, pounding through her fleshy cheek and nose. As she tried to call out, blood spurted from her nose and flooded the back of her throat. Letting go of the bottom of the fence, she reached up and tried to poke her fingers into his face, missing as he moved aside. He loosely lay a sheet of plastic over her head as he leaned back and brought the mallet down again. It was then that the moon disappeared, along with the stars and the smell of dampness in the air. Through closed eyelids, she heard a click followed by a flash of light.

A tear slid down her face as she struggled to take her final breath.

CHAPTER TWO

Detective Gina Harte listened to the man's gentle snoring. She hadn't told him he could stay for the night. The longer he lay there, the more she wanted him to go home. Her fingers itched to push him out of her bed and tell him to leave. As she lay there under the quilt cover, naked and irritable, she stared around the dark room. Time ticked on. Before she knew it, she'd be back at the station having had no sleep. She checked her phone. It was almost one in the morning.

The man stirred and reached across her breasts as he snuggled in closer. This was too cosy for her. She didn't want to spoon in bed with some stranger. 'Hey,' she said as she shook him gently.

He lifted his hand and wiped his eyes. 'I must have fallen asleep, sorry. I tell you something, your bed is comfortable. It's soft and warm, just like you.' He reached over, stroking her hair as he went to kiss her. She turned away, receiving his kiss on the side of her head. He began kissing her neck and she felt him harden beneath the quilt. It wasn't happening again, not with him.

'I think you should go,' she whispered. He continued to caress her, his hands moving further down.

'You're so hot.'

As he tried to crawl on top of her, she pushed hard. Turning on the bedside lamp, she watched as he grasped at the quilt, trying to stop himself from falling over the edge of the mattress. 'Whoa. You should have just said something. No need to pull a stunt like that on me. Although, it was rather erotic. I like a woman who can fling me halfway across a bedroom.'

'I did say something. I said, I think you should go. You were too busy listening to your penis to hear me.'

He slipped out of the bed and grabbed his jeans from the floor. 'Sorry, I genuinely didn't hear. Anyway, I thought we had a great time last night and I didn't hear you complaining then.'

He may have had a great time but Gina certainly hadn't. He didn't quite do it for her and she doubted a second run would be any different. 'I'm sorry. I just don't do stay overs. You know how it is. I need my space.' That wasn't entirely true. No one had compared to her boss, the department DCI, Chris Briggs. Out of the three lovers she'd encountered since subscribing to Tinder, not one had done it for her.

'Get out more. Try it, you might actually have a good time,' Jacob had said to her as he showed her all the women he'd been paired with. Watching him swipe had almost given her hope that it could work and, to a degree, Jacob had been successful with the matches, at least on a casual basis. She'd laughed it off while in his company, even pushed the notion to the back of her head, but the winter had been lonely. She barely saw her daughter and granddaughter, and, after spending Christmas and New Year alone, she vowed to go out and look for some company. Briggs appeared to have moved on, accepting numerous dates, none seeming serious. She had to make the same effort. Her thoughts turned to Briggs, her superior and the man she'd had a brief but passionate affair with. Keeping their relationship a secret had become burdensome on both of them, especially Gina.

As her latest Tinder match slipped his jumper over his head, he paused and looked across at her. 'Is it something I said, or did? I really like you and I thought—'

'Look, you didn't do anything wrong. We had a fun date. Dinner was good and we had a laugh. That's where it ends.

Thank you, err...' She clicked her fingers as if trying to remember his name. His playful expression turned into an overemphasised frown.

'Rex. My name is Rex, Gina. You really are something.' He lifted the pile of clothing in the corner of her bedroom and began throwing her crumpled shirts and trousers across the room while he searched for his missing shoe. 'Bloody hell. I can't find my other shoe.'

Gina slipped on her dressing gown as she stepped out of bed. 'Rex, I didn't mean to give you false hope. You're a decent guy and—' The sound of her mobile phone ringing and vibrating across the bedside table interrupted her mid-sentence. 'DI Harte.' She paused as she listened to DS Jacob Driscoll.

'DI, no way! Where the hell is my shoe?' Rex asked as he began to search under the bed.

'Company, guv?' Jacob asked.

'Button it, Driscoll. I'll be there within the hour.' She ended the call and grabbed a pair of black trousers from the wardrobe. 'You're going to have to leave now. I have to go to work.'

He stood, holding the shoe in his hand, his grey-peppered brown hair stuck up in tufts at the back of his head, resembling a pineapple. 'You're bedside manner leaves a lot to be desired. I didn't know you were a detective inspector.'

'I don't give everything away on a first date.' She buttoned up her shirt, stood at the bedroom door and pushed it open, waiting for him to leave.

'Will I hear from you? I'd like to see you again. Call me.'

She followed him down the stairs, rushing him along. A major crime scene awaited her attention and she didn't have time to flirt or go along with any form of small talk with a man she'd only met a few hours ago.

'We'll see,' she replied with a smile as she pushed him out of the front door, slamming it closed. A few minutes later she heard his car revving up, then he drove away. 'Although, I probably won't,' she said as she ran back up the stairs. She had a couple of minutes to sort out her straggly hair, have a quick wash and get to the crime scene.

CHAPTER THREE

'Ah, DI Harte. Follow me and stick to the stepping plates,' Bernard, the crime scene manager said as he led her along the back path, the onset of light rain beginning to seep through his white forensics suit. She peeked through a gap in one of the fences. The houses were set a long way back from the path which would have given their perpetrator a safe distance to attack the woman, far away from the sleeping inhabitants. Lights were still being switched on as the residents realised something was happening. One of the officers had probably started knocking on doors to see if anyone in the houses had witnessed anything.

At the far end of the path, blue lights continued to flash even though the vehicles were now stationary. She heard a back door open and smelled smoke travelling in the air. The curtain-twitchers would be out in force within minutes, all taking to Facebook and Twitter, trying to find out what was happening.

She tucked her creased shirt into the back of her trousers and pulled an elastic band from her pocket, tying her damp frizzy hair into a loose ponytail. Her mind flashed back to the mess she'd left at home. She was sure that Rex had got the hint and wouldn't contact her again. She was also certain that she didn't want to repeat the experience. Loneliness now seemed to be the favourable option to a string of meaningless and unsatisfying encounters.

The stepping plates had been positioned on a small strip of grass that divided the pavement and a thick mass of tangled shrubs and trees. Beyond the trees, all she could hear was the sound of an occasional late night lorry, trundling along the road, heading for the nearby industrial estate. She almost burst into a jog trying to keep up with Bernard. His height and gangly-legged frame made him look like he was walking at a leisurely pace. Each of his steps equalled three of Gina's.

In the distance, she watched as the crime scene crew set up portable lighting and another CSI began to erect a tent, a bit late for the rain that was now coming down. Keith, Bernard's sidekick, was making a few notes in his pad as he circled the body. Their assistant, Jennifer, snapped away, taking photos of everything. The light cast from the portable lamps flickered as insects danced in front of it. Gina lifted the inner cordon and entered the scene. Keith passed her a crime scene suit, which she quickly slipped on over her clothing, followed by gloves and shoe covers.

She gazed down at the corpse. Cheek and nose smashed to a pulp, hair entangled in blood and graze marks over her legs. The straight, dark-coloured dress the victim had been wearing had ruffled up to her waist but her underwear seemed to be intact. She had no shoes on. Gina scanned the scene and spotted one of her shoes against a garden fence and the other a little distance away from it. Stilettos. She noticed the woman's wedding ring. Someone had to be missing her. Gina closed her eyes, trying to divert her focus away from the mess that was the woman's face, but closing her eyes hadn't made it any easier.

'Alright, guv?' DS Jacob Driscoll asked as he approached from behind and started putting on his crime scene suit.

'I've been better. Whoever did this is an animal.'

'That would be unfair to animals, guv.'

'You're not wrong. I didn't see you pull up when I did.' Gina brushed a stray hair into her hood as Jacob zipped his suit up.

'I parked the other end of the path, came in the other way. You were on another planet when I walked down.'

'Yeah. For a moment, I hoped I was, but no. Some earthly being has committed this atrocity and it is down to us to get them.' Gina swallowed and looked away. 'Any witnesses?'

Jacob glanced back up the path and pointed. 'A woman who was taking her dog for its last walk of the night found the body.'

Gina registered the woman standing with her dog at the side of the road with PC Smith. 'Great. We'll catch up with her in a minute.'

'I'd definitely give it a minute. When I passed she was heaving in the gutter. I can see why.' Jacob stared at the body then glanced away, shaking his head.

Bernard said a few words to the crime scene team and headed back over.

'Bernard, what can you tell me from your initial observations?'

He scratched his beard cover and shifted his gaze to hers. 'She has been bludgeoned with a flat-ended instrument, at a guess, I would say a hammer or mallet. Her body had been dragged along the pavement. As you can see, the skin on her legs and feet has been scraped off and our initial tests show blood on the pavement coming from that direction.' Gina glanced in the direction, noting that an alleyway led onto the path a short distance back. The rain seemed to ease off a little before stopping altogether. 'She also seems to be missing a cutting of hair. It was a neat cut, done with sharp scissors. She is missing a fingernail too. We will continue searching but so far, this is all we have. We only set up a short while before you came.'

'Any thoughts on time of death?'

'On first inspection, it happened no longer than two hours ago.'

'Did she have on her person anything that can help us to identify her?' Gina asked.

'Not that we know of. Her jacket pockets have been checked. The contents have been bagged. There was just a set of keys, that's all. Oh, you can't quite see from the angle she's positioned in, but she has a small faded butterfly tattoo on her ankle. It looks like she's had at least one session of laser removal but not recently.'

Gina felt a shiver prickling on the back of her neck as she imagined the scene. Closing her eyes, she tried to picture the sequence of events unfolding. The woman would have been walking in heels, maybe from a night out or from a friend's house. Maybe she'd been on a date. There were no pubs or clubs close by. As she walked in the dark, had she heard someone following her or was she with her attacker? Maybe her attacker walked her home. Maybe a stranger had seen her walking alone and followed her, seizing the opportunity to attack. A weapon was used. Did the attacker have this on their person? If so, it wouldn't have been a spontaneous attack. Why this woman? She needed to know who lay before her. A crime scene investigator nudged her out of the way as he finished erecting the tent, finally covering the body from the public's prying eyes. She was certain that none of them really wanted to see what had happened on their own doorsteps.

'Right, let's go and speak to our witness.' Jacob pulled his hood down as he left the inner cordon and led her over to the stepping plates.

The witness looked to be in her early forties. She leaned against the wall of the end house, her greyhound patiently standing beside her, oblivious to its owner's suffering. PC Smith met Gina and Jacob a short distance from the shocked-looking woman. 'Alright, guv. She's not doing too well. Paramedics have checked her over and she's in shock. She's slowly coming too, but she's not good. She lives in one of the flats just down the road caring for her sick mother, so we've sent an officer over to sit with her mother while we get a statement. Also, our officers are knocking on doors, appealing for witnesses.'

Gina glanced over and saw a paramedic sitting the woman in a wheelchair. Her sweaty hair and glassy eyes showed Gina exactly what she'd been through. 'Do we know her name?'

'Vicky Calder, forty-two years old.' Smith zipped up his fluorescent jacket and stepped aside.

As Gina approached, her knees clicked. She crouched in front of the woman. 'Vicky? Do you mind if I call you Vicky?'

The pale woman wiped a tear from her eye as her gaze met Gina's. She shook her head. 'I was just walking Sprinter, my dog, and—'

Gina noticed the woman shaking. 'DS Driscoll, would you grab a blanket or something?' Jacob nodded and walked over to the ambulance, jogging back with a foil blanket. Gina placed it over the woman's knees.

'Thank you.'

'Can you tell me what happened, Vicky? We need to catch whoever did this.'

She nodded and cleared her throat. 'We live in a flat, Mum and I, and when the dog needs to go, I have to take him for a walk. Normally his last walk is around eleven but he was whimpering to go out again. I threw my clothes on and thought I'd quickly go round the block and—'

'You're doing really well, Vicky. What happened next?'

The woman shook her head and let out a whimper as she sobbed. 'It had just started raining so I'd hurried.' She paused. 'He was there as I came through the alleyway. I saw a shadow of a person stooping over before dragging her along the pavement. I couldn't move, or shout. He heard me, then he let go of her and ran. A few seconds later, I heard a car start up and drive off. It could have been me. If I was out with Sprinter just a few minutes earlier, it could have been me—'

Gina noted down that Vicky had described the perpetrator as a he. 'Can you be sure it was a man?'

Vicky shook her head. 'He walked like a man and seemed stocky. It was dark, that's all I could see. I was frozen to the spot, but the dog wouldn't stop snuffling in the verges and the man heard and spotted me. As soon as he knew I was there, he ran.'

'What time was this?'

'I can't remember. I didn't even look at the time before I left the flat. I think it was gone half twelve. I'd been looking on Facebook at that time.'

Gina felt her feet begin to deaden but she wasn't about to stand. She needed to keep Vicky talking to her. 'Can you remember anything else about him?'

She shook her head, teeth chattering as she tried to think. Jacob removed his overcoat and placed it over her shoulders. 'Here you go. This should warm you up.'

A couple came out onto the street in their dressing gowns and began staring. 'Could one of you please bring a hot drink out?' Gina shouted over to them.

They nodded and the woman went back into the house leaving the man to find out more. If people were going to stand there, she couldn't stop them, but she could at least get them to help.

'Going back to the attacker, can you give us a description?'

Vicky shook her head. 'It really was too dark. He was taller than me. I'm five foot tall.'

Gina looked at the pavement, her own legs beginning to wobble after holding the same position for so long. It was likely that most people were going to be taller. So far, their perpetrator was likely to be male and over five feet tall.

'I can't tell you any more. I don't know anything else. Is the woman okay? Will she live?'

Gina stood, her legs no longer able to hold her position. 'I'm really sorry, but the woman you found was dead when officers arrived at the scene.'

Vicky wiped her eyes. 'I thought so. I just hoped—'

The neighbour came back out with a mug of something hot. Gina thanked her and passed the drink to Vicky. 'Here you go. Try to have a few sips, it will warm you up.' Gina nodded at the paramedics who came back over to assist. Vicky removed Jacob's coat from her shoulders and passed it back.

'We'll need you to give us a formal statement. An officer will help you home in a minute. Can you do that for me?' Gina asked.

'I'll do anything to help catch the bastard who killed the poor woman.'

'Here's my card in the meantime. If you remember anything at a later date, however insignificant it seems, call me.'

As Gina turned back towards the scene, Bernard came running around the corner. 'We've found a handbag!'

CHAPTER FOUR

Jacob pulled into the cul-de-sac, where several detached houses filled the end of the road in a curve. All houses were in darkness, including the one that they needed to visit.

'Have you noticed something?' Gina asked as he pulled the handbrake and switched off the engine.

Jacob ran his hand over his short brown hair as he stared at the house. 'No one is waiting up for her. The house is in darkness.'

'Correct. Either they're not in or they've gone to bed, but no one is at all worried that Jade hasn't come home. She had a phone in her handbag, fully charged and ready to use. Not one person had called to check that she was safe. Maybe I'm overthinking all this and her husband wasn't expecting her for whatever reason but it's nearly four in the morning.' Gina fanned her face and took a deep breath. 'No one is going to do this for us. I suppose we'd best take a deep breath and go deliver the bad news.'

They walked down the block-paved drive and knocked at the door. A bedroom light flickered. They listened as the occupant's footsteps led the way down the stairs. 'Did you forget your keys?' a man's voice boomed out as he opened the door wearing nothing but a pair of tight boxer shorts. He was obviously comfortable with his body. Jacob looked away from the man's rippled torso and glanced at the wall.

'DI Harte and DS Driscoll. Are you Mr Ashmore?' Gina held her identification up.

'Yes. What's happened?' He ran his hands through his full head of blond hair before stroking his designer stubble.

'I'll explain if you could just let us come in a moment.' Gina didn't want to break the news on the doorstep that his wife's body had been found.

He stepped aside and gestured for them to enter the kitchen.

Gina felt her heart begin to race as he followed them through the hallway into the large open plan kitchen. His pink cheeks began to drain of colour. 'Would you like to sit down, Mr Ashmore?'

'No, I don't think I would. Just tell me what's going on.'

'I'm afraid we have bad news. We have found a body at the back of Gilmore Close and we believe it may be your wife, Jade Ashmore. I'm so sorry.'

The man wobbled slightly. Jacob pulled out one of the bar stools and the man fell into it. 'It can't be her. You've got it wrong.'

'I know this is hard for you, Mr Ashmore. Is there someone you'd like us to call? Someone who can be with you.' The house was in silence. She wondered if anyone else was upstairs. She knew they had a child.

'Who the hell would do something like this? Are you sure it's her?'

'Did Jade have a tattoo?'

He gasped for air, held his head in his hands and began pacing across the kitchen tiles. 'A small butterfly on her ankle. She hated it and was having it removed.'

'It's her, Mr Ashmore.' Gina had seen Jade's driving licence that she'd kept in her purse. The one side of her face matched the photo perfectly. A confirmation of her identity was merely a formality. 'I'm so sorry to deliver such bad news—'

'How did it happen? Did she have an accident?'

As Gina shook her head, her stomach began to turn. Her mind flashed back to the moment she saw Jade's body and the damage to her head and face. 'I really am sorry. She was attacked and didn't pull through.' She didn't want to say that Jade had been brutally murdered. 'We will need to know where she went last night. We will also need to know where you were.'

He stopped in front of the bi-fold doors, his reflection staring back at him. He kicked one of the kitchen chairs that were neatly placed around a six-seater table and let out a roar before wiping his teary eyes. 'What am I going to tell our daughter?' he said as he sat on the edge of the table, shaking his head. 'How can someone have hurt her? She wouldn't hurt a fly.'

Gina hated having to continue pushing him for answers but she needed to know where he'd been that night and she needed to get the investigation gathering momentum. They didn't have time to wait. Her throat began to dry up. 'Can we make you a drink?'

He shook his head.

'May I have a glass of water?' she asked as she headed over to the sink.

He nodded. 'I can't believe she's gone.' He clenched his fists and began to tremble as the news sank in.

Jacob stood at the other end of the kitchen table, unable to offer anything further. As Gina took a gulp of water, she caught her own reflection in the kitchen window and tried to focus on what lay beyond. Deep within the darkness of what would be the garden, all she could see was Jade's face, blood oozing onto the pavement and no sign of the eye that had once been on the right side of her face. She saw the mother that would never again come home to her child. A tremor began to build in her hands. She placed the glass on the draining board before she spilt it. It was a chilly early morning and she was tense. Questioning the husband wasn't going to be easy. 'Mr Ashmore, can you tell me where your wife went last night?'

'We went to a party at a friend's house. Her name is Dawn.' The man grabbed a tartan throw. He slumped into a chair at the kitchen table as he pulled the blanket around his shoulders.

'Do you have a surname and address for Dawn?'

He nodded, grabbed his phone and scrolled. 'Her surname is Brown and her address is 27 Houston Close. It's one of the large houses on the new-build estate, just a few roads away from here.' The man wiped his nose on the back of his hand.

'I know this is difficult, but we need to catch whoever did this to your wife. Getting as much information now—'

'You don't have to explain. I know. I want whoever did this caught.' He wiped the corner of his eye.

Gina sat opposite him at the kitchen table. 'What time did you arrive at the party?'

'We arrived about half seven. It only takes a few minutes to get there if you know the area. We walked.'

Gina watched as Jacob began taking notes, the sound of his pencil scraping across paper almost made her teeth itch. 'Tell me what happened after that.'

'We were the first there, apart from our host, Dawn. A few minutes later, her partner Steven arrived with a box of beer and wine. Then there were two more couples. I've never met them before so I can't tell you much about them. I did recognise one woman, a young woman called Aimee. I've seen her around with her boyfriend. They live close by too. I think everyone lived close by as they all walked. I can't remember when the rest arrived. We were ushered into the lounge where Jade and I sat together and talked. We were quite nervous.'

'Nervous?'

'Yes, we didn't know anyone except Dawn. It's always a bit nerve-wracking meeting new people. Jade was a bit tense. She's not exactly a social butterfly, preferring to stay at home and watch a film. I encouraged her to go to the party, said it would be good for us to get out. As it happened, we all had a good time. Couples split up and were talking to others. People migrated out to the garden where some smoked.'

'You came home without her?'

The man began messing with his phone. She could tell he was holding something back. 'We haven't been in the best place lately, as a couple. You know, things go a bit stale. Jade kept moaning about going home. I topped her glass up a couple of times and asked her not to ruin the evening for me. She basically snubbed me, which is her thing. I get short, she gets all passive-aggressive.' A tear slid down his cheek. 'It was obvious she was pissed off. Anyway, I had a few to drink and at around eleven thirty I told her I was going and I left her there.'

Jade was the one who wanted to go home yet Noah Ashmore left first. It seemed a little odd to her. She pictured Jade, a little merry from the wine she didn't often drink, chatting away to strangers. Had she been trying to show him she could have a good time without him?

'Did you come straight home after that?'

'No, I ended up outside, talking to Aimee for a while. We walked as far as the woods and I left her there. I suppose I just used her to sound off a bit. She could tell there was some tension going on between Jade and me.'

'So, let me get this straight. You left at about eleven thirty and walked towards the woods. Is that the woods that back onto Houston Close?'

He nodded as he linked his fingers.

'How long did you spend walking?'

He shrugged his shoulders. 'About half an hour, I guess.'

That was a lengthy time to sound off to someone he hadn't met before that night. Jacob scrawled away, making lots of notes. He glanced at her, she glanced back.

'What happened then?'

'I walked home, relieved the babysitter from her duties and went to bed. I just assumed that Jade would turn up when she'd made her point.'

'Her point?'

He held his arms up, the tartan blanket held open making him look as though he had wings. 'That she was capable of having a good time.' His hands dropped back into his lap.

'I'm sorry, Mr Ashmore. I know this is hard but it's really helping us. Can you tell us when you arrived home and when the babysitter left? We will also need to know who babysat.'

'Tiffany left at about twelve twenty, twelve thirty, maybe. I arrived home, paid her and she left. She lives a few doors down. She studies childcare and she loves Lilly, our four-year-old.'

'What number does she live at?'

He looked up at her with glassy eyes. 'Really?'

'Yes, Mr Ashmore. We need to know where she lives.'

He stood, stomped out to the living room and looked out of the window. 'I don't know the number but she's one, two, three doors down, on our right. She lives with her dad. You don't need to disturb her tonight, do you?'

Gina glanced at Jacob and nodded as Noah Ashmore walked back into the room. 'I'm afraid we do.'

'But she wouldn't know anything. She just babysat then went home.'

He flinched as Gina broke the silence. 'What happened is serious, as you can appreciate.'

'No shit. You're telling me. I've lost my wife, and not only that, we'd fallen out. I have to live with that forever. The last memory of my wife was her being mad at me. She died being mad at me! We have a daughter. What am I going to do?' The enormity of the situation dawned on the man as his shoulders crumpled. He fell into the chair, trying to hide his sobs.

'Daddy,' a little girl called. The tiny patter of feet came downstairs and a bleary-eyed four-year-old clutched a comfort blanket as she looked up. Noah gasped for breath and looked away, doing all he could to control his emotions. 'Who are these people, Daddy?'

Noah wiped his face and turned to his daughter, scooping her up and holding her tight.

'Are you sure we can't call anyone to be with you?'

He shook his head. 'I just need to be with my daughter for a while. I'll call the family then. Please catch whoever did this?'

Gina nodded. 'I'll leave my card here, just in case you can remember anything else. We'll call you later today about making a formal statement. Do you have a photo of Mrs Ashmore that I can take with me? We will be putting out an appeal soon but we'll be in contact with you if and when that goes ahead.'

He leaned over to the cabinet, holding his daughter with one arm, and slid the drawer open. He pulled out a small album and dropped it onto the table, then opened it to the third page. 'Please take that one. She liked that photo of herself.' He placed his daughter down as Gina fought to extract the photo from the static-ridden plastic cover. 'Just find who did this to her, for me and this little girl here,' he said as he held his hands over the little girl's ears. 'Right, Daddy will take you back to bed now.'

Gina's stomach turned as they let themselves out. 'I hate this part of the job. Hate it!'

'Do you think he's holding something back? He looked a little cagey when you mentioned the babysitter.' Jacob turned the page on his notebook.

'I know what you mean.'

CHAPTER FIVE

Tiffany Gall came down the stairs wearing a fluffy onesie, her dyed black hair stuck to one side of her face. She squinted as she came into the light, passing her father who stood anxiously, waiting for the kettle to boil. 'Come through, officers,' the man called, as he laid out four cups.

Gina and Jacob followed Tiffany into the kitchen.

'What's going on, Dad?' Her voice reminding Gina of that belonging to a young child.

The man placed the coffees on a mat in the middle of the kitchen table. 'I think you should take a seat, sweetheart.'

'What's happened?' Tiffany pulled several strands of hair from her face and glanced at Gina.

Gina felt a trail of sweat begin to itch on the nape of her neck. Tiffany had obviously been close to the family. 'We're sorry to tell you that Mrs Ashmore has been attacked only a few hours ago. Unfortunately she didn't make it.' The girl glanced at the detectives and then at the table.

'But... I saw her only a few hours ago.'

'I know, and I know it's a lot to take in. You were close to the family and their daughter Lilly?'

'Is Lilly okay, and Noah?'

'They're both fine.'

Tiffany nervously began pulling at a few strands of her hair. 'I babysat for them occasionally. I suppose we were friends. They've lived on this road since I was in my early teens.' The girl went silent and began to sob.

Her dad ran over and embraced her.

Gina swigged the hot coffee, needing caffeine more than ever. 'I know this is hard and that you were close to the family but we need to catch the person who did this to Jade. Can you just tell me as you remember, what happened from when you arrived at the Ashmores' house to when you came back home?'

From what Noah Ashmore had said, Mrs Ashmore hadn't come home with him but Gina wanted to make sure. Jacob flicked the pages in his notebook, ready to jot down what was said.

The girl nodded as her dad passed her a tissue. She rubbed it over her reddening eyes as she began to relay the events of the evening between sobs. 'They told me to get there about seven, which I did. When I arrived, Mrs Ashmore was just finishing getting ready in the bedroom and Noah was in the living room, watching something on the TV. Lilly was curled up in one of the armchairs, holding her favourite storybooks. I joined her and continued reading until way after they'd gone out. They shouted bye as they left and told me they'd be back late, maybe after midnight. I put Lilly to bed at about eight thirty and read to her some more.'

'After that?' She was coming to the bit Gina wanted to know more about.

Tiffany shrugged. 'I plugged my earphones in and listened to a bit of music while I played on Facebook.' The girl stopped talking and stared into space.

'Tiffany?'

She flinched as she brought her attention back to what Gina was asking. 'That was it. Noah came home and said that Mrs Ashmore was still out. He gave me twenty pounds and I left. That was it.'

Gina made a note of her own. Whenever Tiffany spoke of the family, she referred to Noah by his first name but his wife as Mrs

Ashmore, never Jade. *That was it* – there was more to this evening than Tiffany was telling them. 'How did he seem?'

'Do you think he killed Mrs Ashmore?'

'We're not saying that, Tiffany. We're just trying to establish what happened.' A warm smile spread across Gina's face as she hoped to put Tiffany at ease.

'Right. He wouldn't hurt anyone.' The girl paused.

'The lovely police lady just needs you to tell her anything you can think of, sweetheart,' her dad said as he placed a loving hand on his daughter's shoulder.

Lovely police lady. It wasn't the most accurate description of her role or title but she'd let it slip as she'd just delivered such bad news.

'When he came home, Noah, he seemed fine. He looked like he'd had a couple of drinks and stank of wine. He wasn't drunk, just slightly merry, I'd say. He waffled on for a few minutes as he took off his coat and sat in the living room. Mostly, he talked about how they'd had a little fallout, but then he said that all would be good, that she'd be home in a bit and things would be back to normal. He asked if I could come and help out with Lilly the next day if Mrs Ashmore wasn't up to it. He thought she might have a mega hangover. I said yes, took the money from him and then I left. That really is all I know, officer.' The girl pulled the hood of her onesie over her head and began biting her nails.

'What time did Mr Ashmore arrive home?'

She shrugged her shoulders. 'I can't really remember. It was after twelve, maybe about ten past, quarter past.'

Gina placed her card on the table. 'If you think of anything else, please call me immediately.'

'Thanks, officers. She'll call if she remembers anything else.'

From the corner of her eye, Gina watched as Tiffany lifted her feet off the tiled floor and hugged her legs. That girl wasn't telling the whole story.

'Wait, there is something. It's about Mrs Ashmore.' The girl dropped her crumpled tissue on the table.

Gina and Jacob resumed their positions, waiting to hear what she had to say.

Tiffany's father put his head in his hands. 'Sweetheart, what is it now?'

'Dad, it's okay. Something did happen earlier tonight. At one point I got a bit spooked. I heard a creaking sound in the garden and nearly shit myself.'

'Language, Tiffany.'

'Sorry, Dad. I was scared. I thought there was an intruder in the garden.'

Gina could see that the girl was trying to work out whatever she'd seen for herself. 'What did you see?'

'Someone in the summerhouse.'

'Who?'

'Jade. She came out of the summerhouse looking a bit of a mess to be fair. I hid behind the curtain with the kitchen light off, hoping that she hadn't seen me. She glanced around the garden and left out the back gate. I just closed the curtains and waited.'

'What time was this?'

'Just before Noah came home.' If Noah had just arrived home as his wife was leaving out the back garden, he couldn't have been the one to attack her – that's if Tiffany Gall was telling the whole truth.

'Would this strike you as odd behaviour for Mrs Ashmore?'

'Very. I don't know why she'd come home then go out of the back gate.' Mr Gall placed an arm around his daughter. 'I should have called her to see if she was okay. If I had, she might not have gone back out and got attacked. But she looked like she was on a mission. She headed out that back gate pretty quickly, even leaving the summerhouse door open and the gate flapping in the wind. When Noah arrived home, he popped out to close both.'

'Why didn't you tell us this before?'

The girl took a sip of her coffee. 'I don't know. I told Noah when he came home and he seemed in a mood and I didn't want to get him into any trouble.'

'Why would this get him into trouble?'

She shrugged her shoulders. 'I don't know. It's silly really, isn't it? If he arrived home just as she was leaving out the back, he can't have hurt her, not that he would. He's a genuine guy, a nice guy. I don't think she appreciated him.'

Gina felt her heart rate pick up. There was more, she knew it and she'd already guessed. Either Tiffany had an infatuation with Noah or they were having some kind of relationship. 'Could we speak to Tiffany alone, Mr Gall?'

'No, she's my daughter and she needs a parent with her.' The man slammed an empty cup on the side. 'Sweetheart, you don't have to say anything else.'

'She's an adult at nineteen and doesn't need a parent with her when speaking to the police.'

'It's okay, Dad. Just go to bed.' The man stood in silence for a moment before admitting defeat and leaving the room. They all listened as his heavy footsteps reached the landing.

'I thought you might not want your dad to hear my next question. Were you having any kind of relationship with Noah Ashmore?'

Another tear slipped from the corner of Tiffany's eye as she nodded. 'I told him I love him. I kissed him once, last week, and he didn't stop me. I don't know how it happened but it just did. We were in the garden. Mrs Ashmore had gone out and Noah was just about to leave. They'd called me to look after Lilly. I was helping him move a pot in the garden that Mrs Ashmore had insisted on moving and then it happened. We kissed. He told me how much he thought about me too. I knew they argued so it was just a matter of time before they were over, at least that's what I thought.

'When he came back tonight, he confirmed he'd had enough of it all and that there was more to life. He seemed really dissatisfied. I asked where they'd been and he said they'd just gone to a friend's. I told him about Mrs Ashmore in the summerhouse and he just shrugged it off, saying that she left earlier and had drunk a few glasses of wine and probably staggered there, not wanting to embarrass herself by coming home. He said she'd probably gone to walk it off and would be back later. I asked about us and he said he couldn't think and virtually shoved me out of the door.'

Gina felt a rush of excitement running through her body. Where had Tiffany gone after leaving the Ashmores' house? Maybe she'd gone looking for Jade. 'Did you see anyone else around when you left Noah last night?'

Tiffany's gaze met Gina's. 'Creepy Colin. Noah's neighbour. He saw us kissing in the garden and he saw me when I left Noah's. Whenever I see him, he gives me the most revolting grin.'

'Tiffany, where does Colin live?'

'Next door to Noah. He's always watching what everyone is doing. He thinks we can't all see him peering through the gaps in his curtains.' Tiffany shivered.

CHAPTER SIX

'Forensics have just pulled up.' Jacob stood to the side as Gina walked from Noah Ashmore's house to meet Keith coming out of his van with his toolbox. He stood on the roadside putting his forensics suit on. Another car pulled up and a crime scene assistant stepped out and met him.

'It's the summerhouse, you say?' Keith flinched as he straightened his back out. 'I feel as though I'm being dragged from pillar to post tonight. Straight from one scene to another. That's how I roll.' So did Gina, but she wasn't going to enter into a conversation about it. As he zipped the suit up, he arranged his comb-over under the hood and proceeded towards the gate to the side of the house. Noah Ashmore stood just inside the hallway, now dressed in jeans and a jumper. Neighbours had filtered onto the street and were being encouraged to go back home by PC Smith.

'Yes, just head through the gate. I'll follow you. It was the last place she was seen alive.' Gina followed him alongside the house and into the garden. As they stepped in darkness on the uneven slabs, Gina thought back to Tiffany and what she'd told them. Her father had confirmed that she'd arrived home at about twelve thirty. She'd woken him up as she'd left her key at home. One of the other neighbours had confirmed that they heard her knocking on the door and calling her dad through the letterbox.

'Ooh, nice place.' Keith placed his toolbox down on the patio and began erecting a portable battery light.

The garden had to be about forty foot long. A neat path led from the patio, dividing the turf until it reached the summerhouse.

It looked to be the size of a small bungalow, two rooms reaching from one end of the fence, almost to the other, leaving only a small gap that led to the gate. The light came on and Keith brought it closer. The summerhouse was decorated with dark tartan curtains. One side looked as if it was used as a playhouse for Lilly, the toys on the windowsill giving its purpose away. The room on the right looked a little more sophisticated. Gina crept closer and shone her torch through the window. There was a comfortable settee and a coffee table. A small and well-equipped bar adorned the other end and was finished off with several bar stools. She pointed the torch to the floor. 'Keith, there seems to be a mound of throws on the floor.'

He gently opened the door and led the way. Gina pulled on a forensics suit, gloves and boot covers and followed him in. He flicked the light on. 'At least the light works.'

'It looks like someone has just got out of bed, the way all these blankets are arranged. What's that?'

Gina pulled on the nylon and slowly revealed a pair of tights. She couldn't pull them any further. They'd caught on the bottom of a bar stool. 'There's a smell about this place. It smells… sweaty. I can smell perfume hanging in the air.' Two empty glasses sat on the bar, one was on its side with its contents splashed around it. Gina leaned over the glasses and inhaled. 'Wine, white wine to be precise.' A cork lay next to the half-empty bottle of Chardonnay. 'Bag these glasses up. We need to find out who she was here with.'

After a few minutes, they left the summerhouse. Keith began cataloguing the samples and wine glasses as Gina gazed around the garden.

A neighbour peered out of his bedroom window. Gina didn't need to ask his name, from Tiffany's description she knew this had to be creepy Colin.

He pushed the window open and called to them. 'I see things, I do. I bet *you* want to know just what I saw last night.'

CHAPTER SEVEN

Gina wiped her feet on the mat outside Colin Wray's front door. The dawn chorus ended as Jacob closed the door behind them.

'Coffee?' Colin asked as he grinned at her, exposing his toothless mouth.

'No, thank you.' She'd have loved another dose of caffeine but one look at his home had put her off. The smell of stale laundry and cigarette smoke hung in the air, almost making her feel sick. Stomach rumbling, she followed the man into the lounge and sat on one of the armchairs, ensuring that Colin couldn't sit next to her. Jacob had no option but to sit next to him on the sofa.

'Okay, can I take your full name?' Colin's eyes travelled from her legs to her breasts. 'Your name, please?'

'Sorry, I don't get many visitors.' Gina could see why. 'It's Colin Wray. Call me Colin.' His tongue ran across his gums as he eagerly waited to be questioned.

'You said you saw something earlier this morning, or was it last night? What was it you saw and when?'

He leaned forward and opened his legs, almost touching Jacob with his knee. Jacob inched across the sofa as if trying to escape. Colin just widened his legs further. 'Not a lot happens around here that I don't see. I don't sleep well. I'm retired and a lot of the time, I'm bored. She's a bit of alright that one next door, a yummy mummy I think they call 'em. All legs and hair. Pleasing to the eye. I'll admit, if I hear her door go, I check the window for a look. Just a look though. I'm not getting into any trouble with any birds.'

'So you spy on her?' Gina felt her fists clenching. Referring to the woman she saw on the pavement, her head smashed to a pulp, as a bird, in such a disrespectful manner was making her blood boil.

'Don't be daft. I just look out of my window if I hear things and it's often her. I see things and I feel sorry for her, you know, always arguing with her husband.' Colin widened his legs further.

Jacob stood and stretched. 'Sorry, I'm feeling a bit achy. Carry on.'

'I know the little tart a couple of doors down has been having it away with Jade's hubby. I saw them kissing in the garden when Jade was out, tongues the lot. I know her type, dresses in tight jeans, asking for it she was. He's a married man and she led him astray.'

Gina felt her hands begin to tremble and her neck redden. Never once did men like Creepy Colin blame a grown man for manipulating an impressionable girl. In another life, she'd have liked to punch him but any perception of disrespect towards him could lead to a complaint and after spending the past few months proving that she could cope with her work, she wasn't going to give DCI Briggs any excuse to start asking her if she was okay every five minutes. She wasn't undertaking any more counselling. 'Mr Wray, please just tell me what you saw!'

He rolled up his pyjama bottoms and began picking at a piece of skin on his feet, then flicked it across the crumby brown carpet. 'Got ya, you bastard! In a rush, are we?'

'Look, Mr Wray, we haven't got time to play games. During the early hours of this morning Jade Ashmore was found dead and I want to know what you saw or we'll be taking this down the station.'

'Hold your horses—'

'No, Mr Wray, you don't get to tell me to hold my horses. What did you see? If you keep me here any longer, I'll assume you're withholding information in a murder enquiry.'

The man leaned back into the flat burgundy cushions and sighed. 'I don't know what time it was, before or after midnight. I heard her back gate go. They really need to oil it, it's always creaking when the wind blows. I watched her enter the garden with a man and they went in the summerhouse. Under the moonlight and with the faint glow coming from her house, I could see that the man she was with wasn't her husband, Noah. He was taller, slimmer and had long hair. Anyway, it struck me as odd. I've never seen Jade get up to much, it's normally her husband who catches the eyes of the ladies.' The man fanned himself with his hand. 'What happened next will blow your mind. Her palms slammed against the window. I opened my window a little so that I could hear. He was slamming into her from behind. He didn't last long and I think towards the end she was trying to push him off but he wasn't getting the hint. As soon as he was done, she pulled her dress down, they had words and she pushed him out of the way before leaving. She looked angry, maybe upset.' The man stared into space and smiled. Gina's stomach turned. He'd been unashamedly spying on Jade Ashmore as she struggled to get this man off her, that's if he were to be believed. 'Really slamming her, he was.' A grin spread across Colin's face as he stared at the wall ahead, obviously reliving the moment in his mind.

'Slamming into her.'

'You know, getting a bit of how's your father.'

Gina took a deep breath. 'They were having sex. Did it look like he was forcing her?'

'Nah. It looked like she was playing a bit of hard to get from where I was standing. They were role playing, fantasy, whatever. Yes. That's exactly it, Detective.'

'And you could tell all that from your bedroom window in the dark?'

'Yeah.' The man grabbed his tobacco and began rolling a cigarette. 'Mind if I smoke?'

When they found the man who'd been with Jade, she'd definitely question him hard about his conduct as well as Jade's murder. Colin held his cigarette up and shrugged his shoulders. It was his house. Gina glanced at Jacob and nodded. 'Can you tell me any more about this man?'

'Oh yes, I recognised him straight away.' Gina's eyes widened, identifying the man in the summerhouse would certainly make their job easier. 'He's with a much younger girl, everyone talks about them. I saw them once at my local, the Angel Arms. It was months ago now. He's got to be in his late forties, she looks like she's in her teens. I'm sure she's not but she looks like a hot young thing. Too hot for him.' A shiver ran down Gina's spine. There were too many people like Colin Wray in society. She was judging him and she wanted to judge him. He was all that was wrong with the world. This young girl he was describing was nothing but a piece of meat to him.

'Do you know his name?'

'Rhys. She is Aimee, the lovely Aimee. I see her around and if I was just a few years younger, I'd make a play for her. Always polite, that girl. Says hello if I see her in the shop. Lovely looking girl who knows how to flaunt it. Drives that man she's with mad with jealousy sometimes. I've heard them arguing when they've been in the shop together. Anyway, it was him.'

'Did you see them leave?'

He scratched his feet again. Gina wished he'd leave his crumbling feet alone as a smell rose up. 'She left first, straight out of the back gate. I thought it was odd. He stood in the doorway of the summerhouse doing his shirt up. That's when I got a good look at him. I didn't see him leave. He may have left then or he may have stayed a little longer, who knows?'

'What did you do then?'

'The show was over so I went to bed and that was it.'

'Was there anyone with you?'

'I live alone.'

'So no one can verify your whereabouts at all last night?'

He shook his head and puffed on his roll-up, blowing circles of smoke into the air. A red-skied morning began to illuminate the room. The thought that he may have left his house quickly to follow Jade crossed Gina's mind. She made a note to do a background check on Colin Wray. He may be in his seventies but she could tell he had strength. He didn't appear frail in any way at all. She wanted to know exactly what the man was capable of.

CHAPTER EIGHT

'Right, huddle round.' Gina waited for everyone to take a seat at the main table before going through what they had.

DC Harry O'Connor licked his lips as he shoved the last piece of doughnut into his mouth. 'I've got to pack up eating cakes.' He undid his top button and patted his stomach.

DC Paula Wyre smoothed her straight black hair down as she grabbed a pen from the middle of the table. 'You, give up cake, never. You know you love it.'

'I'm with Paula, that's never going to happen.' Jacob leaned back comfortably, one foot on his knee as he chewed the end of his pen. PC Smith scraped a chair across the floor at the other end of the table, removing his hat as he fell into a seat.

The side door creaked as DCI Briggs entered and leaned against the doorway. Silence filled the room until Gina's phone beeped. She pulled it from her pocket and felt her heart begin to hum as she caught sight of the sender's name. She turned it on silent.

'As you can see, I've written all that we have on the boards. Early this morning, thirty-four-year-old mother of one, Jade Ashmore, was found dead at the back of Gilmore Close. Bernard and Keith are still processing everything from the two scenes but I'll come onto that in a moment. Suffice to say, they won't be with us this afternoon. I also realise that most of you have been up all night knocking on doors, speaking to witnesses—'

Briggs took a step forward. 'What did Bernard say?'

Gina handed a pile of reports to Jacob who took one and passed the rest around the room. 'All the information we have so far is collated in this report. We've also updated the system with our finds so far. Time of death. Our witness, Vicky Calder, said she saw a man moving the body not long after twelve thirty this morning. The Ashmores' babysitter, Tiffany Gall, saw Jade Ashmore leaving their summerhouse just before Noah Ashmore arrived home. She confirmed that this was between midnight and twelve fifteen. Until the post-mortem results tell us any different, we are working on the knowledge that Jade Ashmore was killed between midnight and twelve thirty.'

Everyone was flicking through the notes Gina had prepared. She pulled a strand of hair from the side of her mouth and tucked it behind her ears. 'After attending the scene, it looks clear that Jade had been attacked at the back of Gilmore Close and dragged a few feet before being interrupted by our witness. This is where she died. There is no evidence to show that she had been killed somewhere else and then moved. Our killer wouldn't have had time for that.' She paused. 'A small chunk of her hair had been cut away as you can see.' She pointed to the photos on the board. 'Also, one of her fingernails was missing. It seems possible that the killer could have removed it, maybe as a trophy, along with the hair. Maybe it was ceremonial, just a thought.'

Jacob leaned forward and placed both feet on the floor. 'Whoever did this must have been in quite a state looking at the injuries.'

'Bernard's first instincts suggest that the murder weapon is something flat-ended. If you look at the edges of the wound, you can see an imprint on the one side of her forehead.'

The right side of Jade's face had been pounded. The flesh on her cheek hanging off, exposing bone and muscle. Gina swallowed and turned away from the photo. She'd had a doughnut for breakfast at the station and skipped lunch. The feeling of emptiness in her stomach combined with the photos filling the board were making the doughnut repeat on her. She undid her top button, hoping to alleviate her indigestion. 'Looking at the blood spatter, we can see a tiny stream along the fence that looks to have come from her broken nose. She must have been leaning up slightly. After that, nothing, apart from what was pooled around her. It had rained a little before the tent was erected so some of the blood had started to run. We found no murder weapon at the scene, no footprints. One thing we could tell was that the spatter wasn't consistent with the scale of her injuries. It would have been messy. The perpetrator must have covered her up during the attack. What with? We have no idea at the moment. Did they come specifically for Jade Ashmore or was Jade Ashmore simply in the wrong place at the wrong time?'

Paula Wyre flicked over to the next page in the report. 'Her injuries are brutal, guv.'

Gina's gaze followed the board until she stopped at the photo that Noah Ashmore had given to her. A photo of Jade as she was before. Her shoulder-length mousy brown hair framed a heart-shaped face, petite nose and large hazel-coloured eyes. 'We have several witnesses. I've already mentioned Vicky Calder who was out walking her dog and the babysitter, Tiffany Gall. But there are more. Seventy-eight-year-old Colin Wray. He is the Ashmores' neighbour and, from the statements, he is known as a bit of a creep.'

Jacob dropped his pen on the table. 'He's definitely a bit creepy, guv.'

'We interviewed him, my notes are there to read. Tiffany admitted she had a crush on Noah Ashmore and a short while ago, she kissed him in his garden. She also saw Colin watching them. Colin also admitted that he'd watched Jade Ashmore in her summerhouse with a man just before she was murdered. I'll come onto that in a minute. Colin has no alibi and lives alone. Did we find out anything further about Colin Wray?'

Jacob nodded and opened his notebook. 'I checked to see if he had a record and he does. Minor assaults on younger women involving inappropriate touching, antisocial behaviour – trying to look through his neighbours' windows, etcetera, and they were all women. He even has a conviction for stealing underwear from a washing line which sounds like such a cliché, I know. This happened where he last lived and was probably why he moved.'

The afternoon sun shone between the branches of the tree in the car park, drowning the board in light. Gina walked over to the window and pulled the blind. 'Smith, did any of the neighbours see anything? I know you coordinated the door to door at both locations.'

He yawned and wiped the sleep from his eyes. 'The team knocked on doors all morning but no one saw a thing.'

'So, nothing new to go on there. Okay, what we do know is that Jade and Noah Ashmore were attending a party on the evening of the fifth of May at 27 Houston Close. There were other people at the party and the host's name was Dawn Brown. We had Paula take an initial statement from her, which we will follow up on soon. Can you give us a rundown?'

Wyre nodded as she crossed her legs. 'She can't remember when Jade left the party or who with as they'd all had a few drinks. She remembered there being a bit of tension between Noah and Jade, and she remembers him walking out with Aimee, which corroborates Noah Ashmore's version of events. She also gave us a list of first names. That list contained the name of a man called Rhys, who attended with his partner, a woman called Aimee.'

Gina smiled. It seemed to be coming together, they just had to find out who Rhys was and where he lived. She knew from what Colin had said that Rhys was local. 'That at least ties up with what Colin Wray said to us. He said he recognised the man coming out of Jade's summerhouse and that he knew him to be called Rhys.'

Flipping over a few pages in her notebook, Wyre studied what she'd written and nodded. 'Dawn Brown also seemed very vague when it came to her guests. She doesn't seem to know them that well, saying they all lived close by and she just wanted to get to know some of the locals better. She didn't even know their surnames or where they lived. She said she just met them out and about, at the shops or on the High Street, and had asked them over on that date. In fact, she wasn't much help.'

'Now that sounds weird to me already. We need follow-ups on all the attendees. We need to locate this Rhys. I know you've made a start, Wyre, but can I leave that one with you? As soon as you have anything, let me know. I'll be paying Dawn a visit too. O'Connor, will you assist Wyre?'

Gina's phone beeped again. Thinking it might be Bernard with further information, she snatched it out of her pocket. Her face began to redden as she placed it on the table face down. Chatter began to fill the room as each of the detectives and officers prepared for the afternoon ahead.

Briggs walked over, smiling as he stood beside her. She returned his smile as he passed her a piece of paper. 'Here you go. I've prepared the press release and I'll pass it to Annie. We really need to put out an appeal for witnesses. Apart from that, Harte, you're the Senior Investigating Officer. Keep me updated. Call me if you need anything.' All that remained was the smell of his musky aftershave, the one she'd always loved. After all that had happened, she still thought about him, a lot. She doubted she'd ever stop. She grabbed her phone and replied to her messages.

Sorry Rex, I can't meet for a drink tonight. Have a lovely time though! Gina.

He'd been a mistake, not like the mistake she made with Briggs, a real mistake. Some mistakes were not made to regret but Rex was. A message pinged back. He wasn't getting the hint.

O'Connor looked away from his screen and grinned. 'The council have come up trumps. We have an address for one of our party-going couples.'

CHAPTER NINE

Diane pulled at the creaky wooden gate, trying to force it closed with her stiff fingers. Pain shot through her knees, almost causing her leg to buckle. That old rotten gate was as creaky as she was.

The wood had warped over the years and seasons, and she'd never had it fixed, never had the money or the skill required. Not that it mattered. She'd always felt safe in her little house at the end of a terrace in such a quiet area. She gasped as she reached the back door and turned the key in the lock, pushing the shopping through first.

She dropped the bags on the kitchen table. One from the food bank and one full of all the reductions she could find at the supermarket. Turning up in the afternoon sometimes paid off and today it did. A variety of vegetables for less than a pound in total. With the tin of corned beef and stock cubes from the food bank, a stew was on the menu for later. As she grabbed the fresh loaf, laden with price-reduction stickers, a bright envelope caught her eye.

The post had already been delivered before she'd left for the shops. It had to be a hand delivery. The pink envelope lay on the doormat. It wasn't her birthday so who would send her a card? At least it looked like it could be a card. She hobbled along the hallway and flinched as she kneeled. The latest flare up of arthritis had been one of her worst.

The envelope wasn't even sealed. She pulled out a pink card. On the front, the large letters wished someone a happy birthday, but it wasn't her. If she found out who it belonged to, maybe she could post it to them. It was probably meant for one of her neighbours, someone had obviously posted it through the wrong letterbox.

She gently opened it, hoping to find out who it belonged to. As she read the cut out letters, she gasped. Staggering back into the kitchen, she switched on the main light. 'It can't be,' she whispered under her breath as she lifted up the fingernail from the fold of the card. Seven years ago, that was when she last saw her friend. Since then, her friend had been nothing but a memory, silent in all ways. There had been no calls, no letters, no visits. She'd simply vanished.

There was a knock at the front door. Her heart slammed against her chest and she gasped. 'Samantha?' She made her way back towards the front door and peered through the spyhole and held her chest as her heart rate began to slow down. 'Oh, it's you,' she said as she opened the door.

He walked in with a big smile and a large bag of food. 'I'm glad to see you're so pleased to see me. I come bearing goodies.' She peered into the bag and spotted the crisps and chocolates she loved so much. Any other day she'd be thrilled.

'I thought you were someone else,' she muttered.

'Hey, you okay? You look like you've seen a ghost.' As he led her to her seat at the kitchen table, she knew he'd spotted the card. 'It's not your birthday.'

'It's not for me.'

'Shall I take it to where it belongs when I leave?'

She shook her head. 'That won't be necessary, bro.'

'I wish you wouldn't call me bro. It sounds so silly at our age.' He began to pack the food away, piling it up in the empty cupboards. 'You know it pains me to see you like this. You need to get out more, meet up with friends. You do look peaky. You're not in debt again, are you? You know I'm always here to help.'

And he had been. He'd helped her find a new home, one that her benefits would cover. He'd nursed her through a heavy depression after losing her job. For that, she would always be grateful to him. He began to wipe the surfaces with a cloth and piled the washing-up into the bowl. 'Look at the card.' She pushed it along the table, open at the text.

As he leaned over and read it, his mouth dropped open. 'Your friend Samantha. Who would send a card to her after all this time?'

Tears began to well up in the corner of Diane's eyes as she shrugged. 'Maybe someone knows something. What do I do?'

'Nothing. It's just someone playing a prank. She knew a lot of people and lots of people knew you were friends.' He turned the hot tap on and began filling the washing-up bowl. The musty room began to smell soapy and clean. 'You need to forget her and move on. You've been going on a lot lately, about her, and where she might be and I'm sick of hearing about it. I'm sick of hearing about her. She wasn't the perfect person you always made her out to be. She left you remember.'

'She vanished. It's a bit different. And she never got in touch. She wouldn't do that to me.'

'Yes, like people never let you down and do things you wouldn't expect them to do. People abandon people all the time and she was no better than anyone else.' He threw the little sponge into the soapy bowl.

'She didn't abandon me. You can be such a cynic.' Diane's brow furrowed. 'Anyway, why would someone do this? You know, send a card. I searched for her for years. Nothing. And now someone chooses to send me this. They've gone to a lot of effort, cutting out all these letters from a magazine.' Her bottom lip began to tremble. 'I'm scared and you don't seem to be taking this seriously.'

He turned off the tap. 'Look, Diane. I'm not going to say it again, it's just someone playing a stupid prank. People love playing pranks. Someone out there is having a laugh and you're falling for it.' He placed her usual tablets out on the side. They were all ready for her to take. He leaned over and removed the clump of straggly grey hair that hid her face and placed it behind her ear. 'That's better, I can see you. I've put a new hairbrush in the drawer too. Eat the chocolate, put some weight on and sort your hair out. I don't have to worry about you, do I? I never want things to be like they were before.'

'No, you never have to worry about me.' She pulled down the sleeve of her coat, the scarring on her wrist now concealed. She knew he was a worrier and that scar was a constant reminder of what she'd put him through during her last episode. 'But I am worried over why someone would leave this in the card?' She held the tiny fingernail in the palm of her hand.

He dropped the plate he was wiping, causing soapy water to cascade over the sides of the sink and onto the floor. 'You're being stupid now. Just throw it in the bin and forget it. Here.' He grabbed the bin and removed the lid. 'In the bin with it.' She placed the nail back inside the card and dropped it into the bin. 'Problem gone. Maybe it's time to accept that Samantha has gone, just like that stupid fake fingernail. Right, are you going to help me? I have to get home soon and we have to get your dinner on.'

'I can make my own.' She wanted him to leave and he could sense it.

'Don't get all het up over that stupid card.'

She looked away, remaining silent. If he thought the card was just a prank then he was clearly working against her.

'Do it yourself then! Talk about ungrateful.' He wiped his hands, grabbed his coat and slammed the door as he left. He'd come to visit with all the best intentions and, as usual, he'd left on a bad note. She didn't know how she managed to do something to upset him every time, after all he did for her. Her pained heart felt as though it might explode as tears filled her eyes. She was all alone, again.

Hobbling over to the bin, she removed the lid. The card had slipped amongst all the rubbish and old food, the rising stench almost making her gag. Samantha was out there somewhere. Her friend, the daughter she never had. She reached in, yelping in pain as she pulled the dirty card out and wiped it over with the dishcloth, making sure the little nail was still inside. She dried it off and hugged it close to her chest. *Where are you, Samantha?*

As Diane swallowed her sleeping pill, she stared at the card on the kitchen table. After her brother had stormed out of the door earlier that evening, she'd sat in silence, staring at the card.

She clasped her awkward fingers over the small box that she had fished out from under the stairs. She opened it, pulling out a photo of her and Samantha at the café in Sanders Park, Bromsgrove, after they'd just been for a walk. They'd become close. Diane had appreciated the company as her arthritis worsened. Samantha didn't get on with her family and Diane never had anyone to speak to, except her brother. They'd formed an unlikely bond – the recluse and the party animal. Samantha would ask advice of Diane when it came to men, Diane being more worldly-wise would try her best to answer. Over time their friendship deepened – Samantha became the daughter that Diane never had.

A heavy tear plopped onto the photo that so badly reminded her of her loss, then she gazed back at the card. Who would send her that? Letters cut out from some magazine. Tear after tear began to wet the photo. She closed the box, the memories contained in it were still too painful.

Holding back her emotions wasn't working. As she burst into tears, she picked up her anti-depressants. She wouldn't need them in the morning. She needed to feel, to think, to work out what she was going to do with the card in front of her. Her sleeve slipped down. She'd hurt herself and no one cared. She'd cried for help and no one had listened. Tablets, that's all she'd received as a replacement for human kindness.

She shivered as she picked up the nail. There was no telling whether it really belonged to Samantha. It was perfectly trimmed and clean, like someone had just polished it. Just like her brother had said, someone was probably playing a prank on her. She opened up her little box once again and delved to the bottom, pulling out the dried up nail varnish, the same one Samantha used all the time, the same shade Diane had bought her for her twenty-sixth birthday. Holding it up, she could see the shade was the same. Whoever was pranking her knew Samantha really well. She yawned and her eyelids began to droop. Her bed was calling.

She had to do the right thing but that would have to wait until tomorrow.

CHAPTER TEN

The log burner crackled and Ebony, her cat, lay out in front of it, enjoying its warmth. It hadn't been too cool that evening but the emptiness in Gina's house had left her cold. She took another crisp from the bag as she read over the case notes again. She and O'Connor had headed straight over to Aimee Prowse and Rhys Keegan's address but no one had been home, so they'd left a card. The appeal had aired and Gina hoped that maybe something would come from it.

She glanced at the messages on her phone from Rex. What had she been playing at? She'd heard Jacob mentioning Tinder. He'd had a few dates and shared with her how much fun he'd had and she'd been curious.

It had been months since she'd had any meaningful company. Her daughter Hannah had moved house and was now living in Gloucestershire. Given that they were emotionally distant, she wondered if she'd moved on purpose to get away from her. She missed Gracie, her granddaughter, dearly. The log burner was no substitute for a family but it helped. The crackling sound eased the emptiness of deafening silence. The warm flickering flames and shadows licking the walls made her feel less alone.

Staring at the photos of Jade on her laptop screen, she shuddered as she bit into another crisp. As she glanced up, she almost choked as a face peered through the lounge window. Her pounding heart sent blood whooshing around her body. The man smiled and waved. She closed her laptop screen and hurried to the door.

'What are you doing here? I'm working.'

Rex held the bottle of wine up. 'I just wanted to thank you for a lovely night.'

'I said I was busy and I am busy.' She stood in the doorway, hoping he'd apologise and leave. How dare he turn up unannounced? 'Look, Rex. I'm sorry if I gave you the wrong idea, I'm not looking to get involved with anyone at the moment so let's just leave this here. Go home, enjoy your wine and check out Tinder. There are lots of other women who I'm sure would love to meet up with you, go out, share this wine.'

'I really like you, Gina. You've barely given me a chance.' He paused and smiled. 'Anyway, I came over because I've lost my belt. I think I left it in your room. I'm sorry to disturb you.'

'Okay, wait there.' Leaving the door ajar, she ran up the stairs in her little cottage and searched through her clothes and under the bed, eventually finding the belt against the wall. As she gripped it, she flinched. Terry had once thrashed her with his belt. Laughing the house down as Hannah screamed in her crib. Not wanting sex was never an option and he showed her that. With trembling hands, she left the bedroom. Her ex-husband, Terry, was gone and he could never hurt her again. She'd made sure of it.

'Here you go.' Rex took the belt from her then he headed towards his car.

'Thanks. I'll message you,' he called as he quickly entered his car and closed the door before she could reply.

'Please don't,' she whispered under her breath.

CHAPTER ELEVEN

Aimee stared at the card that the police had left and turned it over. With the lights off, she gazed out into the darkness of the back garden. The rickety shed creaked every time the breeze picked up. Rhys had promised to fix it, he'd also promised to fix the kitchen cupboard, the lock on the bathroom door and the back gate. He always promised but never delivered. Nicole had constantly told her she was too good for him and that she'd changed since they'd been together. Slamming her hand on the worktop, she could see how his controlling nature had been so subtle at the beginning. He'd just seemed over-loving, overprotective. He made her feel safe and cared for. She didn't feel safe any more. She now felt abandoned and suffocated at the same time.

She tried to call Rhys but once again he didn't answer his phone. She shivered as she thought about Jade, the quietest woman at the party. Sitting alone, she'd kept herself to herself, not mingling at all. Aimee would never forget the look on the woman's face when her name was matched with Rhys's. And, since then, she hadn't heard a thing from Rhys and Jade had been murdered. It was all over the papers and the police were trying their best to contact her and Rhys. She screwed up the card and threw it in the bin. She needed it all to go away.

She almost crashed into the chair as the neighbour's dog began to bark like it was being attacked. 'Get in, Barney,' called the neighbour. With shaky hands, she pushed the kitchen window open a little further. Barney wasn't a noisy dog most of the time.

Her heart pounded. Maybe there was someone out there, lurking around the back of the fence. She swallowed as she thought of Jade and the fact that her killer was still out there. Her heart pounded as she leaned in closer to the window, staring out. A bang came from nowhere, followed by a rustling noise.

She slid the kitchen drawer open and gripped a small vegetable knife, before crouching down behind the kitchen sink. Someone was coming, she knew it. She screeched as her phone lit up. 'Rhys!' she shouted, keeping one eye on the back door.

'It's me. How are things going back home?' Her lodger, Nicole, sounded so fresh and happy in Tenerife.

Her eyes watered up as she took a few deep breaths to calm herself. Her panicked breaths turned into laughter.

'Aimee, hun, are you okay?'

'Yes, I'm being stupid. I just got creeped out by Barney next door.' Maybe that's all it was. The rustling of leaves could be nothing more than someone passing the back of her fence. It led to a bus stop and to the rest of the estate. Jade's murder was sending her reactions into overdrive.

'Easy done. Anyway, I'll be home soon to show you my embarrassing pics.' She paused. 'Aimee, I can always tell when there's something wrong. What's up?'

'Now's not a good time, I'll have to call you back. I'll text you later. Sending love and hugs.' She ended the call before Nicole had the chance to say another word. She loved Nicole dearly, they were best friends, but now wasn't the time to chat, especially when she had no idea what to say.

Loosening her grip on the knife, she wiped the beads of sweat from her forehead as she tried to call Rhys once again, this time his phone was actually ringing.

'What?' he snapped.

'Where are you? We need to talk.' The kitchen door flew open, Aimee's heart threatened to explode in her tiny chest. As her vision focused on the face standing in front of her, she stared back, wondering if he was capable of killing Jade. 'Don't come near me,' she whimpered as she held the knife in front of her chest, hands shaking and tears streaming down her face. 'What did you do to her?'

'Aimee, I didn't do anything. She left me in the summerhouse, I finished getting dressed and then I left. She was fine when I saw her last, I swear.'

He took a step towards her and she poked the knife into the air. 'You haven't been home since. The police have left messages and keep trying to call. I didn't know where you were and it's all over the news. If you didn't kill her, why didn't you come home after? I waited and waited in the dark, hiding when the police knocked. They came for you and you weren't here. I waited for you to call. That's when I saw what had happened. Someone on Jade's street posted an RIP on Twitter before the sun even came up. All this happened and not a word from you—'

'I didn't do it, but hey, you've already sentenced me in your head!' He clenched his jaw and took another step forward.

'Were you rough with her? I know you Rhys.'

He shrugged his shoulders. 'You've already convicted me in your stupid little head, and I expected more from you.'

'You forget how well I know you. Stay away from me. I'll use it.' Face wet with tears, she began to sob. She knew he didn't believe her.

He snatched the knife from her hand and threw it on the floor behind him. 'Look at you, holding a knife up at me then making out I'm the dangerous one. You would have, wouldn't you? Maybe you killed her.'

With only the moon and the glow of a street lamp filling the room, she shook her head as she sobbed. 'As if. Why didn't you come home?' She slammed through the kitchen door and ran up to the bedroom, slamming the door and burying her head in her pillow.

Rhys burst in and began rummaging through his drawers. Snatching a handful of clothing, he made a huffing noise as he stuffed the pile into a bag. 'No one's pinning this on me, least of all you! I'll be back for the rest of my stuff soon.' He crept up and lay beside her. 'I'll prove to you that I had nothing to do with Jade's murder.' She didn't believe him. He couldn't give her one good reason why he didn't come home and he'd even had the nerve to accuse her.

'I wish we'd never gone to that party,' she whispered as her body stiffened at his touch; warm breath tickling her neck as he kissed her. She closed her eyes hoping he'd leave.

As soon as the door slammed, she burst into uncontrollable sobs, sobbing for the life of a woman she barely knew and for the man she loved but no longer trusted.

CHAPTER TWELVE

Tuesday, 7 May 2019

Gina flicked between her screens and the report on Jade that sat on her desk. As she delved deeper into Jade's life, more things to consider ended up in her *to do* pile. Jacob knocked and gently pushed her office door open. 'You're here early?'

'I can't stay away from the place, guv. I love it so much.' He placed a coffee on her desk. 'Here, O'Connor sent you this. Made by his wife's fair hand. Apparently it's healthy, it's got nuts in it.' He dropped a serviette containing a cereal bar next to the coffee.

Gina took a bite. Given that it tasted of butter, just like all of Mrs O's bakes, she doubted it was healthy. 'Ooh, thank you.'

'Any updates on the Ashmores?' He took the seat opposite and slurped his drink.

'There were a few reports of noise on file, coming from their house. It seems that they argued a fair bit.'

'Did she work?'

'A little at home. She was a graphic designer but had given up her job to work from home since they had their child, four years ago. She must have felt so isolated.' Gina nibbled another piece of the cereal bar. When her daughter Hannah was a baby, she'd felt all alone, trapped in her house with Terry holding the invisible key. She coughed as she swallowed a few crumbs down the wrong way.

'Have a swig of your coffee, guv. I'm finding them a bit crumby too.' She nodded and slid the report across the desk where he began reading it.

On Jacob's advice, she gulped her coffee and closed her eyes. She couldn't let Jacob see her panic. She took a breath in through her nose, held her breath and exhaled. If the neighbour's reports were right, she knew just how Jade would have felt. *At least Jade didn't kill her husband, like me.* Willing thoughts of her abusive ex-husband, Terry, to go away, she stood and walked over to the window, staring out at the old tree in the car park, its roots pushing the concrete upwards, spilling over and creating the most charming looking trip hazards. She concentrated hard on the morning sun, the birds flying back and forth, landing on branches. She tuned in to Jacob tapping on her desk.

Terry was gone and her life had been good since. *Right, back to it, Harte.*

She knew the pathologist's report wouldn't be completed for a while but she made a mental note to ask Bernard if there were any signs of physical abuse on Jade Ashmore's body.

Her phone beeped and she instantly felt her heart rate speed again as she saw a text from her Tinder date. That man wasn't taking hints. She'd have to be even blunter, maybe even ruder.

'Can I take this report with me, guv? I'll go through it too.'

'Of course. Task O'Connor and Wyre to chase up Rhys Keegan and Aimee Prowse again. We've had all units on alert for his car but nothing has come back so far. I want to know what went on in that summerhouse. I know the Ashmores' creepy neighbour, Colin Wray, saw him there but he also saw Jade leaving a few minutes before Rhys did. It's strange that we haven't managed to find him since. Even stranger that Noah was with his partner, Aimee, at the same time.'

Jacob nodded. 'Totally agree. I'll pass all that on. Shall I tell O'Connor that the cereal bar was a bit crumby?' He gave her a smirk.

She smiled back. 'Don't you dare.'

As he left, she read the text.

I know I messed up, with the wine and leaving my belt, but I really like you, Gina. When you showed an interest in me on Tinder, I was thrilled, so thrilled. I don't exactly know where I went wrong or what I might have done to upset you, but can we start again?

She placed her head in her hands. She thought he would be like the other men she'd met. They went out, she went back to his and that's where it ended. Gina didn't do relationships. She'd tried with Briggs, her boss, but that had left her lost. They could never be together working at the same station and neither would ever leave. She rubbed her throbbing temples. Briggs was the one. He'd never know it, but he was. Another text came.

I'll prove myself. One more chance? I can be a great guy, you know. I'm good at cooking, like long walks, log fires, cats…

She laughed. He certainly had done his research. Briggs had moved on, he had gone on dates, she had to move on too. Her smile turned into a frown. Rex seemed to want so much more than she thought she'd ever even contemplate giving. She'd given her heart away only twice in her life, one had been a controlling psychopath and the other had been a professional no-go. She swallowed as she put herself in Rex's shoes. He liked her, went out with her and slept with her, all the time hoping that it would lead somewhere.

Really, she'd used him just to ease her loneliness and now he was wondering where he went wrong. She typed out a message.

I need time to think. X

Her phone went, it was Jacob. 'Looks like one of our witnesses has finally got in touch.' She smiled as he finished talking.

CHAPTER THIRTEEN

'Come in,' Gina called. Wyre entered. Her crisp black suit matched her newest crisp-cut black hair, a cut that almost resembled pictures she'd seen of Egyptian goddesses. Gina brushed down her crumpled shirt and leaned back. 'I see a smile. You've got something, haven't you?'

'We have just had a call from a lady called Diane Garraway. Seven years ago, a friend of hers went missing, a young woman called Samantha Felton. I just emailed you the missing persons file.' Gina glanced at her inbox and true to her word, the email had already arrived. She clicked on it, then into the link and a photo appeared on her screen. Missing since the fifth of May 2012. No sightings of her since.

'Unless she has new information, I don't see where we can go with this one at the moment. We really have to prioritise the Jade Ashmore murder case.'

'You haven't heard the best of it yet, guv.' Gina could see a glint in Wyre's eye.

'Spill the beans, Paula.' Gina linked her fingers and flexed them out in front of her.

Wyre flipped open a page in her notebook. 'It would have been Samantha's thirty-third birthday yesterday. Diane received a card to Samantha, the letters contained in it are cut out from bits of magazine. Now, here's the intriguing bit, if that wasn't enough already. A small, whole fingernail was also included inside the card, the shade of pink is what Diane believes matches the one that was Samantha's favourite. She thinks it's a fake nail but she isn't sure as it's been thickly varnished.'

'Jade Ashmore was missing a fingernail, the smallest one on her right hand. For the nail to turn up on the same day of Jade Ashmore's murder is more than a coincidence.'

Wyre nodded. 'That's what I thought. Someone's playing a game with us, I think.'

A flash of thoughts filled Gina's head. The image of a fingernail being tugged away from skin made her wince. 'I need to speak to her. Fancy an outing this morning?'

Nodding, Wyre flipped her pad closed. 'Definitely.'

'We can collect the card and send it to Bernard.'

'That sounds like a plan. I mentioned to Diane that we would need the card. She told me she's touched it several times and it's even been in the bin at one point. She could have potentially ruined any evidence contained on it.'

Gina exhaled and slumped back. 'Definitely not good from a forensics point of view. Maybe Bernard can get something from the nail, that's if it's not fake.'

The phone on her desk rang. 'Bernard.' As he spoke, Gina nodded as Wyre tried to listen to what he was saying. 'All we have is the neighbour's word for it then. Thank you.' She slammed the handset down and stared at the phone.

'What was that, guv?'

Gina shook her head and tapped her fingers on the desk as she thought. She selected the other tab on her computer. The list of suspects was huge. There was everyone at the party and the host, Dawn, still hadn't provided all their details. Jade's neighbours, including Colin Wray and Tiffany the babysitter, both may have had opportunity. She also had to still consider that the attacker could have chosen Jade at random on that night, that he was merely an opportunist. 'Gather everyone up for an immediate briefing. We need to discuss Noah Ashmore further and I want to know why we still haven't found Rhys Keegan!' She slammed her fist on the desk, seething that this man was managing to dodge them.

'At least we have his girlfriend Aimee.' Gina glanced at the note on her electronic diary. They were due to go to Aimee's house after lunch. Speaking to her was all good and well but she wanted Rhys Keegan. It was time to step up the search.

CHAPTER FOURTEEN

Wyre closely followed Gina along the tiny uneven path that led to Diane's house, the last small house in the row. Peeling paint flaked from the walls and the overgrown front garden looked like it probably hadn't been tended to in years. A wheelie bin half-covered the front door and Gina wondered if the grimy windows and brown net curtain had ever been washed. The area seemed quiet even though it was only a few streets back from Cleevesford High Street; she would have thought it might be busier, but there was no further access by road and only a small path that led to the primary school.

She knocked twice and rubbed her sleepy eyes.

'Coming.' They waited as the woman with the slightly croaky voice struggled to unlock the door. Finally winning the battle with her keys, she eventually opened the creaky entrance as she swore under her breath. The May sun shone through the woman's long thin grey hair. She looked to be in her seventies but Gina knew she was only in her fifties. Sallow skin clung to her pale face, making her look malnourished. Wrapped in two thick cardigans, Gina wondered if she was stifling hot underneath all that wool. 'Come in,' Diane Garraway said as she beckoned them through with a shaky hand, the bones of her fingers swollen and gnarly, reminding Gina of a weather damaged tree stump. 'I'd offer you a drink but my hands are too cold,' Diane said, leading them to the lounge.

'I can make a drink. Would you like one, Ms Garraway?'
Wyre asked. Gina smiled at her. They could both see that Diane
Garraway needed more help than she was receiving.

'No, I'm fine. I have one on the go. Take a seat and call me Diane.'

Gina pushed the old cushions aside and sank into one of the
armchairs, Wyre sat on the other. The heater clicked and began
whirring into action. It was warm outside and the heater was
on. Gina shivered. Despite all that, the house was cold. She now
knew why Diane was wearing all those cardigans.

Wyre removed the lid from her pen and turned to a fresh page
in her notebook.

'You called us because of a card you received that may be
linked to your missing friend, Samantha Felton.'

Diane trembled as she reached for the card on the arm of the
settee. The picture on the front was of a flower. A butterfly had
landed on one of its petals and the words *happy birthday* filled
the header section. Gina pulled a pair of blue gloves from her
bag. 'May I take a look?'

The woman nodded and handed the card to Gina. 'The nail
is inside so be careful that it doesn't fall out. I didn't know what
else to do with it.'

Gina opened the card. The *Dear Samantha* was made up of
letters cut from a magazine. Flecks of bin juice littered all sides
of the card which wasn't ideal. The generic message that the card
company had printed continued. *Have a wonderful birthday
and may all your dreams come true.* The three words cut out of a
magazine that followed made her shiver – *Ha Ha Ha!* Someone
out there thought it was funny to send a card to a missing woman
and then post it to of one of her best friends. It was definitely a
sinister gesture. She stared at the fingernail, so clean and pink.
Nail varnish wouldn't stay on for years, Gina knew that. After
a few days it often peeled and chipped away. Whoever sent the
nail and card had to have painted the nail recently.

'That was her favourite colour. I bought the same nail varnish for her and gave it to her as a birthday present on the day she disappeared. Rose Petal Pink. I have some here.' She reached into a small box and pulled out a dried up bottle of nail varnish and handed it to Gina. Gina used her phone to photograph the front and the inside of the card, after which, she placed it in an evidence bag. She then did the same with the nail before giving the bags to Wyre for logging and sealing, ready to send to the lab. 'I keep my reminders of her in this box.'

'May I take a look?' Gina asked. The woman handed the box over. Gina began flicking through the photos and cards. 'Can I please take some of these photos? I'll get them back to you. It would be nice to get a clearer picture of who Samantha was.'

Diane nodded. Gina passed a batch of photos and cards to Wyre.

'How did you receive the card, Diane?' Gina could see that the woman was struggling as she watched Wyre logging the card as evidence. Her reddened eyes told Gina that she'd been crying before they arrived.

'I went shopping yesterday, just the food bank and the supermarket on the High Street and I came home through the back door, like I always do. I put my bags in the kitchen and spotted a pink envelope on the hall floor. It had been posted through the front door. Our postman had already been round earlier that day so I knew it wasn't post. I assumed it was a card. What else could it be in a pink envelope?'

'Do you have the envelope still?'

The woman's brow furrowed as she tried to recall what she did with it. 'I opened it in the kitchen somewhere, I think. Maybe it's on the side, or even the table.'

'May I go and have a look for it?'

Diane nodded then took a sip of her drink.

Gina headed towards the kitchen, entering a tiny, cluttered room, full of mismatched cupboards, doors not quite aligned to the carcases, one even hanging off. A collection of old dead plants adorned the windowsill and the worktop was covered in packets of tablets. Gina recognised them to be anti-inflammatories, paracetamol and antidepressants. She shivered as she searched for the pink envelope. Bending down, she spotted it under the half-opened drop-leaf table. She reached down with her gloved hand. 'Here we go, found it,' she said as she went back into the warm sitting room and handed it to Wyre.

'Did you see anyone around, either on your way back from the shops or hanging around the front of the house?' Gina sat back down.

Diane shook her head and used her index finger to wipe the end of her nose. 'No one suspicious. I passed people when I came back from the shops but no one memorable. No one looked out of place and I didn't really look out the front window when I picked up the envelope. I'd say no.'

'Have you heard anything from Samantha since she was reported missing or have you received anything like this before?'

A tear slid down the woman's face. 'No. If I had, I'd have called you.'

'I'm sorry, I can see this is difficult for you.' Gina swallowed the lump that was forming in her throat. She could see how difficult this was for Diane. 'Maybe you can tell me a little bit about your relationship with Samantha.'

She pulled a tissue from one of her sleeves and wiped her eyes. 'Samantha lived close by and I'd seen her while out shopping a few times. I've lived alone all of my adult life and I struggle to make friends. I worked in a shop until my arthritis made it impossible. I've had it years now, wouldn't wish it on anyone. I didn't want to go out much, I mean look at me. I can barely dress myself, let alone make an effort.' She paused and stared at the floor. 'I suppose I've always been a bit of a loner. I was lonely too and found myself smiling at people while out, hoping that one of them would talk to me and no one really did, apart from Samantha. Whenever I saw her, she'd do all the talking, about places she had been, was going, her university work and her boyfriend. This was just when I bumped into her. We then started going to the café if we bumped into each other, just for a chat and a piece of cake. We really got on. I'd listen to her talk about her relationship and she filled a gap in my life. Soon, she was at my house every other night, sometimes I'd make an effort to prepare some food, sometimes when she could see I was struggling, she'd bring food. We'd watch telly together and if she stayed late, she'd sleep in my spare room. She became like a daughter to me. We were that close. I had this dream back then, that one day she would finish her course, get a good job and meet someone decent. I thought maybe she'd have children and that maybe they'd call me Nanny. She called me her Mumsy and would always kiss me goodbye—' Tears began to flood from Diane's eyes.

'I know this is hard but you're doing really well, Diane. We have on record that she was seeing someone called Derek.'

'Ahh, the married man. I did tell her that he'd never leave his wife. I should know, I've been there in my twenties. I wasted several of my best years on a married man so I was in the best position to advise her. Derek was just spinning her a yarn. He was never going to leave his wife and kids. She'd go out partying and meeting other men, all to make him jealous, but he never cared.'

Wyre scribbled a few notes. Gina knew they already had this information on Samantha's missing persons file. From what she'd read, Derek had an alibi on the night Samantha was last seen, but that alibi was his wife.

'Do you know anything about the other men?'

Diane blew her nose. 'No. I know she used to go to Cleevesford Social Club. They had the occasional live band night and regular discos. She used to go there, said she'd met some guys while out for the night. She often made me laugh with her stories. She'd dance with them, flirt with them but then she'd send them packing. She was all about the fun on the night. People had her all wrong. I overheard people talking, angry that their husbands and boyfriends had shown too much of an interest in her. She had an infectious presence. People noticed when she entered a room. Her long golden-coloured hair was always beautifully styled. Her flawless skin and slim figure made her look so youthful. She was also so good-natured, always spoke to anyone. She was such a trusting young woman, too trusting. I told her that people weren't as nice as they seemed, that they pretended, but she just told me I was too cynical.'

Gina looked down at her feet. Too many people let their guard down in life, she had been guilty of that too. In her teens and early twenties, she'd have trusted anyone, she still worried that she too often saw the good in people. Her mind wandered to Rex. Should she trust him? Did she want to trust him? She didn't even know if she really liked him in that way. She squinted and pinched the top of her nose, trying to snap out of her thoughts. 'She's lucky to have had you in her life.' Gina wished she still had her own mother to talk too. She could do with a Diane in her life. She couldn't think about her mother now. After an aggressive form of cancer took her, she'd never allowed herself to overthink what she'd lost, simply enjoying the good memories she carried around.

'I was lucky to have her in mine. I don't think I'd be here now if it wasn't for her. She came into my life just when I needed a friend.'

Diane looked away and wiped her eyes again. Wyre had finished filling out the details on the evidence envelopes, ready to take them to Bernard. After all these years, someone had come out of the shadows to remind them that Samantha was still missing. Had they done that on the night of Jade's murder? In Gina's mind, there had to be a connection between Jade and Samantha. They would have been about a similar age and may have even gone to school together. Maybe they socialised together. She shivered, Jade was dead. Their witness saw a man dragging Jade's body towards the road, then he abandoned the body when he was disturbed and drove away. She snapped out of her thoughts. He was trying to take Jade Ashmore's body away from the scene. Had he done the same with Samantha?

'There is something else,' Diane said.

Gina leaned forward in her seat.

'It's probably nothing and I don't think I mentioned this before. I know Samantha dated a couple of other men to make Derek jealous. After meeting with one of them, both times she came to see me after, she stank of cigarettes. I know she wasn't a smoker, so it must have been him. She didn't even drink a lot when she went out. Do you think she's still alive?'

'I can't answer that. I wish I could. We only have her down as a missing person. A body has never been found but no one has reported seeing her since.' Gina could only hope that her instincts about Samantha were wrong.

The fingernail link was a strong one. He killed Jade but what had he done with Samantha? Gina felt a shiver shoot through her body as she typed out a quick message to Jacob and pressed send.

Get everyone in the incident room, we're on our way back. Emergency briefing.

CHAPTER FIFTEEN

'Thanks for getting here at such short notice.' Gina walked straight into the incident room, dropped her jacket over one of the desks and headed to the boards at the front of the table. Jacob and O'Connor looked like they were racing to finish their sandwiches. Gina inhaled and her nostrils quickly filled with the smell of egg, tuna and strawberry milkshake. 'Right, Wyre and I have just come from Diane Garraway's house. I know Wyre sent you a brief update as we were heading back, didn't you?'

'I did, guv.' Wyre rolled the sleeves of her pristine blouse up and dropped her notepad on the desk.

'So you all know about the card and the fingernail. These have just been catalogued and sent off to the lab. I want to consider the theory that the Jade Ashmore murder may be linked to Samantha Felton's disappearance. There are too many coincidences for my liking. As we know, Jade Ashmore was missing a fingernail and then, what seems to be the fingernail of a missing woman turns up on the same day. Whether it's a real nail is yet to be confirmed but as soon as I have the results back, you'll all be informed immediately. During the press release, it wasn't mentioned that our victim had her fingernail removed so this isn't common knowledge.'

O'Connor held up his hand.

'Yes,' Gina said.

'Are we thinking that the same thing happened to... err,' he glanced down at his notes, 'Samantha Felton, seven years ago?'

Gina took a deep breath. 'Samantha is registered as a missing person. A body has never been found. We know Jade's killer was attempting to drag her away towards his car. If he follows a pattern, this may suggest that he kills them, takes them away in his car and disposes of the body later. Where he takes them, I can't begin to guess. Quite often, the public come across bodies in cases like this, while out with their dogs, walking in the countryside, fishing, jogging, etcetera. If a victim has been buried in a shallow grave, it's not long before animals dig them up. Samantha could even still be alive. Maybe Jade's killer didn't mean to actually kill her. It's too early to decipher his intentions yet. Jacob, you were going to delve into her file, what did you find out about the original report?'

Jacob sucked on a straw as he finished off the small bottle of milkshake then wiped his mouth with a tissue. 'As you know, she was reported missing by Diane Garraway when she didn't visit the day after her twenty-sixth birthday. This was on the sixth of May 2012. Diane had prepared a small birthday lunch for around noon and Samantha hadn't turned up. After trying to call several times, she walked the two streets to Samantha's flat and there was no answer. Her curtains were still drawn and Diane worried that she was sick so she let herself in with a spare key that Samantha had given to her. When she didn't find her friend there, she was worried and called the police. Nothing was found out of place in her home. A few days later an appeal was put out on local news and although there had been vague calls, they all came back with nothing. Samantha had essentially vanished and she's never been seen since, she's not used her credit cards or bank cards either.'

Gina walked in front of the boards, scratching her head as she thought. 'What do we know about Samantha?'

'She was a first year mature student at Birmingham University, studying law. She had a wide social circle as you'd expect any single person to have.'

Gina paced as she mulled over what Jacob was saying. Single did not mean outgoing but she knew in this case he was right. In Gina's own case, it meant occasionally desperate for company but happy being a recluse the rest of the time. 'Elaborate on that a little.'

'She was a member of the Cleevesford Social Club. She went to the Angel Arms pub on the High Street regularly and often met with the other students in Birmingham. In the report, Diane says she was always out and she had a boyfriend.'

Gina nodded. 'Married man, Derek Alton. Back then he was in his late forties and married with two children. The neighbours regularly heard her shouting at him, giving him ultimatums. That wasn't all. Diane said she'd been dating other men, which in her view was mostly to make Derek jealous in the hope that he'd leave his wife. Diane also said that Samantha was seeing someone else just before she went missing. She often smelled of smoke after meeting him. She maintains that Samantha wasn't a smoker but thought that maybe the person she'd been with was.'

Gina flinched as Briggs entered, piercing the silence as he cleared his throat. 'Anything back from forensics?' As he strode past her, he did the two buttons up on his suit jacket and took a seat at the end of the table.

'I spoke to Bernard before we went to see Diane. He has confirmed what we thought we knew about the murder weapon. It was made with something flat that resembles a mallet, like the ones that are used for knocking tent pegs into the ground.'

Briggs rubbed the light stubble on his chin. 'Do we have Noah's statement on file?'

O'Connor nodded. 'He came in and gave us a formal statement. It's on the system. He has also been calling, asking what we've been doing to find his wife's murderer.'

'Thanks, O'Connor.' Briggs rubbed his eyes and smiled.

Gina wondered for a second if her ex-lover was looking after himself or his lack of grooming was due to him having too much of a good time and burning the candle at both ends. Her stomach flipped a little. She almost wanted to slap herself for still thinking about him in that manner. His gaze caught hers and within a second it shot to the board. Gina checked her watch. 'We have to get to Aimee Prowse's house. I don't want to miss her and I want the opportunity to see the home where Rhys Keegan lives. At the moment he is one of our prime suspects being the last person to see Jade alive. There has been no sign of him since the night of her murder. Any news on his whereabouts?'

Everyone shook their head. 'Not a thing, not on him or his car. It's like he's just vanished,' O'Connor said, his shiny bald head reflecting the orangey strip light above.

'O'Connor, I want you to delve further into Dawn Brown, the party host. I need to be prepared before I visit her. I want to know who she's in relations with, what she does for a living, anything you can find out. Wyre, give Bernard another call and see if there are any further updates. I know they're fire-fighting the workload but this case needs to jump the queue. I need the post-mortem to be done as soon as possible.'

PC Smith passed the door of the incident room as he headed to the kitchen.

'Smith,' she called.

'Huh.'

'If there are any sightings of Rhys Keegan, I want you to contact me immediately. Anytime of the day or night.'

He nodded. 'Of course, guv.' He continued towards the kitchen.

'Right, I'll catch up with you all later.' Her mind wandered back to Samantha as she thought about a previous case, that of missing woman Deborah Jenkins. She'd been kidnapped and falsely imprisoned for many years, but she had been alive. Her heart began to hum with excitement. She thought of the young woman that was missing, the law student with her whole life ahead of her. She thought of Diane, the lonely, ill woman who missed Samantha more than anything. Unless they found a body, there was still hope. 'There is a chance Samantha could still be alive. Don't waste any time.'

She grabbed her jacket and nodded to Jacob to follow.

CHAPTER SIXTEEN

There she is again – it gives me so much pleasure to watch Aimee. It's safe to enter now, her session with the grumpy old woman has begun. Private yoga today. My hands tremble with excitement as I follow the side of the house and peer around the wall. I've missed you my lovely little personal trainer and I've missed the smell and feel of your house.

I love the way you do downward dog in your conservatory gymnasium, it's a sight I've seen on many occasion. It's a small, but well kitted-out mini studio – you have a good eye for design and layout. It's a shame the rest of the house isn't as nice. Your client isn't as good at downward dog as you, no one ever is. She's not dedicated like you. You deserve to look that good, all firm, young and delicious.

As I open the back door, I know you won't hear me over the chiming of recorded bells, the ones you play as you enter the meditation stage. I have until the count of eight. That's the way you do things, isn't it? You like doing it all your own way. I know you better than you know yourself. That's what intimacy means in a relationship.

The kitchen is quite dismal, not like the conservatory – actually, it's more of a lean-to that runs along the other side of the house that you spent so much money doing up, the bit your clients see. The house is so mismatched, old with extensions, misshapen but quirky.

Your fridge is almost empty like it always is. You have this lovely house and no food in the fridge. I inhale and all I smell is celery. You wear designer gym wear but there are holes in your everyday shoes.

I wish we could have met in a different way. I wish we could have a little meet-cute, like in the movies. That moment when our gazes meet across a crowded shop or café. You won't like me to begin with. Maybe it's raining and you're all dishevelled. Your bouncy caramel coloured locks will be tight as they'll be wet. I'll bump into you as you wrestle with your umbrella, knocking something out of your other hand, maybe eggs. You'll sound off as I gaze into your big blue eyes, then you'll realise that you've just been a prize bitch towards the handsome stranger. I'll offer you coffee and you'll burst into laughter and apologise. That's how it should have been. A man can fantasise.

You sound a little bell, bringing me gently out of my thoughts. The chiming stops.

Your hallway is dark and a collection of junk is piled up under the stairs. As I head up, the middle step creaks. I stop and listen as you make *aum* noises from your lean-to. You didn't hear a thing. Just like the other night when you were staring out of your kitchen window into the darkness ahead. I could see you. You really need a new fence you know, but I suppose money's tight. Security isn't your priority and you're certainly not very alert, but I already know that. I mean, you don't always lock your back door, even when a woman from your neighbourhood has just been murdered – silly girl.

The smell of your hairspray fills the landing and I love it, I love everything about you. One day, it will be me and you; until then, I'm a man and I have needs, but you're my special girl.

A knock at the door fills the quiet house. In a panic, I take the last step onto the landing and head into your lodger's room, slipping behind the door. Who comes at this time of the day? You don't book more than one client in at a time. I hold my breath as you pad along the hallway and open the door. Sweat beads form at my brow. No way – detectives? That's all I need.

CHAPTER SEVENTEEN

'Aimee Prowse?' Gina held her identification up and Jacob smiled.

The young woman wiped a bead of sweat from her brow. Her flawless skin sported an amazing post-workout glow. 'Come through. Sorry, Sally,' she called towards the conservatory. 'Can I call you later to book you in for another session? You're doing really well. Keep practising and stay focused. Remember your breathing.' The young woman's eyebrows arched as her customer flung her handbag over her shoulder.

The client brushed past Gina and smiled as she headed towards the front door. 'Thanks, Aimee. We'll speak later – definitely book me in for another session.'

'What is it you do?' Gina felt a tingle run down her neck as she spotted Aimee's perfectly manicured nails. Her thoughts flashed back to the nail that had been delivered to Diane.

'I'm a personal trainer. I also manage all the Parkruns in the area and have a collection of private clients. Sometimes I rent space at the gym in Cleevesford but I do run a few sessions from home. Are you interested in getting fitter?' Aimee grabbed a purple hoodie from the coat hook, pulled it on and led the detectives into the lounge.

Clothes were strewn over the settee and several half-filled glasses of water were dotted around the room, some dustier than others. 'Definitely not,' Gina replied as they took a seat on the large corner settee. She thought of Wyre and how much she'd probably love to have personal training sessions to make her perfectly sculptured body even more sculptured. Gina was more about crisps and lazing around when she wasn't working. The thought of being vigorously trained made her shudder. Her gaze wandered to the far end of the room where a sliding door led to a wide lean-to, equipped with gym balls and mats. Wind chimes hung from the ceiling and a light wooden floor completed the natural look. Pretty stones and crystals adorned the shelves. 'We need to speak about the night of Sunday the fifth of May.'

Aimee looked away, folding her arms as she hugged her body. The young woman suddenly took on a child-like appearance. Her frame so petite, she could have easily been mistaken for a teenager. Her fluffy caramel-coloured curls had escaped from her ponytail and were concealing her eyes. Gina shifted in the seat so that she could face Aimee head on. At twenty-four, she was just a little older than her daughter, Hannah.

'It's terrible, what happened to that woman.'

'It is, and we're trying to find out as much as we can, which is why we're here. We need to catch whoever did this to her. Until then, there's someone really dangerous out there. Tell me about the party. What happened that evening?'

Aimee peered through a gap in her curls. 'You know about the party?'

Gina caught Jacob's eye. Something in Aimee's reaction had suggested that this party wasn't all it seemed. Noah had mentioned the party and he'd mentioned talking to Aimee at the end of the night. He'd also mentioned his falling out with Jade. 'We know.' Gina knew this was a bluff but she was sure Aimee wouldn't catch on. She solemnly nodded, waiting for her to continue.

The woman shook her head and closed her eyes for a second. 'I went with Rhys, my boyfriend. It was just a party at Dawn's house. There were a few other couples and there were nibbles. We had wine and that was it.'

'Nibbles and wine. We know it was more than that?' Another bluff. 'How do you know Dawn?'

She shrugged her shoulders and looked away, staring at the artificial orchid in the pot that sat on her window ledge. 'I don't know Dawn. We hadn't met until that night. Rhys said we were going to the party. He arranged it and I just went along.'

'How did he know Dawn?'

A tear slipped down Aimee's cheek and she shook her head.

A flutter of excitement sent endorphins through Gina's body. She was on to something. 'It's really important that you answer my questions. Aimee, a witness saw Rhys with Jade on the night of her murder and we've yet to locate him. You can see how this looks. So, how did he know Dawn?'

Aimee pulled her sleeve over her hand and wiped her eyes. 'He met her on the internet. We were all there to swap partners. Is that what you wanted me to tell you?' She inhaled deeply and let out a controlled breath. 'I wasn't really sure about it but Rhys said we should give it a go and I guess I just went along with it. I sort of wanted to do something different too so it wasn't all his fault.'

It was all starting to make sense. That's why Dawn hadn't known all of the details of those who had attended her party. They were all newly acquainted. 'I'm not here to judge you, Aimee, but I need to know what happened that evening. Can you talk me through everything, from when you arrived?'

The young woman's cheeks reddened. 'We got there just before eight, I think. I can't be too sure. I was a bit drunk. I don't drink often and I'd had a couple of glasses of wine to loosen up before we even left home. The first hour was spent mingling with the others, then Dawn came out of the kitchen with two glasses. Men's names in the first and a location in the second, women picked. We didn't discuss who or where with anyone. We were meant to just make eye contact with our random partners, leave the house and they followed us women out to the secret locations.

I've never done anything like this before and I'd hate it to get out to my clients. I've worked so hard to get high profile people on my books. Are they going to find out?'

Gina couldn't reassure her either way. 'Who were you paired with and where did you go?'

'I got Noah. I don't know his second name. He left just after me and we walked to the woods together.'

'Did you see Rhys leave?'

She shook her head. 'I was so nervous about what was happening, all I thought of was myself. I was jittery and my head was everywhere. I liked Noah and was glad I got him over the others.' She paused. 'I only caught a brief glance of Rhys when he left. I remember being angry at him as he didn't look back. So much ran through my mind. I thought he didn't care. I questioned what the hell I was doing but at the same time I wanted it when it turned out to be Noah.' She began to rock gently on the end of her seat. 'I was with Noah for about half an hour. That's all it took from start to end. We parted sometime after midnight and that was it, the end. I headed home and so did he, at least I think he did. I didn't go home with him.'

'Was anything said?'

She stared into space. 'Not really. He mentioned that Jade hadn't been too happy with him and he was likely to be in the doghouse when he got home. He didn't look overly worried.'

'Aimee, I know this is hard, but have you heard from either Noah or Rhys since the party?'

She shook her head. 'After, I came home for a bit but didn't hear anything from Rhys. I got anxious and had no idea where he'd be. When he wasn't home by about six in the morning, I basically pounded the streets, sick with worry. I haven't seen him since.'

Jacob cleared his throat as he turned a page in his book and began to scribble a few notes.

Aimee walked over to the window and began playing with the potted orchid. 'He wouldn't have hurt her.'

Gina would reserve the right to challenge that statement until she'd had the opportunity to speak to the elusive Rhys Keegan herself. If he had nothing to do with Jade's murder, why had he vanished before anyone even knew she'd been murdered? Why hadn't he come home after leaving the summerhouse? Gina made a note to do a background check on Rhys. 'Has he called you since the party?'

Without turning to face Gina, the woman shook her head. 'That's all I know. It really is. I haven't seen or heard from him.'

Gina's thoughts flashed back to creepy Colin Wray. 'We have a witness who saw Jade Ashmore with Rhys and there's something a little sensitive I need to ask you.'

She nodded and wiped her brow.

'Is he ever forceful or rough with you?' Gina wondered if there was anything in what Noah's neighbour, Colin, had described. A slight tremble washed over Aimee as she reached for one of the many glasses of water. She took a sip from the dusty glass. 'If you need any help—'

'No. Thank you, Inspector. He's not like that. We went to a party, got off with other people, he's missing and she's dead. Have you ever thought something might have happened to him? I don't know any more.'

Gina took a card from her pocket and placed it on the coffee table next to one of the old glasses of water. 'If you hear from him or he comes home, you need to contact me immediately.' Aimee's gaze flitted from the window to her lap, to over Gina's head. Gina could tell that she was probably hiding the fact that she had seen him since. 'As it stands, Rhys is a prime suspect in a murder enquiry.'

The sun shone through the window, highlighting the dust motes in the air. As Aimee turned, she nodded and forced a smile. 'Of course, I'll call.'

*

As Gina and Jacob headed towards the car, she stopped. 'Of all the things they could have been hiding, it had to be a partner-swapping party!'

'Well played on getting that out of her.'

'I just knew something was off. Did you believe her, about not seeing him after the incident?'

'No, guv. I think she's holding onto something for sure.' He slumped into the passenger seat of the car as Gina buckled up. She placed her phone on the dashboard holder and typed the address of their next destination into Google Maps.

'She's covering something up, covering for Rhys. Noah never once mentioned the nature of the party. It looks like Jade Ashmore picked Rhys Keegan at the summerhouse out of those glasses. What we need to know is what happened to the rest of the party. Let's go and pay the host a visit. It's Dawn Brown, isn't it?'

Jacob nodded. 'Yes, she has a boyfriend called Steven but that's all we know.'

A message flashed up on Gina's phone.

Hello sexy. Dinner later? X

'Sounds like you're on a promise later, guv.'

'Shut up! This guy just doesn't take the hint.' She felt her face burning up as she smiled with embarrassment.

'Okay, not saying another word.' He made a pretend zip action with his fingers pinched across his lips. She shook her head and smiled as she drove. 'Is he nice?'

'I thought you weren't going to say another word, Driscoll.' He stared out of the window, a smile on his face.

'At least one of us has a life.'

'Shush.'

'Okay!'

As they pulled out of the road she mulled over the message. She'd deal with Rex later.

The party ran through her mind. She could see people turning up, uncomfortably sussing each other out, some of them entering into things they weren't comfortable with. Her smile faded. She felt a shiver run through her body as she thought of Terry and that one incident she'd never spoken about in her life, an incident she'd buried so deeply in her mind until this moment. An incident that was so surreal, it almost felt like it should have merely been a dream.

Taking a deep breath, she indicated left and joined the main road on the outskirts of the estate.

CHAPTER EIGHTEEN

I check my silenced phone and there are no new messages. I have all the time in the world and a part of me hopes that Aimee goes out so that I can make my escape. In slow motion, I place it in my pocket.

My heart feels as though it will fly from my mouth as I hear her jogging up the stairs. First the detectives arrive and now she's closing in on me. With each step, I can hear her gasping for breath. I know she gets easily overwhelmed and after hearing what the detectives had to say, I can only guess at what's going through her head. I like that she takes risks in life, that she's game for a bit of fun. I am too. It's exciting.

As she reaches the landing, I hold my breath. She can't catch me behind her lodger's bedroom door, it would ruin everything. I listen as her whimpers turn into uncontrollable sobs.

'Answer your phone,' she yells as she storms through the bathroom door, slamming it closed. She won't get an answer, of that I'm sure.

I hold my breath as she passes me on the other side of the door, so close, the smell of her sweet sweat fills my nostrils. I exhale. Phew – that was close.

The sound of the shower brings a smile to my face. As she steps in, I creep along the landing for a quick look at her bedroom and my stomach flutters. Her underwear lies on the floor. I pick up the pink pants and rub the soft material across my rough face. *I'll be back soon.* I drop them and tiptoe out of the room, past the bathroom door and begin the careful journey down the steps.

The shower goes off. That was quick. I step again and the step creaks.

'Rhys?' she calls.

My heart bangs against my chest. I need to get out the back door before she comes out. She can see the front path out of her bathroom window. I carry on down the stairs not making a sound until I reach the hallway. Holding my breath, I pick up the pace as I reach the back door and open it.

'Rhys, is that you? I know you're there,' she calls. I exhale as I dart out of the back gate. She can't see me, not yet. I scurry off into the distance as the neighbour's dog pounds against the fence, barking like it's the end of the world.

My phone lights up. *Oh, hello.*

CHAPTER NINETEEN

Gina pulled up on the drive of the new townhouse, right behind the caravan. 'This is a nice new estate, guv. I see myself living somewhere like this in a few years, wife, couple of kids, nice garden.'

'You hate gardening and you're not that keen on kids either.'

Laughing, Jacob leaned down and grabbed his satchel from the foot-well. 'You know something, you're always right. Big mistake that would be. It wouldn't be so bad if kids came with a volume button.'

Gina glanced up at the house as they stepped out of the car, heading up the drive, taking care not to brush against the newish Land Rover Discovery. The new build, three-storey, end of terrace semi was neatly finished with a Juliet balcony on both upper floors. The curtains at all of the windows matched the lead-grey colour of the front door. Window boxes finished the look off beautifully. The parked up caravan looked to be a little older than the car and house but it was large and clean.

Jacob pressed the doorbell and a woman answered.

'Dawn Brown? DI Harte and DS Driscoll.'

She nodded and stepped aside. Gina inhaled the smell of new house as they entered the airy hallway that led to the bright kitchen. All other doors were closed. Dawn knew exactly what she wanted them to see. Calculated move or did she simply value her privacy?

'I have all the names for you. Here you go.' She slid a handwritten list of names across the island in the middle of the kitchen.

Jade and Noah Ashmore.
Aimee Prowse and Rhys Keegan.
Maggie and Richard Leason.
Myself (Dawn Brown) and Steven Smithson.

Gina gasped for breath as she took a step back. She needed air. Jacob's gaze met hers as she opened the back door.

'Can I get you something, Detective?' the woman called.

Gina shook her head as she practised her breathing exercises that the counsellor had taught her to do. 'I'm fine, thank you. I just swallowed the wrong way down. I'll be okay in a moment.' A small lie that would buy her a few seconds until she could expand her contracting airways. Breathing in through her nose, she held and then exhaled.

'Excuse me a moment.' Jacob left Dawn and followed Gina into the garden. 'What's going on, guv?'

She couldn't hide the fact that she was shaking or that she was in a mild panic. Sweat glistened on the end of her nose. She felt her neck burning up and knew full well that she was reddening.

'It's nothing. I just recognise a name on the list, but I'm okay now.'

'Which one?'

'It doesn't matter.' She took a final deep breath and smiled. 'Let's go back in. That woman must think I'm barmy.' She stepped back into the kitchen. 'I'd love a glass of water, Ms Brown, thank you.'

As Dawn ran the tap and reached for a glass, Gina tried to match her with Steven. They weren't a match in her head. Steven had always gone for much younger women, normally with a naivety about them. Dawn looked like a mature, independent woman and certainly didn't come across as a pushover. Steven, her ex-brother-in-law, the man who knew what she was like back then, when Terry was alive. The man who knew her old self, the woman she'd tried so hard to escape and forget. The woman he'd enjoyed taunting and keeping in her place, watching on as Terry abused her, knowing and encouraging his brother to continue. She'd once been so fearful of them both.

Dawn placed the glass in front of Gina. Her ash blonde bob, bouncing as she walked. Her green eyes searching for some kind of reassurance that Gina wasn't going to possibly throw up on her gleaming kitchen floor.

'Thank you.' She gulped down the water and smiled. 'That's better. One of our detectives spoke to you on the phone so you're fully aware of why we're here.'

She nodded as she fidgeted with her jeans, the ones that were at least a size too small. 'It's about what happened on the night of the party. I don't really know what I can tell you. We had a party at mine, everyone left before midnight and that was it really.'

'We know about the party,' Gina said, hoping that Dawn would be prompted to say more. If Dawn thought she'd be able to fob them off with neighbourly wine and nibbles, she had another think coming. 'You also know that one of your friend's was brutally murdered on the night of your party.'

Her shoulders slumped. 'It wasn't my idea.'

'Dawn, we're not here to judge you at all. A woman was murdered. We're here to find out what happened and who killed her.'

She slumped onto one of the bar stools on the other side of the island and picked her lips. 'I don't know how we ended up having the party, that's Steven and me. I suppose it was something he wanted to try so I went along with things.'

'Tell me a bit about the evening?'

Gina wondered if Steven had chipped away at her self-esteem, threatening to leave her, telling her what to wear and calling her names. Had he followed this with the deepest of love messages until she'd become dependent on him, relying on the love-bombing cycle that he'd carefully honed, his tried and tested method?

Gina knew that Dawn was an estate agent, a successful one at that. She didn't need Steven for anything, but life can be lonely when you've been divorced. Maybe she didn't have a huge social circle. Gina had checked her out that morning. On paper, Dawn didn't look the type. Gina also knew there was no type and that Terry and Steven were very alike. The woman tugged her oversize top down. Gina could see her vulnerability. She didn't want anyone to see her stomach falling over the stupidly tight jeans. She walked around her own home in little heels, unbalanced and clearly feeling the pinch in her toes. She was in a constant state of waiting for Steven, living in fear of him leaving her for someone younger and fitter. Gina knew him too well.

'I was so nervous, I think I drank a whole bottle of wine throughout the early evening. Partner swapping was Steven's idea. He'd never tried it and said he'd always wanted to.' Gina knew that was a lie. 'I went along with it. He'd found some local people who were up for some fun, as he put it, and he arranged it all. He did it to get closer to her but he won't admit it.' Dawn's index finger pointed at one name on the list. Aimee Prowse. 'He'd seen her around the estate and when he discovered she was on the forum, I just knew it. You know when you can tell. I tried to change his mind about the evening but he kept going on about how I promised him that I'd be more adventurous. I thought he'd maybe dump me if I didn't at least give it a go. I didn't know what to do. Two marriages have ended on me. I thought maybe it was me and he was right.' A tear slid down the woman's blotchy face. She slammed her hand on the worktop, walked over to the fridge and pulled out an opened bottle of rosé wine and poured a glass. 'Want one?'

Jacob and Gina shook their heads.

'I need something. I can't cope with all this.'

'You mentioned a forum. Is this on the internet?'

She nodded and topped up her wine glass. 'It's a website called Swap Fun. Check it out. I can't believe I actually allowed him to upload our profiles for all members to see. I love him and I know I'm a fool—' The woman burst into tears. 'I don't want to screw up again. I'm forty-seven. I've had enough of going it alone. I've had enough of failing. I just want to be happy and be with someone who loves me. Is that too much to ask for?'

'Of course it's not, Dawn. Is it okay if I call you Dawn?' Gina asked.

The woman nodded and slammed the wine glass down. 'Anyway, the last thing I remember of that night is leaving with Richard.'

'Where did you go?'

Crimson blotches spread across Dawn's face, giving away her distress and embarrassment. 'The caravan. We were in there from about eleven thirty, maybe later or earlier. I'm not sure. I don't want to talk about it either. All I know is he was with me about that time and we'd both had a few.'

'Tell me a bit about Steven and Aimee. You mentioned that he already knew her.'

She shook her head and brandished a false smile across her face. 'Oh he fancied her something rotten. She'd jog around the estate in Lycra, bending and stretching. She's the estate's most famous personal trainer. I think all the men around here get an eyeful. It's also common knowledge that she likes older men and I think stupid Steven thought he was in with a chance. He threw it in my face a lot, telling me that I should book some sessions with her, get fitter, get my hair done better and wear better clothes.' She sipped the last of the wine. 'I ashamedly prejudged her until that night. I could see she was nervous and I could see that she was so relieved she hadn't picked Richard or Steven. When she nodded at Noah, I was happy for her but Noah's wife Jade looked mortified that she'd ended up with Aimee's Rhys. Anyway, off they all went. I went with Richard, Steven tootled off with Maggie. I was so happy he'd been disappointed, but that's another story. After it was over, I came back in my house and had a shower. That's all I can tell you.'

'What time was that?'

She shrugged and sipped her wine. 'I have no idea.'

'Where's Steven now? Does he live with you?'

'Yes, but he comes and goes as he pleases and he still has the tenancy on his flat. He goes there when we argue. If I ever dare ask him where he's going he just accuses me of being controlling. I can pass a message onto him when he answers my calls or comes here.'

Gina picked up the list and passed it to Jacob. 'Did he come home after the party?'

'I didn't see him. I think he must have gone back to his flat.'

Jacob folded the list, placed it in his notebook and smiled. 'Thank you, Dawn. You've been really helpful. We'll need to know the address of his flat too.'

Gina wrote down the number of the station on a piece of paper and tore it from her notebook. She'd normally leave her card, but not this time. 'Please tell Steven to get in touch with us if in the meantime he comes back here. Is he at work?'

'No, just out. He doesn't work at the moment. He got sacked from his last temp job.'

Nothing had changed. The Steven she knew then was still the same Steven. Gina knew he latched onto women, used them for as long as he could get away with and then moved onto the next.

As they left the house and headed towards the car, Gina spotted another text.

I'm a prize idiot. I'm sorry about the message earlier. I get it – totally. You don't want to see me again. Sorry. Rex. X.

'Come on, guv. We best get this list back to the station. So which name on the list did you recognise?'

'Steven,' she replied.

'Do you know him well?'

She released the handbrake and reversed off the drive. 'He's my dead husband's brother.' She let that information swim around her head for a while. The dead husband was dead because she'd pushed him down the stairs. She'd killed him and, since then, she'd been trying to forgive herself. She'd never forgive him for the pain he'd put her through though – ever. 'Give base a call and get someone over to his flat, if not, get them to keep checking back. We need to get his version of events.'

'Guv!' Jacob yelled out as Gina kept reversing, narrowly missing a van that had turned into the road. The driver slammed on his horn as Gina slammed on the brakes, gripping the steering wheel. 'Didn't you see it coming?'

'I just missed it, sorry. Are you okay?'

'Yes, all good. He was whizzing around too fast anyway. Back to the station or do we grab lunch?'

'Lunch is for wimps. Let's get back and we can eat vending machine food like real detectives.' She plastered on a fake smile as she drove, hiding her worry that Briggs may remove her from the case. Why did Steven have to be on the list? She silently swore under her breath as they headed back.

CHAPTER TWENTY

Her finger hovered over the delete button as she contemplated what to do about the text she'd received. She'd been harsh with Rex. Maybe just another meetup as friends would be fun, no funny business, just a drink. The thought of going back to her house alone that night sent a shudder through her body. She was stronger than she'd ever been. She'd dated other men recently and she'd had an okay-ish time with Rex. She needed to make an effort or she'd end up as needy as Dawn or worse; as needy as she once was all those years ago with Terry.

Briggs walked into her office without knocking. She placed the phone, face down on her desk. Her previous lover standing in front of her while she was thinking about her most recent one-night stand. He filled her office with the smell of his aftershave, a smell she'd enjoyed on her pillows in a past life. Sadness was etched around his eyes. She knew he'd been dating. Since his brief fling with Annie in Corporate Communications, there had been a couple of others. He'd been seen at the cinema with a woman and out at a restaurant with another. Was he hopping around like her, trying to find a connection with another person, never finding success? In another life, they'd have been the perfect couple but in this life, they were both in a serious committed relationship with the job, one in a superior position to the other. Soon realising that they couldn't have both, they'd settled for awkward friendship.

'You know one of the witnesses then?'

She nodded and sat back, her gaze catching his. 'Yes, Steven. He's my ex-brother-in-law.'

'As it stands, I want you on the case. You're a brilliant detective and I know you need to immerse yourself into it from the core. I don't want you to interview him though, everyone else, yes, him, no. Let the others do it. You can watch from behind the mirror but that's it. Are we clear on that?'

'Yes, sir. Thank you.'

He shrugged his shoulders. 'What for?'

'For keeping me on the case. You could have taken me off.'

'I trust you not to compromise this investigation. You're my best detective and I know you won't let me down. Was he around when—' He shook his head. 'I shouldn't have asked.'

Gina felt a familiar pressure building up in her forehead. 'It's okay. You want to make sure I'm up to it, I understand. He was around and he knows all about me, about my past, about my relationship with his brother. He stood by and watched while he beat me, even encouraged it. He is a sadist, a complete piece of shit but as you said, it won't be me who interviews him.'

'I'm here you know, if you need to talk.'

She forced a smile as her heart pounded. Now was not the time for a chat about all the bad things that had happened in her past, and she definitely wouldn't discuss the memories that damn party had conjured up. *Please leave,* she thought, but he was still standing there, fixed to the floor, waiting for her reply.

'I think, given the circumstances, I will be Senior Investigating Officer on this case. I'm happy for you to do all that you normally do but run things by me, especially when it comes to Steven. You can run with forensics though. Whatever you need, I approve.'

'Thank you, sir.' She knew being SIO would be out of the question now that Steven was involved. 'Anyway, how's things with you?'

'Okay, you know. And you?'

'Okay too.' They both knew the other had been dating but neither person was going to ask. An uncomfortable silence filled the air. Images of him making love to her on her living room floor flashed through her mind and her stomach flipped. For a moment, she was sure he could see what she was thinking. She looked away. 'I'm trying to get out a bit more.'

He nodded and smiled as he left. That was it. That was all he was leaving her with. A nod and a smile.

She grabbed the phone and dialled the extension for the incident room. 'Wyre, can you investigate a website called Swap Fun, maybe set up a fake profile and look into it a little. Check out the list of witnesses and get a flavour of what they're about.'

'Will do, guv.'

'Has anyone found Steven Smithson yet?'

'No, guv, uniform dropped by his flat and left a card. Nothing so far.'

Briggs's words ran through her mind. *I'm here if you need to talk.* Maybe he meant well or maybe he just wanted her to make the same mistakes again and fall back into his arms, picking up where their secret relationship had left off. He wanted her to get bored with unfulfilling dates, to live a lonely life working at her kitchen table with only her cat, Ebony, for company. That wasn't going to happen even though she often fantasised about being with him again, if only for the odd night. Fantasies were for teenagers and she wouldn't be seduced into ruining her career, all to fulfil her silly fantasies. She didn't need to talk. She needed to get out and forget him. She pressed send on the message to Rex that she'd typed out just before Briggs had knocked. She had to get him out of her head.

CHAPTER TWENTY-ONE

'Another tequila?' Rex called as he ordered at the bar. He pulled his casual checked shirt down over his belly as he waited for her answer.

Gina giggled as she shook her head. 'I have work early in the morning and I can't afford to turn up with a hangover.'

He burst into laughter. 'I think the hangover is already a given.'

'I'll have a coffee.' He nodded and continued speaking to the young barman.

The pub in Stratford-upon-Avon had been a good call. It was warm and inviting, busy but not crowded and the garden had a lovely view of the river. She glanced out of the window, taking in the lights that reflected in the shimmering water. She turned her head and smiled. The warmth of the wall lights coursed through Gina's veins, or was it the tequila? As midnight drew ever closer, people left and the place really was thinning out. A bell rang, calling last orders.

'Right, your turn. Ideal night of passion.' He placed a wedge of lime in his mouth and pulled a funny face.

'We're not still playing this game, are we?' Gina stared at him before bursting into fits of laughter. She daren't tell him it involved someone else, Briggs. He knew exactly how to turn her on. 'I don't have any set ideas.'

He pulled the lime from his teeth and slammed the shot down his gullet. She began sipping the hot coffee in the hope of sobering a little. 'Cop out! You never thought of threesomes or booty calls?'

She almost spat her coffee out. 'Aren't you a booty call?'

He moved his eyebrows up and down and grinned. 'I hope so. Which phone box shall we head to? I've never done it in a phone box.'

She threw the tiny biscotti that had come with the coffee at him. 'In your dreams. That's so not on the cards.'

'I forgot, Inspector. I suppose it's more than your job is worth but wouldn't that add to the excitement? Yuck, I've had enough tequila. Right, I need a slash, then I suppose we best call a taxi. So, it's no to the booty call. You didn't dismiss the threesome idea. You're a dark horse, Gina. Back to yours?' He hurried towards the men's room, not giving her a chance to answer.

The warm fuzziness seeped out of her like an Arctic blast. He was not coming back to her place. She'd made it clear that having a laugh as friends had been her only intention. She shook her head as she thought of the evening and how it had developed from general conversation to flirtation. Again, she'd totally given him the wrong impression.

His words swam around her head, propelling her back to the night Terry had brought home a prostitute and held a knife to her throat. The look in his eyes had said, *do as I tell you or you're in for it.* She closed her eyes as she recalled the night she was trying so hard to forget.

'That's better. Did you call a taxi?' Rex said as he wiped his damp hands on his jeans.

Gina opened her eyes and wiped the tear that had slid down her cheek. That particular memory had been buried for such a long time. Now, it was back with a vengeance.

'Dryer didn't work, I didn't pee on my hands, if that's what you were thinking.'

She forced a smile. 'I've called two taxis, one for you and one for me. Oh look, mine's just arrived.' She finished her lukewarm coffee and put her jacket on, fighting with her drunken jellied legs as she walked towards the taxi driver. Her instinct had been right about Rex. He wasn't right for her and he didn't really want to be just friends. She held a hand up to him, waving as she left, not once looking back. He'd presumed wrongly when he thought he was going back with her. As she opened the door to the taxi and got in, a flood of tears filled her burning red cheeks.

She'd never eradicate the memory of that night and what happened next. She thought of Jade Ashmore and Dawn Brown. Had they been pressured into things they didn't want to do? Maybe Steven, like Terry, had brought Dawn a few surprises home and maybe she just wanted to forget. Steven, like Terry, wasn't the type to take no for an answer. She suddenly felt sick. Did Steven know about that night and would he twist it and use it to shame her over the course of the case? She swallowed. She wasn't going to throw up, not tonight.

'Where to?' the driver asked as he reset the meter, ignoring her tears.

CHAPTER TWENTY-TWO

Wednesday, 8 May 2019

I just can't sleep. I've had a little drink, tried a few deep breathing exercises of which I know Aimee's a fan, but they didn't work on me. Aimee with two e's. I even love the way she spells her name, it's so… her. I thought it wasn't real, the name, but it is. That is how it's spelled on the electoral register. I like her parents, they created a real individual.

I needed to see her. It's way past midnight, one, maybe two in the morning. Who knows? Who cares? I certainly don't. That's why I'm standing knee deep in the tangled shrubbery at the back of her house.

She's given up pacing and staring at her phone. The main light in the bedroom, flashes on and she stares out of the window. I hold up my phone and take a sneaky photo through the gap in the fence. Another photo of the most beautiful girl I know.

Standing in darkness, I remain still, hoping that she won't look my way. I doubt she'll see me. I've been there in plain daylight, right in front of her and she's failed to acknowledge my existence. *One day, my darling, one day.* I know exactly how to charm a woman, it's tried and tested. I also love that you don't mind sharing as I'm not an exclusive kind of guy. But, when I saw your profile, I knew you were more special than the rest.

I step back a little further as she steps forward, inquisitively searching for any sign of life. *Don't be scared, my lovely. Everything will all work out fine.* She places a hand on the window and stares out as she cries.

I remove what's left of the tiny spliff from my pocket and place it between my lips. As she closes the curtains, I light up, inhaling the relaxing drug. I feel the muscles around my mouth relaxing into a gentle smile.

Now, I'm ready for bed but there's something I must do first. *Goodnight, my sweetness. Sleep tight and dream lovely things.*

CHAPTER TWENTY-THREE

The tight room swelled and contracted, like a beating heart, trapping her deep in its central cavity. Ba-boom, ba-boom, ba-boom.

'You can do better than that, my little flower,' Terry yelled as the knife glinted in the candlelight.

'Please, Terry, no. Please.'

He leaned over from his chair, knife tip pointing at her chin.

Walls closed in. Redness filled her closed eyelids as the sharpness of the knife tickled her ribs.

From the cold stone floor, she prised an eye open.

Darkness, nothing but the blackest darkness surrounded her. She reached out into the nothingness. Screaming – it was almost like the atmosphere was absorbing the sound. She should hear her gasping breaths and chattering teeth – nothing.

Screaming and screaming but no one can hear, no one ever heard her screams.

Gina jolted up in bed and gasped for air as she tussled with her sweaty sheets. Her head pounding in unison with her hammering heartbeat. 'Leave me alone,' she yelled as she grappled for the lamp, tears filling her eyes, panic filling her heart. Flashes of the red pulsating room filled her mind and fuelled the panic.

Light – there was light. Hot, she needed to remove her soaking wet nightshirt. Nausea. She stumbled out of bed and ran across the landing to the bathroom, leaning over the sink and splashing her face with water. The rancid taste of tequila mixed with coffee at the back of her throat made her cough. Deep breaths. She was safe in her home and she was there alone. She splashed herself again and her heart rate began to calm. Images of her nightmare flashed through her fuzzy head. She removed a strand of sweaty hair from her mouth and staggered towards the shower and crawled in.

Standing under the showerhead, she sobbed hard, letting all the shame and fear roll down her cheeks, mingling with the cleanliness of the scorching hot water, flowing over her dirty memories. Slamming the flat of her hand over and over, against the steamed up tiles made her want to hit harder. She wanted to feel something, anything, even if it hurt. Just not fear. Anything was better than fear. The look in the prostitute's eyes as Terry had held a knife to both of them while humiliating them was back to haunt her. Just when she thought she'd sent these memories packing, they'd come back like an unwelcome visitor. Only this time, she wondered if this visitor would ever leave.

She felt along her ribs and touched the tiny scar where he'd jabbed the tip of the knife into her and she gagged with disgust. It had happened and it was real, regardless of how deeply she'd tried to bury it. What exactly did Steven know?

CHAPTER TWENTY-FOUR

As Diane padded down the stairs, she shivered. The cool breeze met her face as she reached the bottom. She pulled her thick dressing gown across her body and tied it up at the waist.

The hairs on the back of her neck began to prickle. Turning slowly, she felt her stomach drop. Light from the downstairs toilet filled the hallway. She would never have left the window wide open. 'Hello,' she whispered as she peered into the room. Toilet seat down, soap and towel untouched. Maybe she had left the window open or maybe it had blown open. The catch was loose anyway. It had never happened before but there could always be a first. She made a mental note to call the landlord. It would be the second time but she was sure his tardiness in getting it fixed was merely an oversight.

Her knees made a clicking noise as she leaned over the toilet to close the window.

She headed to the living room and opened the curtains. Greyness filled the sky. Leaning down, she turned her little heater on. It would take her all morning to warm up now, costing money she didn't have. She knew she only had several pounds left in the meter and it had to last. She glimpsed at the photo next to the television. She'd drifted off while thinking about Samantha and what might have happened to her. The smiling young woman looked into her eyes, just like she had always done in the past. Diane tried to imagine her voice but recalling it was becoming more difficult. She was slowly forgetting what her friend sounded like. She picked the photo up and gripped it to her chest, hugging it closely, just like she had done with Samantha on a few occasions.

She wiped her eyes as she headed towards the kitchen. Five in the morning. It was no time to get up. Maybe she'd get a cup of tea and go back to bed instead of sitting in the living room. Maybe she'd stay in bed, not get up all day. Finally she'd become sick of looking for reasons to get up. There were none. As she flicked on the kettle, something caught her eye.

There were many things on the kitchen table. Salt, pepper, sauce and vinegar. A few bills and some junk mail. But, she definitely hadn't left a photo on the table. She took a deep breath and began to shake as she crept closer. Someone had been in her house, she was right all along. While she had been in bed, struggling to sleep, an intruder had crept in through her bathroom window, walked across the hall and into the kitchen. She tried the back door. It was unlocked. She'd definitely locked the back door before going to bed.

She picked up the intruder's gift and held it in her hand, twiddling it between her thumb and index finger, shaking as tears slid down her cheeks. First the card and nail, and now this.

CHAPTER TWENTY-FIVE

Gina rubbed her tired eyes as she waved at Jacob in the distance. She watched as Keith came out of Diane's house with a couple of filled sample bags. Her disturbed sleep had left her feeling fuzzy and the few tequilas that she had drunk with Rex the night before were the cause of the nauseating throbbing that hammered through her head. Drops of rain dotted her face.

As her gritty eyes focused, she stared at the lock of hair through the clear evidence bag that Keith was cataloguing. 'What do we have?'

He flinched as he straightened out, his back once again playing up. 'Hair, blonde hair, about three inches in length. There are some roots but I hope there's enough to run the sample through the DNA database.'

'Check them against the fingernail that was sent in the card.'

'Will do.'

'Anything else?'

Jacob interrupted. 'We arrived not long before you. Diane reported that she woke up about five in the morning, came downstairs and noticed that her downstairs toilet window was open. Then she spotted a photo and a neat lock of hair in her kitchen. The intruder must have left them.' He did the buttons up on his anorak as he stepped back to stand under the front door canopy to avoid the heavy downpour that was building up.

'I've taken all the samples I need from the downstairs toilet and the kitchen. I'll get them straight over to the lab.' Keith dragged his thin long strands of grey hair that had flopped over straight back across his balding head.

'Thanks, Keith. Where's Diane?'

Jacob pointed towards the living room where the woman was being comforted by PC Smith. He smiled as Gina entered and stepped aside. The little heater hummed as it chugged out very little warmth. 'Hello, Diane.' Gina sat on the settee next to the frail-looking woman.

'There was someone in my house last night. I didn't even sleep well. How could I not have heard a thing?' The woman began to tremble. Gina passed her the toilet roll from the floor. Diane pulled a few sheets and wiped her eyes.

Gina shivered, knowing exactly how it felt to have someone sneaking around your home while you slept. In a previous case, that had happened to her. It took a long time for her to feel safe, for her home to feel untainted by a presence that wished to harm her. She knew exactly how Diane was feeling.

'I know this is hard, Diane, but can you talk me through what happened this morning?'

'I've already told the lovely PC here. I didn't hear or see any more,' she said as she blew her nose.

Gina nodded for PC Smith to follow her through to the kitchen.

'I'll be back in a moment.' The woman nodded and sipped on a cup of tea.

Smith picked up his hat from the chair and followed her through to the kitchen. 'As you can see, she's very distressed. When I got here about an hour ago, she was almost hysterical. We quickly determined that the intruder got in through the broken bathroom window. The catch is damaged. At night, she's been pulling the window closed but it hasn't been secured.' She followed Smith along the hallway until they stopped at the small room.

'The window's quite large and not too high up. I think I could easily fit through it. The intruder obviously came through, stepped on the toilet and bingo, they're in.'

'Any footsteps on the toilet seat?'

'No, ma'am,' Keith said as he passed by with Jacob. 'It looks like whoever broke in cleaned up after. There is nothing around the window frame, no traces of caught clothing, fingerprints, etcetera. Not even a hint of a footstep on the flooring or toilet seat. This person cleaned up after themselves.'

Her gaze travelled from the small water closet, along the hallway and towards the kitchen. She followed the intruder's steps until she reached the kitchen table. Junk mail filled the one side, charity appeal after charity appeal. Pamphlets with special offers on heated booties, magazine holders and impractical footstools were scattered everywhere, all brandishing a free gift to anyone who placed an order.

'The photo and lock of hair were found here.' Smith pointed at the chair that was closest to the door.

'So the intruder breaks in and leaves a photo of missing woman, Samantha Felton, along with what we're thinking might be a lock of her hair.'

'It matches to the colour in the photo, guv.'

Keith smiled as he came back into the kitchen. 'Right, I'm going to head back with the samples.'

'I need to see the photo,' Gina said.

He passed it to her, secure in its plastic cover, all labelled up.

She placed the photo down on the table and stared at it. A scene from a party, maybe. She saw the back of a man dancing with Samantha, one of her legs hitched up and wrapped around his waist, clearly laughing as she tried to grip him. 'I wonder who the man is, the one she's dancing with. More so, I wonder who took this photo.'

Maybe the photographer or her dancing partner was her cigarette smoking lover. Maybe the photographer was Derek. She squinted as she tried to look further into the detail of the grainy photo. It had to be a pub, social club or a bar. Burgundy material-covered chairs everywhere, dark wooden rectangular tables adorned with beer mats, drinks and empty packets of peanuts. Along the wall and behind a row of tables was a long bench. People laughed and drank as some danced and had fun. One face stood out. This woman wasn't laughing.

'There's something familiar about this woman.' Gina turned on the kitchen light and held the photo up. It was a few years ago. The woman was much slighter and her hair was longer but there was no mistaking her face. Gina dashed back to Diane in the living room with Jacob close behind. 'Do you recognise this woman, this one here?' She pointed at the photo.

'Sorry, I've never seen her before. Who's doing this to me, first the card and now they break into my home?'

Gina clenched her fist as she thought of what Diane was going through. Finding the intruder was key to solving everything. Someone out there was leaving a trail of breadcrumbs. Where they were leading, she had no idea. Why they were leaving them? That was a mystery too. She now knew for certain that Jade Ashmore's murder was related to Samantha Felton's disappearance. Why else would the intruder leave a photo of Samantha dating back to all those years ago, especially a photo showing Jade Ashmore watching her? Between the photo and the nail, she was more than certain.

Gina flinched as someone tapped on the door. Looking up, she saw a big smile emphasising two tiny dimples on PC Kapoor's face. 'I've just been doing door to door, guv, and look what I have,' she said, screeching in her Brummie accent. The tiny officer waved a disk in front of her face. 'One of the neighbours has CCTV covering both sides of his house after his shed was broken into a couple of months ago.'

'Well done, Kapoor.' Gina took the disk and placed it in her file. 'Carry on with the good work. If you see Smith, tell him I'm heading back to the station in a moment.'

Diane looked up with reddened eyes. 'Will I be able to see who broke into my home?'

'I really hope so. We're going to take this footage back to the station and give it a thorough examination.'

Gina's phone began to ring in her back pocket. After a struggle to remove it, she enthusiastically accepted the call. 'Bernard, what have you got? Excuse me a moment, Diane.' She left the room and stood outside. 'Fire away.'

He paused for a moment. Gina imagined him stroking his ever lengthening grey beard as he scanned his notes. He was looking more like Gandalf with every week. 'The fingernail that you sent in.'

'Yes?' Gina felt her heartbeat humming under her shirt.

'It is Jade Ashmore's nail. A little bit of skin was still attached to the nail and it is a definite match. It looks like our perpetrator trimmed it and painted it pink.'

CHAPTER TWENTY-SIX

'Coffee and walnut slice, guv? Made by Mrs O's fair hands.' O'Connor entered the incident room with an old biscuit tin full of cake.

'Smells lovely. That's breakfast sorted. Thank her for me.' She took a slice before he headed to his computer. Gina took a bite of the sugary sponge as she stared at the boards. 'Right, gather round,' Gina called as she slotted the disk into the computer. Wyre, Jacob and O'Connor headed over and filled the tiny space at the front of the room. As the computer whirred into action, Gina pressed play and the footage started. She fast forwarded to seven minutes past three in the morning. 'I've already had a brief look.' She pressed play.

They all watched as the grainy figure in a dark coat, hood up, scurried past the front of the house. As with a lot of domestic CCTV, they all knew it wasn't going to clearly identify their person. Gina paused the footage just before the figure went out of shot. 'We can see what I think is the outline of a white envelope. As for shape, I would say we are looking for a male. The coat is quite thick looking. He also appears to be wearing a small backpack.' Gina pointed to the small mass on the back of the figure. 'Keith has already examined the scene and taken samples. He also said that our perp had cleaned up well, no footprints on the toilet which was the entrance point, no fingerprints on the window or catches, again suggesting that gloves were worn. We are still waiting for results to come back on the hair sample.

Initial thoughts are that this belongs to Samantha Felton. The fingernail that was delivered to Diane's with the card had a bit of torn skin attached to it, even though our perp went through a lot of effort to clean it well. It is a positive match against Jade Ashmore. We have also confirmed that Jade's nail was painted in Samantha's favourite colour. Confusing, I know.'

Gina began to fast forward the footage. 'When does our perp leave?' Jacob asked.

'This isn't shown. I can only think that this person left in the other direction which matches what Diane said. Her back door was unlocked even though she locked it before going to bed. Smith and Kapoor have yet to find any further witnesses or CCTV, but I live in hope.'

Jacob took a seat at the main table and everyone else followed. Gina turned off the CCTV footage and joined them at the head of the table. 'Given that we now have a photo of Jade and Samantha together as well as a sample of Jade's nail turning up at Diane's, which happens to be painted in Samantha's favourite nail varnish colour, we are working on the premise that our intruder is responsible for Jade's murder and Samantha's disappearance. I want this person found. Follow up on everything, however small, and delve into all our partygoers' lives. Wyre?'

'Yes?' Wyre finished writing and looked up.

'How did you get on with researching the Swap Fun website?'

Wyre bit the end of her pen as she flicked back a few pages. 'I've created a profile and I've been trying to strike up conversation. I've had three pervy messages asking if I'm basically up for a booty call, an invite to a dogging event and two dick pics. As for the partner swap forums, I'm waiting to be accepted. I'm randomly joining in with the open threads, trying to gain their trust and hoping that it won't be long until they bite and let me in. I obviously haven't used a photo of my face when I set the account up. This won't seem odd as many people don't.'

Gina slid across the floor on the wheels of her chair and opened Wyre's Swap Fun account for all to see. The photo she'd used for her profile showed the back of her head while wearing a long blonde wig. She'd finished her creation off with a pair of sunglasses, sitting on her head. It clearly showed that her application to join the Cleevesford Swapper Forum was still pending. 'As soon as they let you in, call me. I want to know what these people get up to. You and O'Connor carry on with that and the processing of any information that Smith gets back to you with. Jacob?'

He looked up and nodded. 'Yes, guv?'

'We need to pay a visit to Maggie and Richard Leason. Find out their side of it all. So, finish your cake and get ready to leave.'

He began chomping on the cake that O'Connor had given to him. 'I'm ready when you are.' He wiped the crumbs from the side of his mouth as he swallowed the rest of the cake.

O'Connor kept flicking his pen lid, annoying Gina. In her mind she was reaching over and snatching it from him.

'Guv?' Nick the desk sergeant entered with a huge bunch of pink roses. The little diamantés in the centre of some of the buds glinted in the shaft of sunlight that escaped from the dark clouds.

The room went silent and everyone turned to see him place them on the table. 'They're for you, guv,' he said as he smiled and left the room.

'Ooh, who's the mystery man?' O'Connor asked as he dropped his pen lid on the table.

'There is no mystery man.' She walked over the other side of the room and pulled the card from the bunch of flowers, opening the envelope.

'Mystery woman?'

O'Connor was pushing it. She felt her shoulders stiffen as she opened the card. 'For the last time, there's no mystery anyone so button it and get to work on finding our murderer.'

He left the main table and headed back to his desk.

'Right, to Richard and Maggie Leason's then,' Jacob said as he slipped his jacket on. 'Nice flowers.'

'There is no mystery lover,' she said as her cheeks reddened. 'At least there isn't any more.' She grabbed the flowers and placed them upside down in the waste bin. As soon as she got into the car, she was going to message Rex. How dare he humiliate her by sending her flowers at work? She didn't work in an office or a shop, she was a senior detective, commanding respect from her team. Getting sent a bunch of pink flowers with a silly card containing only a love heart drawn in it, was nothing short of thoughtless. She had her doubts and now they had been confirmed. As she screwed the card up and threw it in the bin, Briggs walked through the door.

'I've just caught up with everything. Are you off out to interview the Leasons now?' Gina went to nod and stopped as she watched Briggs's gaze fall on the flowers. 'Are those flowers in the bin?'

Her neck prickled and her red face totally betrayed her cool calm voice. Briggs now knew she was dating. He also knew things weren't going well as she'd binned a bunch of flowers. He was a senior detective too, she couldn't fool him for a second. Her mind flashed back to the night she'd slept with Rex and her stomach turned.

'What a waste,' he said as he walked over to the boards and began examining all the information and photos. She could tell he was analysing the situation and didn't want her to see that he was. With a shaking hand, she grabbed her bag. In another life, she'd have liked to place a hand on his shoulder, for him to turn around and hold her tightly in his firm arms and kiss her. But that other life didn't exist and the situation was what it was.

She scanned the room. No one was looking at her any more. No doubt they were all wondering who had sent her flowers at work and they were probably all wondering why she'd thrown them in the bin. 'We're just going, sir. I'll update you later.' She leaned over and pulled the card back out of the bin and stuffed it into her pocket. She didn't want Briggs to get hold of it once she'd left.

'Right you are, Harte.' His disapproval stung. He couldn't even turn to look at her.

CHAPTER TWENTY-SEVEN

Gina wiped a spot of rain from her nose as they stood outside Maggie and Richard's end-of-terrace house. She glanced up at the old brickwork and the sign. *1 Lavender Lane – 1959.* What a totally opposite style of house to Dawn Brown's. The period house almost seemed dark with its tiny windows and old brown curtains that were still half drawn. She knocked again.

'They probably didn't hear,' Jacob said as he undid the zip on his jacket.

A sound came from the other side of the door as a curtain was swished across and the door unlocked.

'Mrs Leason?'

The woman nodded. 'Maggie, please.' From her notes, Gina knew that Maggie was forty-two and Richard was forty-five.

'Detective Inspector Harte and DS Driscoll. We spoke to you earlier.'

'Come in, Inspector,' she said as she looked at Jacob.

Gina grimaced as she inhaled the stale tobacco smoke filling the hallway. 'I'm DI Harte.' She knew she should have made it clearer. It had been a long time since someone had assumed that the senior colleague was the male she was with.

'Oh sorry. Come through.' The woman wrapped her navy cardigan across her body as she led them into the snug at the front of the house. Her short blonde hair, shaved to within an inch of its life, framed her bronzed skin and large brown eyes. She sniffed and wiped her nose. 'This is Richard.' She held her arm out.

The chubby man stood as she entered the lamp-lit room, his crew cut just a little shorter than his wife's hair. 'Take a seat. Can we get you anything?'

The roaring fire was almost hypnotic and far too warm for the spring day. The room was dark and the ceilings high. It was a cool house. She shook her head and Jacob copied. 'No, thank you. We need to speak about the other night, Sunday the fifth of May and the early hours of this Monday.'

They all sat. Gina and Jacob on the couch and Richard and Maggie on an armchair either side.

'We just went to Dawn's party and came home. We don't know anything apart from that.' Maggie nervously twiddled her fingers.

Jacob pulled his pad from his pocket and waited.

'We know about the party and we need to know exactly what happened that night. We know it wasn't just a run-of-the-mill party. Now you know what we know, what can you tell us about that night?'

Maggie cleared her throat and glanced over at Richard. She opened her mouth to speak then stopped.

It was going to be a long interview with their two witnesses. Gina could tell that they hadn't spoken to each other about that night, including who they went with and what they got up to. 'DS Driscoll, if you take Mr Leason into the kitchen, I'll speak with Maggie.'

'Of course, guv. Lead the way, Mr Leason.' The man caught his wife's eye and left the room with Jacob following.

As a fire crackled, a chunky log dropped on to the rest of the debris. Maggie leaned forward and began moving her attention to a loose thread on her cardigan.

'Maggie?' She looked up, swallowing as she met Gina's gaze. 'Tell me about that night. Where did you end up?'

She pulled a cigarette out. 'Can I smoke?'

Gina nodded. The more at ease the woman felt, the more she might tell her.

'I've started vaping but struggle to stay on the wagon when I'm stressed.' She lit the cigarette and sucked hard before exhaling a plume of smoke, creating a thick fog in the tiny room.

Gina knew her hair and clothes would stink after this visit. As soon as she finished up for the afternoon, she was heading home for a shower. 'Right, back to that night.'

Maggie crossed her short legs and leaned her elbow on her knee as she puffed once more. 'It may surprise you to know that I was really looking forward to that night. I get bored easily and Richard is willing, which makes it easier. I think being a little free in the bedroom is what has really kept us together all these years. We met Dawn and Steven for the first time that night. It was their first time but not ours. Anyway, we drank a bit and smoked until we'd had a chance to mingle with the other guests.' Maggie stared into the fireplace.

Gina also doubted that it was Steven's first time. Dawn's maybe. 'And then?' Gina flipped the page of her pad and waited for the woman to carry on.

'I was pretty blotto if I'm honest but it seemed early, not long after midnight, I'd say. When I got home, I just fell face down on to our bed, only being disturbed when Richard got in and I woke up in the morning. That's it.'

Gina was hoping she'd remember something that might be of use. 'Tell me what you do remember.'

'I remember my husband checking Aimee out, they were all checking Aimee out. Her profile picture on Swap Fun doesn't do her justice. I've never seen such a perfect-looking woman. I understood where they were coming from. I'm not into women but, to be fair, I'd have been happy if I'd ended up with Aimee. Anyway, Richard ended up with Dawn. We don't discuss what we did, that's part of the rules. All I know is he left with Dawn and I left with Steven.'

'Did you and Steven stay in Dawn's house?'

She shook her head. 'Dawn looks after her brother's house. He's apparently working abroad as a chef for the rest of the year so it was vacant. Steven had the key.'

Another location to look into. 'Where was this house?'

'Just on the next road. Fox Close. There was no one there but the house was warm and the lamps were already switched on. Dawn must have gone earlier to prepare the house. Steven was half-cut and lit up a spliff. I shouldn't have said that. Oh for heaven's sake. I'm such an idiot but I don't suppose you care about one silly little spliff. I think one was being passed around earlier that night too.'

Gina made a note. She already knew Steven had a love of weed. He'd always stank of it in the past and she doubted he'd changed his ways. 'You're not an idiot, this is really helpful. This is a murder investigation and you're doing really well.'

'Okay.' She stubbed the cigarette out in a chipped saucer. 'We were there about an hour, I think. I'd had a drag of his weed too and I was pretty out of things which is why I'm struggling to remember. I don't normally do weed. I've only tried it once when we had a weekend in Amsterdam. I don't know why I did it but I did. I was caught up in the moment and wanted to feel good. I fancied Steven, I'll admit that much.' The woman pulled the thread on her cardigan and it began to unravel.

Gina couldn't understand how any woman could find Steven attractive.

'It wasn't good. He pushed me around a little. I don't know if I gave the impression of wanting it rough or whether it was something I did. I mean, I was a willing partner. I thought he would've tried to be a bit more considerate. I tried to tell him what I needed but it fell on deaf ears. Before I knew it, he'd finished. He slapped me on the arse and threw my jeans at me. I'd really like to erase the experience from my mind.' She shuddered.

'Rough?' Gina wondered if he'd crossed any boundaries.

'He didn't hurt me, he just grabbed me and moved me around a little abruptly. After we finished, he casually said he was thinking of Aimee while we were doing it and laughed. I remember feeling my stomach lurch. The weed and wine, and his comment, were swimming around my system and I found the whole experience a little surreal. I threw up in the sink. After I'd cleaned up a bit, I looked up and he'd gone. I grabbed my things, left out the front door and hurried straight home. I had a glass of water and fell into bed. As I said, Richard came home soon after.'

Sweat began to form at Gina's brow. The tiny room was now filled with smoke and heat from the fire and the woman's cigarette. 'What time did he return?'

She shrugged her shoulders. 'I was half stoned, nauseous and a bit drunk. Like I said before, I think it was a little after twelve. We were all around the local area. After the deed, it wouldn't have taken long to get home. He got into bed, snuggled against me for a few minutes and then I remember him snoring, loudly. I did look at the radio clock around then, I think it was about twenty past twelve. Next thing I remember is morning. That's when we heard on the radio that someone had been murdered. We didn't know it was Jade at that point but word gets around quick. I went on Facebook and then we knew it was her.'

'Is there anything else you can remember?'

'No. That's it. We really are sorry for Noah. She, Jade, didn't say much. She looked nervous but she seemed like a nice woman. She mentioned their daughter and seemed quite gently-spoken. It was a shock, you know?'

Gina nodded and closed her notepad. She hoped Jacob would hurry so that they could compare notes. She gazed at Maggie, wondering if there was any way she could have overpowered

Jade. Their witness at the scene hadn't described the perpetrator as short. Maggie looked to be around five feet tall.

A few moments later, Jacob re-entered the room. She could see that he was bursting to compare notes.

CHAPTER TWENTY-EIGHT

Thursday, 9 May 2019

Gina swigged the rest of her takeaway coffee. After another disturbed night's sleep, she needed all the help she could get. She'd sent that final text to Rex and heard nothing back so far. Still seething, she stared at the bin. The flowers would be long gone now. The cleaner would have dumped them in the industrial bin at the back of the building. Gone forever, just like Rex. 'Right, team, thank you for being here so bright and early. I know you're all working your socks off but it's important that we discuss findings to date.' She briefly stared at the crime scene photo of Jade Ashmore. Broken nose, half of her face caved in, the sheer brutality of the attack imprinted in her mind. She swallowed and turned to face the team. She stroked her own hairline, remembering where Terry had once split her head open, just under the fringe that she'd grown.

'We've had to release a further statement as Lyndsey Saunders of the *Warwickshire Herald* kept calling Annie. Corporate Communications have issued a holding statement for the time being, simply saying that we wouldn't be answering any questions and that we'd follow up with a more detailed press conference in due course. We offered our assurance to the public that we are working solid on this. I don't want the press getting hold of any details for the usual reasons.' Gina sighed. 'I don't want anything released about the link to Samantha as yet. The fingernail, the nature of Jade's injuries, they have to remain under wraps. All the public need to know is that we are treating her death as a murder enquiry and to be extra vigilant. We'll keep appealing for witnesses.'

Nodding his approval, Briggs gave her a slight smile. Maybe she'd been overthinking what he'd thought of the flowers. 'Right, I'm taking it that you've all updated yourselves with the case so far. Everything on the system is up to date, the board is up to date and we all have our tasks in hand. Is that correct?'

Jacob, Wyre and O'Connor nodded. O'Connor bit a chunk of nail from the corner of his thumb and flicked it onto the floor. A new habit of his that was starting to grate on Gina. Between the nail biting, pen flicking and chair sliding, he was fast becoming her number one annoyance. He started rolling back and forth on his chair.

Gina stared at him.

'Annoying, guv?'

'Just a bit.' He slid the chair under the main table for the last time and waited for her to begin.

'Jacob, can you give us a brief overview of what Richard Leason said when you spoke to him?'

He rubbed his eyes and read his notes. 'Yes, after finding out he was paired with Dawn, they went out to the caravan on Dawn's drive. He didn't go into great detail about what they got up to but he did say he felt there was someone watching them. He suspected that Dawn wasn't too into him and he openly admitted he was unhappy to have been paired with Dawn. They had a brief but awkward encounter and then he left. He said he went straight home and got into bed with Maggie. He also mentioned that he and Dawn had a few words, and that Dawn was drunk and got quite aggressive. With the thought that someone might be watching them and Dawn's odd behaviour, he felt like he just needed to get home. He didn't clock the time and said that he'd had a fair bit to drink himself.'

Gina glanced at the map on the wall. 'Every one of these people live close by to each other and to where the incident took place. Our witness remembers hearing a car leaving the scene. From what I've read and heard, no one took a car with them to Dawn Brown's house. That doesn't mean that the murderer didn't take the short journey back home to get their car, before or after attacking Jade. They all lived really close to each other. I'm keeping an open mind on that one.' Gina's thoughts wandered back to Steven. Could he have finished up and then hurried back to the house to see what was going on? She knew he drove. Could he have got in his car and gone looking for Jade? After all, he'd know all the locations that went into the glass as he and Dawn had prepared them. Had they all spoken about the locations in conversation that night? 'Moving onto our visit with the Leasons yesterday, that's Richard and Maggie. Just to clarify, we can now confirm that all parties attended this partner-swapping party which took place at Dawn Brown's house.' She pointed at the board. 'We have Jade and Rhys who went off to Jade's summerhouse, Aimee and Noah went to the woods, Dawn and Richard went to Dawn's caravan and, lastly, Maggie and Steven went to Dawn's brother's house. Can you write all that on the board?'

Wyre took the pen from her and began noting that information in a list so that everyone could see it presented in some sort of logical order.

'It's like a game of Cluedo. Partner A went off with partner B in the wherever, then our unknown murderer killed Jade Ashmore with the mallet. That's one piece of information we are now certain of. After speaking with Bernard again this morning, it is absolutely confirmed. A small fleck of wood was also found embedded in Jade's skull. Jade was hit repeatedly over one side of her face with the mallet. We can't rule out other suspects. Jade was wandering around the estate and we think she was heading back to the party to look for her husband, Noah. We can't rule out that Rhys followed her back, he is still our main suspect and he is still missing. We can't rule out Colin Wray, Jade's neighbour, the one Tiffany the babysitter described as creepy. Did he see her leave and follow her? The perp could have murdered Jade and still have had time to come back for their car. I can't emphasise enough how closely they all live to each other and the crime scene.' She gazed up at the map. The pins pointing out the crime scene and where everyone claims to have been at the time, were almost upon each other.

'And the link to Samantha Felton?' Wyre said as she turned her engagement ring around her finger.

'That too. We need to investigate further. There is a clear link between them. We have the photo of Jade attending the same party as Samantha several years ago. Someone broke into Diane's house and planted it for us to find. Who took the photo and how do these women know each other? Is the person who planted the photo the murderer? We can't ask Jade now.'

The landline rang. Wyre walked over and picked up the phone. 'It's Bernard, guv. He has the results back on the hair sample. And that's not all, a cigarette packet found at the back of Diane's house has come up trumps.'

CHAPTER TWENTY-NINE

Next door's Alsatian had been pounding against the back fence for at least half an hour. Aimee wished he'd just take the dog in. The old man called out. 'Barney, shut it, you little shit.'

Aimee grabbed her phone. There were still no messages or calls from Rhys. Her lodger Nicole had tried to call five times from Tenerife and had eventually left a message. She swallowed, hoping that the calls would just stop and that Rhys would come home. Prime suspect in a murder investigation – that was how Detective Inspector Harte had described him. She twiddled the contact card between her fingers, wondering where their investigation was going.

Over the past year her business had been doing really well. She'd gained a local soap opera star and a high-profile music producer on her books. If they found out what she'd been up to, would they still hire her to keep them in shape? All the work she'd put in could be ruined overnight. She'd have to take a job working at a gym again, that's if they'd even have her. Along with the large sum her granny had left in her will, her high profile clients were the ones who had almost helped her pay the final chunk off her mortgage this year and that financial security could all be replaced by another minimum wage job. She imagined the headlines. *Local personal trainer to the celebs in wife-swapping murder scandal.* She yelled out as she screwed up Gina Harte's card and threw it at the windowsill.

'I hate you!' she called as she kicked the door. The more she thought about it, the more she convinced herself that he was capable of murder. He was rough, he was dominant and he did always seem to get his own way. It was his way or no way in their relationship, that's what Nicole had said.

The dog barked and barked. She flung the door open and yelled. 'Shut up.' It made no difference.

She grabbed her phone as soon as it buzzed. 'Rhys?'

'Aimee.'

'Oh, Nicole.'

Her lodger and best friend remained silent for a second. Aimee knew Nicole could tell that she was holding something back. 'I've been trying to call you. I saw on Facebook about that woman being killed. It's just a few roads away. I was a bit worried and when you weren't answering, I thought something had happened. Are you okay?'

She stared out of the kitchen window, through the smeary glass panes. 'I'm fine.'

'You can't fool me, Aimee. How long have we known each other?'

Her friend was right. As she began to speak, the whole story spilled out and tears soon followed.

'Look, just calm down. You've done nothing wrong. You're too good for that loser. Promise me you'll keep away from him if he comes sniffing around. He could be dangerous.'

She wiped her teary face. 'I know, but murder. I'm not sure. I just don't know any more. Urgh, I'm so confused. I want it all to go away. When are you back?'

'Just hold tight. I'm back tonight and we'll get through this together, I promise.'

A smile escaped from Aimee's mouth. Nicole was right, they'd sort it out together when she got home. She was also right about Rhys. He'd been toxic for her and her best friend had noticed the change in her since they'd been together.

Rhys suddenly burst through the door, knocking Aimee's slight frame flying against the far wall. The phone flew from her hand and slid across the kitchen floor. 'Dammit. I didn't know you were behind the door. Are you okay?'

He went to stroke the arm she was rubbing. 'Get off me.' She pushed him away from her as she struggled to stand.

'If that's the way you feel. You know I didn't do anything?' She felt her heart slamming in her chest.

'Help me out here. I need some money. I didn't eat yesterday.' He ran his shaky fingers through his greasy, tangled shoulder-length hair. Eyes red and puffy. A couple of days' worth of stubble.

'Aimee, Aimee. Tell me you're okay.' Nicole's voice filled the room.

'I'm okay, Nicole. I'll call you back in a bit,' she shouted.

'Don't hang up—' Rhys picked up the phone and ended the call.

'Shit,' he said as he began to pace back and forth. He stopped and began rummaging through the kitchen cupboard, snatching a loaf of bread, peanut butter and a few biscuits. 'Money!' The cupboard door he slammed began to lean on its hinges, threatening to fall off.

She sobbed as she rubbed her arm. Pain throbbing from her elbow to her shoulder.

He began opening the kitchen drawers, throwing out the sticky tape, a pack of tea-light candles, some leftover fly strips. 'Where is it?'

He was referring to her money tin where she kept the cash that some of her clients paid. Eventually he reached the correct drawer and smiled as he pulled it out. He snatched the lid off and pulled a roll of ten pound notes out. She really wished she'd been a little more on the ball when it came to banking now. 'Please, Rhys, I need that money.'

'More than me? Look at me.' He placed the wad of cash into his back pockets and kneeled before her, wiping her tears with his fingertips.

He leaned in to gently kiss her. She turned away. More than anything, she needed her life back along with her old self. She needed to go out with Nicole and feel free again. 'Don't come back. I want you to go. Someone saw you pushing Jade around and I know you.'

'You know nothing, you stupid bitch.' He gripped the bottom of her chin in a vice-like grip. Her fear-filled gaze met his until his sinister grin sent a shiver through her body. He began to laugh, releasing her as he straightened her top. For a moment, her vision began to cloud and she was sure she might faint as she held her breath.

Her phone began to buzz along the kitchen floor and a message flashed up.

I'm calling the police.

Nicole had saved her. Rhys stepped backwards across the floor, maintaining eye contact with her until he ran outside. She heard the gate slam closed and the dog barking. Sobbing, she grabbed her phone and called Nicole straight back. 'Don't call the police. I'm okay. I'll see you when you get home.' She ended the call and flinched as she made her way to the kitchen sink and ran the tap, splashing cold water over her sweaty face. She patted her face with a tea towel and sobbed as she felt her face, sure that there would be imprints of Rhys's fingers embedded into her skin.

She stared out of the window at the banging gate, then caught sight of a couple of footprints that had dried in the mud. Rhys had been there watching her, of that she was sure. When she was in bed, in the shower, there had been someone else there. She felt it.

CHAPTER THIRTY

'Good morning. I know you all have the forensics report in front of you.' Gina pulled out a copy of the bound report and held it up. O'Connor flicked through the pages loudly and Wyre cast her gaze over the main page. Jacob grabbed a copy and began flicking through the pages. Keith in forensics quickly nibbled the rest of his apple. He flung the core into the bin and scratched his head.

'I wasn't expecting this at all, guv,' Jacob replied as he popped a stick of gum in his mouth.

She turned to face the board, pointing to the additional information. 'As you can see, the hair that was left at Diane's house is the same colour as Samantha's when she went missing. There were no follicles in which to obtain a DNA sample. This was a neatly trimmed lock that had been carefully preserved.'

Keith half-raised his hand and smiled. 'We can confirm that it is real hair. What really has sealed the link when it comes to the disappearance of Samantha Felton and the murder of Jade Ashmore is the cigarette packet we found at the back of Diane's house.'

Wyre's face was slightly screwed up as she contemplated the evidence in front of her. 'The person who broke into Diane's is the one who killed Jade?'

Keith picked a bit of apple skin from his teeth. 'Got ya!' He smiled. 'Yes, it's looking that way. For those who haven't read that far. The cigarette packet found outside Diane's was covered in Jade Ashmore's prints.'

Gina interjected. 'All the cigarettes were gone suggesting that the perpetrator finished off or removed any remaining cigarettes in the packet before discarding it.' She nodded at Keith, gesturing for him to continue.

'There were several other partial prints on the packet, but these could have been added during the process of packing, distributing and selling them. All prints have been lifted, logged and checked, but the only prints we can actually identify are Jade's. One of the others could well be our murderer's, we just have nothing on the database that is a match.'

Gina glanced at the board. 'Have we matched the prints against any that were found in Diane's house?'

'No matches, I'm afraid. The entrance through the bathroom window was dusted, as were many other parts of the house. None of the prints found in her house match those on the cigarette packet. As always, we have them on file and we couldn't identify anyone from those prints either. They were not on our database.'

Gina sat at the head of the table. 'From the CCTV, it looked like our perp was wearing gloves anyway. Thanks for coming, Keith.'

'Glad to be of help.'

Wyre's screen flashed with a message. She left the table and headed to her computer as they continued to speak.

'Anything else? You've all read the witness statements, I assume?'

Everyone nodded.

'And you all know what you're doing next?'

'Guv?' Wyre headed back to the table.

Gina arched her brows as she waited for Wyre to speak.

'I've just checked two messages. Firstly, we have Steven Smithson coming in for a voluntary interview this morning. Dawn made the call and said he'd be happy to help.' Gina felt a familiar shiver flash across the back of her neck as the colour drained from her face. Briggs had said she wouldn't be able to interview him.

'Make sure you use interview room one.' At the very least, she'd be able to watch him through the mirrored glass. 'And the second message?'

'We've had a call from Diane today. She left a message saying that she remembered something else about the time Samantha Felton went missing. Samantha's mystery lover was a weed smoker. She said she just remembered that Samantha smelt of weed back then. I suppose it was a long time ago and she's not in the best of health.' As Wyre relayed the latest piece of information, the room tilted as Gina almost lost her balance.

'Here. Sit down, guv.'

Jacob pushed a chair behind her and she sat. 'I'm okay. I just need some breakfast.' She smiled at him and he seemed to take that as an excuse for the minor level of shock she was feeling. Steven could well be their murderer and she'd never be the one to make the arrest. Gina's gaze slowly left the table until she met Wyre's. 'And Steven and Maggie were smoking weed when they were together!'

CHAPTER THIRTY-ONE

'You okay?' Briggs asked, the plastic chair creaking as he leaned back.

'Why wouldn't I be?' Gina instantly regretted giving such a short, sharp response.

'You forget how well I know you and I know how hard you're finding this.' Briggs didn't even know a smidgen of what she was hiding. He gave her a sympathetic look as he stared through the glass at her ex-brother-in-law. Steven stared back as if he knew she was watching. 'He doesn't know you're here.'

She felt her fists clenching. Not only was he encouraging of the abuse that Terry had inflicted upon her when he was alive, he was now in the middle of her investigation and had taken her senior investigating officer title away from her. She now had to run everything through Briggs. All of it – his fault. And now he was a suspect, up there with Rhys Keegan. Her mind reeled, could Steven be the brains behind it all and could Rhys be a part of it? So far, she'd failed to link them until the night of the party. There had to be more to it all and she was going to unearth the sorry lot.

'Look, being this uptight won't help.' Briggs smiled.

'I'm not uptight.' They may well have been lovers in the past, but he didn't know everything about her. The small room they were sitting in suddenly felt even more confined. Her elbow bumped into his as she adjusted her seating position.

'Harte, your knuckles are white.'

She returned his comment with a wide false smile and loosened her grip. 'And you know exactly why. I just want to be in there, doing my job.'

'And you are. Your job is to gather enough evidence to convict a murderer. Your job isn't to hinder the case with the fact that you've had some involvement on a personal level with this witness.'

Witness? That was a joke. He was guilty of a lot and Gina knew he had a hidden dark side. 'You're right, sir.' She took a sip of cold water as she stared through the glass.

'Here we go,' Briggs said as he folded his arms and stared through the glass.

Wyre and Jacob entered, sitting opposite Steven. He instantly grinned at Wyre as he unzipped his leather jacket, eyeing her up and down. Gina knew he would put his all into making her feel uncomfortable and she also knew Wyre was too good to fall for his nonsense. He linked his two hands behind his neck and leaned back in the chair as Wyre prepared. His T-shirt rode up exposing his hairy belly and a belt. Gina's heart began to pound as she spotted the buckle, the thick, solid square-covered mechanisms that fixed onto brown leather. It was exactly the same as what Terry used to wear, the same style that had been imprinted on her thighs for days after he'd attacked her.

She placed her fingers in her cup of water and flicked a little on her face as Briggs watched what was going on through the screen. He couldn't see her having any kind of meltdown. He'd been watching her too closely and she couldn't let him pull her off the case on health grounds. It had taken all she had over the past few months to conceal the depths of her anxiety but she had so far succeeded. High-functioning she knew everyone called it. She would continue to function highly and do her work.

Grounding – the counsellor told her to use this technique when the overwhelming feelings of anxiety started up. She felt the desk in front of her, it was smooth and cool. Her fingers brushed the side and underneath, hard chewing gum – gross. She inhaled and the mustiness of the room made her feel slightly queasy, but at least it was real. The little room was always musty regardless of how often it was cleaned. She listened to the voices as Wyre finished with the opening formalities.

'So, go over what happened that night?' Wyre said.

Steven removed his hands from behind his head and leaned forward. 'Oh it was a good one. It would have been better if I hadn't have ended up with that munter, Maggie. Stupid bitch looks like a man. There was only one woman there that every man wanted to stick it in and that was Aimee.'

Gina wondered if Wyre would try to get the interview back on course but she hoped Wyre and Jacob would allow him to continue speaking freely, hoping it wouldn't take long for him to hang himself. She loved their strategy, Wyre leading. She knew they'd both be able to see his character as they entered the interview room. She trusted her team to be vigilant.

Steven shrugged. 'You can't win 'em all. That dick, Noah, with his preened pretty-boy hair and Ken doll body ended up being the lucky one. When I left with the dog, we walked to Malcolm's house, that's Dawn's brother. We lit up a spliff and she looked a bit ill. Didn't stop her though. Stupid cow was gagging for it.' He ran his tongue across his teeth. 'The women are the worst for this you know. They pretend to be all, oh we're so prim and ooh we're not sure, but they love it. Dawn was like that when we met but boy is she a dirty bitch now, you should see her. Maggie was the same too, gagging for it by the time we got to the house. Anyway, we did it against his worktop – slam, slam, slam and she was loving it. When we finished she chucked up in the sink and I left. Couldn't be bothered dealing with some sick bint who couldn't hold her wine.'

Maybe the thought of being with you made her sick. Gina thought that was more the case.

'What happened after you left Maggie Leason?'

Well played again. Steven was trying so hard to get a reaction out of Jacob or Wyre but neither were giving him anything to be joyous about. He was certainly losing the attention battle that he'd instigated.

'It was late, I don't remember what time. I staggered home. I'd had a few draws on the old spliff. I was all warm, post-coital and tired, you know how that feels, Detective?'

Wyre stared back at him, waiting for him to continue.

'Bundle of laughs you lot are,' he said as he smiled at Jacob, seeking some male support.

'Just answer the question,' Wyre said in a firm tone.

'Ooh, angry, are we?' Silence filled the room. Steven sighed. 'I just walked home and went to bed.'

Wyre glanced at the file in front of her. 'Did you go through Gilmore Close?'

'Why would I go that way?' He began leaning back on the chair, front legs repetitively lifting off the carpet tiles, a sickly grin across his face.

'Fresh air to sober up, looking for someone, meeting someone? You tell me.'

He shook his head as he laughed. 'You ain't pinning that on me. No, I didn't go that way.'

'You knew where all the locations were, didn't you?'

'Me and the rest of 'em. We told everyone about all the different locations during the course of the evening. They weren't a secret.'

Gina slammed her fist on the desk as she wondered why none of the witnesses had mentioned that fact. That blew her theory out. If they all knew the locations, they'd all know where Jade could have been. Given that all the locations were as close by as all their addresses, she'd be easy to find in a relatively short period of time.

'Calm it, Harte!' Briggs said as he offered her a mint.

Reluctantly, she took one, unwrapped it and popped it in her mouth.

Wyre continued for a few minutes as Gina sucked on the mint, watching intently. Steven tapped his slightly stubbly chin with his index finger as he grinned before rubbing it in exactly the same way that Terry used to. The similarities were uncanny. She shivered and took a deep breath. Briggs placed a friendly hand over her shoulder and squeezed before removing it. A slight crossing of boundaries but one they were both comfortable with.

'Mr Smithson, you say you can't remember when you got home. Can anyone else confirm when you returned?'

He nodded then stared into space as he tried to recall that night. 'My nosey neighbour, Frank. The bastard never sleeps and is always looking through that spyhole of his. I think he finds me attractive.' Steven sniggered. 'Apart from that, I went back, took my kit off and had a shower.'

Wyre tucked a loose strand of hair behind her ear. 'Did you speak to anyone else after that?'

He tutted. 'What do you think?'

'Did you speak to anyone else after that? Answer the question.'

For a moment, Gina thought he might demand a solicitor or refuse to speak. He was at present only a suspect and they had no direct evidence linking him to the murder.

'Mr Smithson, it's important that you tell us all you can.' *Well played, Wyre – a slightly softer approach could get them what they needed.*

'Dawn kept trying to call me. Stupid woman doesn't know when to give up. I ended a few of her calls. When I woke up in the morning, I had a further several missed calls. At one point I told her to leave it out and hung up. Stupid woman was sobbing down the phone.'

Gina made a note to see if Dawn would give them access to her phone records. She needed to know what time that would have been and exactly what was said. Briggs glanced at her notes and nodded. The interview finally came to an end.

Steven stood and zipped up his jacket as he headed towards the door Wyre held open.

Gina slammed the chair into the wall behind her. Briggs grabbed her arm, pulling her back. 'Give it a minute until he's gone.'

She wanted to throw the chair and break the table. She'd like nothing more than to kick it to death. Instead, she'd breathe it out and wait. Steven knew full well she'd be involved in the case and that she worked at Cleevesford. The lights went off in the interview room as Jacob left and closed the door behind him.

'Gina?' She turned.

'Huh?'

'Do you fancy a drink on the way home? We can have a catch up, talk about the case.'

He brought his hand slowly towards her arm and she stepped out of the way. 'No, I have things to do tonight and I don't think that's a good idea.'

'I was just going to open the door and if you don't want a drink, that's fine.'

He grabbed the door handle. He was nowhere near her and she'd flinched out of his way like an idiot, thoughts of Steven and Terry swimming through her mind and clouding her judgement.

He left first, leaving her alone inhaling the musty air.

'Sir,' she called.

He turned back and smiled.

'Thanks for the offer though. See you tomorrow.' She was going to update her notes, call Dawn Brown to ask about her phone calls and then she was grabbing some chips and going home to work.

Gina pulled her hood over her head as she jogged across the car park, trying to avoid the puddles forming in the tiny potholes. The chip shop was calling. The sick feeling in her stomach was more likely to be hunger.

'Fancy seeing you, Detective,' Steven called as he waited beside the main road. 'Just waiting for the bitch to pick me up.'

She felt her heart begin to race. He'd been waiting for her, she knew it. 'Good for you.' She pulled her car keys from her pocket and pressed the button, unlocking her car doors.

'You can fool them but you can't fool me, Gina. You're like me, aren't you? Like a bit of someone else in the bedroom. Terry told me all about your ways.' He winked and grinned.

Her stomach lurched. Maybe she'd forget the chips. She turned and swallowed forcing away the gagging feeling that threatened to overcome her. What had Terry told Steven about that night? Obviously not the truth. She opened her car door, swallowed and turned back to face him. 'Steven, just go home and stop being a dick.'

'You like dick, don't you, Gina? I know everything.' He paused and laughed, raindrops bouncing off his nose. 'You know it has struck me and our family that you've never properly grieved for Terry. Miss him, do you?' He pointed two fingers at his eyes and then pointed them over at her. 'Your own daughter thinks you're a cold-hearted bitch too, that's why she moved.'

She flinched as if that comment had literally slapped her. Sticking two fingers up at him, she got into her car and drove off without looking back. As she turned out of the car park, she passed Dawn's car. That's why Dawn hadn't been answering her phone when Gina had called her, she'd been driving.

Terry told me all about your ways. Her skin began to itch as she thought back to the night when at knifepoint Terry had forced both her and the prostitute to do things as they cried into the night. Tears flooded her face as she wondered exactly what Terry had said to Steven. The rain fell harder, clouding the windscreen. As she left the town and headed along the country roads, she slammed the brakes on and jolted out of the car, throwing up in the verge, trying to purge herself of all that had happened. She retched until nothing more would come out. Soaked through, she staggered back to her car, sat in the front seat and gazed through the steamed-up window as she yelled and hit the passenger seat until she'd drained herself. One thing she was certain of was that Steven wouldn't win this battle, he couldn't. If he did, she would be finished.

CHAPTER THIRTY-TWO

I watch through the hole in the back fence as Aimee helps Nicole drag her cases through the hallway. Spending time with Aimee is a little trickier now that her dopey friend had arrived back from her holiday. My mind wandered back to how we'd meet.

Aimee would enter the café, coming out of the rain. We'd part after arranging a date. Of course, a date was inevitable. I'd easily be able to impress her as I already knew all about her. I've watched her little fitness videos on YouTube, read her blog, checked out her Facebook page and even tried some of her fitness tips. I've never followed her page or tried to friend her though, don't want to look like a cyber stalker.

The rain has stopped for now. I inhale, enjoying the earthy smell that has been left behind. What I really want to smell is Aimee's soft perfume tantalising my senses. I'd like nothing more than to run my fingers through her soft curls and feel the firmness of her body pressed against mine. My mind wanders all too often.

The two women head towards the kitchen and the shorter chubby woman grabs a pen. Through the open window I hear parts of their conversation. Fish and chips, Aimee only wants fish with no batter, always watching her figure. The good news is, one of them will be going to fetch their food and as Nicole has her coat on, it looks like she will be the one. My stomach flips with excitement.

Nicole flings the back door open and lights up a cigarette. I'd love a cigarette but now isn't a good time and I've been trying to quit. I can smell Aimee's perfume through the smoke, it's only slight but I can detect it. Lilies, I love them. They remind me of someone else but I can't think about her at the moment. I don't want to think about her – there's a time and a place. Aimee scurries around, looking for her purse.

'You're always losing things,' I whisper with a smile.

'Found it! You know, those cancer sticks will kill you. I can't believe you started smoking again when you were away.'

Nicole laughs and taps her friend on the shoulder. 'Oh shut up, Mum.'

Aimee passes her some cash.

'Have you heard from him since?'

Aimee shakes her head. 'No. But he didn't do it, I'm sure of that.'

'You can't keep defending him. I heard what went on and he's well capable of doing it. I've seen him when he's in a mood.'

Aimee steps back into the kitchen, casting a shadow across the garden as she stands in the light. 'I can't talk about this now. Forget my fish.'

I love the rage in her face, it almost turns me on.

'Aimee, Aimee—' Nicole takes a final drag on her cigarette and throws it on the slabs, its gentle glow fizzling out as the damp concrete consumes all its warmth. 'I'll get you your fish anyway.'

It's no use Nicole talking to Aimee, she's already gone in and isn't listening. My back stiffens and I want to stand up straight and to walk it off but it's so quiet. Nicole eventually slams the door at the same time Aimee's bedroom light goes on. Aimee stares out of her window so I press my body against the fence and hold my breath, knowing she can't see me here. The light on the bushes behind me softens as she closes her curtains. I bend once again and stare through the hole. Nicole walks around the house and heads off towards the chip shop. Ten minutes to walk there, ten minutes in the shop and ten minutes back. That gives me thirty minutes alone with Aimee. And the stupid woman didn't lock the back door. This was too easy. 'It's just you and me, Aimee.'

Just as I enter the kitchen door, the neighbour's dog bounds over and starts jumping against the fence. Slipping through the door, I gently close it behind me. Thirty minutes and the clock is ticking.

CHAPTER THIRTY-THREE

Gina lay in bed, laptop screen lit up in the dark with Jade and Samantha looking at her, side by side. Both young, beautiful women with their whole lives ahead of them. One missing, the other murdered. Her head pounded. After feeling so sick, she'd skipped the takeaway that she'd promised herself earlier that day and settled for peppermint tea to settle her stomach which now rumbled away.

Snatching her phone, she checked it one last time for messages before putting it on charge. Nothing. Rex had left her alone. She hoped she'd heard the last of him. She'd made a big mistake giving him false hope with the second date. Another lesson learned. Her finger hovered over the Tinder app on her phone. Several swipes in her favour had pinged up. Maybe a quick glance, to satisfy her curiosity. No – she threw the phone face down onto the bed.

Paws pattered up the stairs and Ebony jumped up on the bed and began nudging her under the arm. 'Hello, girl,' She stroked the short-haired cat as she purred and settled, filling her bed with comforting warmth. Between the cat's purrs and the humming of the laptop, Gina felt her eyelids begin to clamp until she drifted off into a deep sleep.

Aimee lay in the darkness, her face covered in blood. Was she alive? The young woman jolted up. Gina had to protect her just like she'd want someone to protect Hannah. She needed to get her to safety. 'We have to run, get up.' Gina grabbed the woman's arms and tried to pull her from the floor but Aimee wasn't responding.

Aimee's fear-filled eyes opened and stared directly at her. 'Take my hand, Aimee. We have to leave now,' Gina whispered. She rubbed her eyes as Aimee's face morphed into Samantha's.

'Why would you want to leave?' the man asked. She squinted several times until she could just about see her oppressor through the red mist that had begun to fill the room. Steven! He prodded her with a knife, cutting the skin that protected her rapidly beating heart, forcing her backwards into the secret room.

'Samantha, run,' Gina called out. Was it Samantha or Aimee? As Gina stood to run, the door in which she'd fell through vanished leaving nothing but a black wall in its place. A wall with no door, a room with no escape lit by three candles.

A black whirlwind began to form in the middle of the room as Steven howled with laughter. As the breeze gathered like a mini tornado, a chill ran down her spine and the lit candles blew out, leaving her in darkness. She thrashed around, searching for a door before being slashed by the knife and sucked in by the whirlwind. She couldn't hear – the noise filled her head, ringing, buzzing, gale force winds, howling laughter.

'No, get me out. Get me out of here,' she whimpered as she fought against her surroundings, blindly grasping for anything that felt tangible. The floor began to melt and she felt herself sinking and falling, whirling uncontrollably to her end. 'No!'

Ebony meowed and pounced onto the floor as Gina thrashed, tangling her legs in the quilt. Her fearful stare searched every corner of her bedroom for the intruders from her dream as she gasped for breath. Her heart skipped a beat as she caught her laptop before it crashed onto the floor. Several screens flashed up as she randomly pressed the buttons on the keyboard. It eventually rested on the photo of Jade, lying dead on the path. Gina held her breath as she gazed at the screen. Slamming the lid down, she placed it on the floor and held her hand to her chest.

Snatching a tissue, she mopped the sweat that dripped down her forehead. She could guess all night and day as to what Steven thought he knew and it was killing her. She knew it wouldn't be the true version of events and she also knew that wouldn't matter to Steven, the man who idolised his loser brother and believed everything he'd told him.

She looked down and noticed how hard she was gripping her pillow. Gasping, she kneeled up, punching it over and over until she was too exhausted to breathe. She loosened her grip and ran to the bathroom. Hot and sweaty, she turned on the shower and stepped in before it had even warmed up.

Through chattering teeth, she sat in the bath as the water cleansed her, washing away all her self-disgust. Cold turned to steaming hot. Tears mingled with the shower water and all she wanted was someone to hold her and tell her everything would be okay. Closing her eyes, she thought back to when Briggs had touched her arm, his tender touch making her crave him.

Her thoughts then flashed to Steven, so like the brother of his that made her life unbearable when he was alive. Her thoughts settled onto Diane, the pained woman who lived all alone with no one to visit her. Gina didn't want to be a Diane but she could see her future when she looked at the woman. She inhaled the steam and as her mind flitted back to Steven, she could almost smell him, sweat and cheap aftershave with a hint of weed. Her heart rate picked up. Weed. Had Steven been Samantha's lover? Samantha smelling of weed was a big clue. He was connected, she knew it. She needed proof and she was going to get it. Diane was the key to everything.

CHAPTER THIRTY-FOUR

Friday, 10 May 2019

'Jacob, yes. I'm just outside Diane Garraway's house. I'll be in shortly.' She placed the phone in her pocket and knocked on Diane's door. The bathroom window the intruder had entered through had now been boarded up. A few moments later, she heard Diane shuffling along the hallway.

The woman opened the door. 'Morning, Detective.' She moved to the side, allowing Gina to pass her. The dark hallway felt as though it was closing in on them as they almost filled it. 'Sorry, I haven't been up that long. It takes me a long time in the morning to get up.' She tied the belt of her quilted dressing gown. After leading Gina into the living room, she pulled the brown curtains open, letting in all the light that the cold grey morning had to offer. Magazines were strewn over the settee and a bowl that looked as if it had contained soup the night before had been left on the floor. 'I haven't had a chance to clean up.'

'Don't worry about that, Diane. I know it's early so thank you for seeing me. I just wanted to speak to you about Samantha, the man she was seeing, and Derek.' Gina sat at the far end of the settee, close to the window.

'Oh here, I'll turn the light on.' The woman flinched as she tried to stand.

'I'll do it.' Gina placed her notes on the coffee table and turned on the light.

'I'd offer you a drink but I've only just taken my tablets. It'll be a while before I'm good for much.'

Gina checked her watch. It wasn't quite eight in the morning. She knew she'd caught Diane a little off guard and the woman had been good enough to see her. 'Shall I make a drink for you?' Anything that would make her more comfortable when they spoke had to be a good thing.

'If you could just fill the kettle and flick it on, that would be great. I'll be okay soon but I struggle to hold the kettle under the tap. Stupid swollen knuckles.'

Gina smiled and went through to the dark kitchen. Turning the light on, she spotted a half-full beaker of water on the side next to Diane's tablets. Her mind fixed on a packet of tablets she recognised. Fluoxetine – antidepressants. After Terry's funeral, she'd been prescribed a few months' worth. She'd taken them for a while but eventually had come off them. She flicked the switch on and gazed around the small kitchen. Holding her coat over her arm, she followed the smell to the overflowing bin and spotted a fly buzzing around it.

'Did you find the kettle okay?' Diane called out from the living room.

Gina swallowed as she took in the decay and clutter around her. Diane was only a few years older than her but she was virtually immobile and totally alone since Samantha had vanished. Gina pushed her thoughts out of her head. She couldn't get involved. Diane was one of many with problems in the town, one of many struggling with money and not getting the help and care she needed, one of many living with a chronic long-term condition that affected her everyday life. There was nothing Gina could do apart from find out what happened to Samantha. 'Yes. It's boiling.' She turned off the light and headed back through the hallway.

'You want to know about Derek, then?'

Gina nodded and picked her notebook and pen back up. 'Yes, I'm just trying to get a clearer picture of Samantha. From speaking with you and reading her notes, I know she was a clever young woman who enjoyed going out. She lived alone and was seeing a married man called Derek.'

'He strung her along, you know. People had Samantha wrong. They knew she was seeing him, even his wife suspected but I'm not sure how much she cared. Samantha told me it was more about the kids and him not being able to leave them. I tried to tell her that he was stringing her along but what can I say, she believed him and loved him.'

'You said she was seeing someone else. Did she see other people?'

The woman stared beyond her, fixing her vision on a scratch in the paint on the wall as her forehead crumpled as she thought. 'People called her names, like slag, marriage wrecker. I heard them while I was out and about. I may be falling apart in every other way but my hearing is spot on. I heard people when I went to the café, to the shop or even huddled on the streets. Everyone knew her. All the men had a thing for her and all the woman hated her. I knew her better though. She was just a kind-hearted, trusting girl who wanted to be loved. She loved Derek. The others were just there to make him jealous.' She paused. 'She played a stupid game really but she was led by emotion. I know people thought she was more calculating than what she was, that she played with people's feelings. She broke the hearts of a few young men who fancied their chances, none I know the names of, she just told me about them as she fished for advice.'

'Advice?'

Diane let out a little laugh. 'She'd say she was talking about a friend of hers but I knew it was her. She reminded me a little of myself. I bet you can't believe I was ever attractive, can you, Detective?'

Gina cleared her throat and smiled. She wasn't going to answer that question. 'Tell me more about the other men?'

'Some really liked her, some were just one-night stands. Samantha never felt fulfilled or loved. She was looking for something she couldn't have when it came to Derek. I don't know what she saw in him. He wasn't particularly attractive and he certainly wasn't as intelligent as she was. He came with so much baggage too and, worst of all, he was using her really. As for the others, there was no one memorable. Sometimes she'd go to the pub or a party and end up with someone. Rumours would go around and she and Derek would argue. He didn't want to commit to her but he soon objected when there was someone else on the scene.'

Gina's phone beeped. She glanced at the message. It was Jacob wondering how long she would be. She turned the phone over to remove the distraction. 'Tell me what you know about the last man she was seeing. You now say you remember Samantha smelling of cannabis when she'd been with him.'

'He was just some bum, that's what she called him. No one special. She'd seen him two or three times and as I said, she stank of weed when she came here. She was never stoned though. She didn't smoke. I can tell a stoned person a mile off, seen a few in my youth. I know she'd told Derek about the other man. She'd had enough and was about to break it off with him and he was livid.'

'About the other man, do you remember anything else she said?' Gina knew from the files that Derek had been questioned numerous times and had come back clean. A search of his property had given them nothing and his wife had provided him with an alibi on the night of Samantha's disappearance, stating that he'd been at home all night.

The woman stared through the window as a man walked past. 'No. I should have asked her more. I should have tried to protect her. She was vulnerable you know. People didn't see that. She always felt she was worthless and not good enough. She wanted to complete her degree so people would respect her. She walked people's dogs for them if they couldn't get out, checked on her neighbours too. She helped the very people who gossiped about her. I hate people, I really do. They all loved to hate her. They were jealous because she was beautiful and clever and they loved the drama that her life brought.' Diane wiped a tear away. 'You need to speak to Derek again. I don't trust him.'

'Why do you say that?'

She shrugged. 'I said all this at the time. His wife was his alibi on the night of her disappearance. She'd have done or said anything to keep him. Samantha was everything to me and no one understands—' The woman pulled her dressing gown sleeve over her hand and wiped her eyes as she sobbed.

'I'm going to do everything I can to find out where Samantha is.'

'Was.'

'What do you mean?' Did she know more than she was letting on?

'I knew her, better than anyone else. If she was alive, she'd have contacted me, not remained silent all these years. She treated me like her mother, for heaven's sake. She's dead somewhere, dead,' Diane said as tears fell from her chin.

'Oh, Diane, I'm so sorry. I didn't mean to upset you.' Gina ran out to the kitchen and grabbed the kitchen roll. She passed a couple of sheets to Diane.

'Don't be. I know she's gone. Just catch who did this to her.'

Gina nodded. 'I will do everything I can.' She placed one of her cards on the table. 'I know you probably have my card but if you think of anything or you need to talk, just call me. I know this case has unearthed a lot of upset for you.' Gina couldn't leave her without offering a little support even though she knew Briggs would think she was getting too involved if he found out. Maybe she was but Diane wasn't in a good place.

'Did one of the officers call you to talk about home security since the break-in?'

She nodded. 'I have someone coming from the council next week to fit some more locks.' Gina smiled. It wasn't much. They should be offering so much more but funds were a problem. Lack of funding affected people like Diane. A police officer driving by regularly would be preferable but it wasn't going to happen, not with their current staffing levels. Diane going to stay with a relative or friend would also be a good option but after looking at her notes, Gina knew she had no one to turn to.

Gina stayed with Diane for a few minutes and left her with a freshly made cup of tea and a slice of toast. After emptying her bin, she'd left, promising that she'd do everything to find out what happened, and she would. Finding out who killed Jade and what happened to Samantha were the most important things in her life at this moment. Her heart ached for the woman and deep down there was still a glimmer of hope that Samantha was still alive. She wouldn't give up on her that easily. She glanced at the message that Jacob had sent and scrolled down further.

Hurry back, guv. Wyre has finally infiltrated the Swap Fun weirdos! You've got to see this!

CHAPTER THIRTY-FIVE

Gina scoffed the rest of her fried egg sandwich as she nodded at Nick, the desk sergeant, before hurrying through to the incident room. It was just what she'd needed to line her screaming stomach. After the night before, she knew she'd feel sicker still if she skipped breakfast. She caught a glimpse of her reflection in a window. Her dark circles were a giveaway that she'd not slept much that night. Make-up may have hidden them had she been wearing it, but time to preen herself was a luxury she didn't have that morning.

A glimpse into the Swap Fun group was just what they needed. She rubbed her greasy hands together until the crumbs dissipated over the hard-wearing carpet tiles. 'So, what have you got for me, Paula?'

Wyre glanced back from her computer screen and smiled. 'I'm in, guv.' She punched the air and smiled. 'They trust me. I've already had several messages from couples wanting to meet up and jazz up their stale sex lives. The main forum for the meet-ups is full of chat about another one, and guess when it is?'

Gina shrugged her shoulders and leaned over Wyre's screen. 'Tell me everything.'

'You know all that greasy food is bad for you.'

Gina gave the younger woman a comedy stare and they both tittered. 'Whatever.'

After clicking a couple of tabs, Wyre opened up the chat room conversation. 'As you can see, most people don't use their own names. I'm Daisy Dukess.' She shrugged. 'I don't know where that came from but I thought it might sound attractive. Given the ages of the people we've interviewed so far, most of them will remember *The Dukes of Hazzard*. I'm trying to work out who our contributors might be and there are only two I think I can clearly identify at the moment, Stevie Boy and Ames Yogi. I don't think our Steven Smithson made too much of an effort to hide who he was. And Ames is a picture of a pert bottom in jazz pants, I'm thinking Aimee Prowse. She describes herself as a personal trainer and yoga guru.'

O'Connor grabbed a pen from the window ledge and wrote Stevie Boy next to Steven's details and photo. 'Stevie Boy, that's original.' He tapped his foot on the floor, filling the brief silent gap with an irritating sound that echoed through the damp-smelling room.

'Ooh, morning, guv. Coffee?' Jacob placed a tray of machine coffees on the middle table.

'Perfect timing.' Gina grabbed one and took a long swig. Just the tonic she needed to feel more human. 'There's a lot of conversation on this chain. How far have you read back?'

'I've gone back a couple of weeks to catch the lead up to Jade's murder. It mostly talks about the meet-up arrangements. I think anything more risqué is saved for private chat. You'd think it was a Women's Institute meeting or something. People are formal, on their best behaviour and don't really give a lot away. There are several anonymous users who don't even have profile pictures. They are just marked as living in the area.' A message bubble pinged up on her screen. 'Check this out, I have an invite to a private chat.'

'Accept it.' Gina leaned in closer. Jacob and O'Connor rushed over and stood behind them.

'It's an invite, guv. Oh dammit.'

Gina heard Smith whistling along the corridor as he headed out of the kitchen with a cup of coffee. 'Morning all.'

Gina's attention remained fixed on the screen.

PC Smith wandered over. 'Morning.'

'I'll be with you in a minute,' Gina replied as she placed her drink down and read the message.

Hi All.

Just to let you know, we'll be holding a bash at ours tonight. It's an informal drinks evening to get to know the other members in the area. Some of you were already invited a couple of weeks ago but I've resent this invite for the benefit of the new people and those who haven't confirmed their attendance.

I see we have a couple of new people – huge welcome from Swap Fun! I hope you all come along to some of our events and have lots of fun. Anyway, drink and chat starts at eight tonight. As always, don't forget to bring a bottle. There will be nibbles. We look forward to meeting you all. The address and directions are attached to the location tab. You never know, you may meet some new, special friends!

Don't forget to click confirm. I need numbers.

Admin – SwapFunSarah.

Gina spotted that eight people had confirmed attendance and one included Stevie Boy. 'We need to be there.' Gina leaned over and clicked attend on the mouse. 'Hope you've still got that blonde wig to hand.'

'Looks interesting. Is this to do with the Jade Ashmore murder?' Smith asked as he gulped his coffee down.

'Smith, are you busy tonight? You're going to a party.'

He almost choked, spitting coffee down the front of his uniform. 'What? I get off at five, this best be meaty. If it's meaty, count me in.'

Wyre pulled the wig from a bag under her desk and placed it on her head. 'I can't go, the witnesses have seen me.'

'I know, our Stevie Boy has seen you. I'll think of something, just give me a minute. Put a comment in the invite. Tell them that you and your husband, err, Fred will be attending.'

'Fred. Do I look like a Fred?' Smith asked.

'You will do. At some point today, go home and get your party clothes. Not too weird. Smart jeans and a shirt. Shiny shoes. At 6 p.m., I want you all ready to go and we'll all be in the area, in position. Jacob, O'Connor, check out the address and maps, work out our observation points.'

He nodded as Wyre passed him the address.

'It's in a large house along the river in Bidford-on-Avon. Not too far from a boat storage and mooring facility. We should be able to hide our cars there and looking at the map, there are plenty of good vantage points and trees to stay behind.' Jacob clicked on the street view. He was right, it was an undercover surveillance dream.

'Smith, we've gotta go. There's been a call in. Some woman is arguing with another woman about a parking space over at the Co-op and apparently she pushed her.' PC Kapoor's voice filled the room.

'Kapoor? How would you like to do something more exciting than break up a couple of warring motorists today?'

'What?'

'Like going undercover to a partner-swapping party.'

She burst into laughter and took a couple of steps back. 'Are you serious?'

Gina nodded and smiled. 'Send someone else to the Co-op.'

'Yes, count me in.'

'Great. So, Kapoor, I want you to take in the features of every-one who was at the party on the night of Jade's murder. I need you to be able to spot them so please take some time to memorise these faces and names. We need to know who is in attendance. That is your main role.' Gina pointed to the board. 'O'Connor and Wyre will take you through all you'll need to know and what else you'll be looking for. Are you okay with that?'

The tiny young woman nodded and smiled. Gina could tell she was bursting with excitement about being given such an interesting role in the investigation and Gina knew she was ready to take it on. She'd always been attentive, professional and good at her job.

'The only person we can definitely identify on the guest list is Steven Smithson—'

'Is that right?' Briggs asked as he entered. 'That means I'm coming too. As SIO, I need to be there.'

Gina went to speak but then stopped and sighed. She hadn't intended to confront Steven, she was going to stay back, direct the team and observe. Now she was going along with a babysitter. It was no use trying to argue with Briggs. It looked like they would be going together. Her phone beeped with a message.

Gina, haven't heard from you in a while. I miss you and loved our dates. Can we see each other again soon? Rex.

'Guv, these have just been delivered for you.' Nick had left his post to bring the embarrassingly large box of chocolates through to her. He left them on the main table and headed back. Neatly tied with a big red bow around them and a little card attached to the front, Gina felt her face begin to redden as Briggs stared at the unwanted gift. Just when she thought Rex had got the hint. She stomped over to the chocolates and forced them into the much smaller bin, grabbing the card at the same time. She could feel the weight of Briggs's stare on her back and she knew he'd wonder who they were from and why they had been delivered to the station. He'd also wonder why she'd thrown them in the bin. Maybe that hadn't been her best move.

'Can we speak in a minute, Harte? Pop through to my office.' He turned on his heal and left the room.

Wyre, O'Connor and Jacob turned back to their work, trying to relieve her of the embarrassment and Smith broke away from the group with Kapoor and began discussing the evening ahead.

Another message came through.

I was just passing your house. Thought we could do lunch. Can we speak? Rex. XX

Her hands began to shake as she clenched her knuckles. Tension washed over her arms and shoulders and a pain shot through her head. He was now officially giving her a headache, one that could only be cured by his parting from her life. She hastily replied.

Rex. Go home. Leave me alone and don't contact me again. Stay away from my house.

She stared at the phone, hoping there would be no more messages but true to his form, he replied immediately with a crying emoji. She threw the phone in her pocket. She wasn't going to indulge him any further and if he came to her house again without an invite she wouldn't be quite so civilised.

'These look like good chocolates, guv. They've got ganache and hazelnuts in them. Can we have them? It seems such a waste throwing perfectly good chocolates in the bin.'

She nodded. O'Connor fought with the packaging and began chomping on a chocolate.

'I know you have a lot to do, Jacob, but I want the Ashmores' neighbour, Colin Wray, brought in for his voluntary interview. Also, Derek Alton, Samantha's married boyfriend. Contact him and get him here, ASAP. Also, I know Noah Ashmore has been calling. I should have gone back to see him but with all that's happening, I can't fit that in too. Can you get someone over there? Keep him updated. Thank you.' As she headed towards Briggs's office, she opened the little envelope and pulled out a card. It had a little heart on the front and no messages inside. She shoved it back into her pocket as she knocked on Briggs's door.

CHAPTER THIRTY-SIX

'Gina, I know there's something going on and I can see it's affecting you? Take a seat.'

She sat the other side of his desk. 'Whoa, direct or what?'

'If it affects your ability to do your work, then I'm going to be direct about it. How else would you expect me to be? Would it be best if you kept your personal life separate from your work life? It really doesn't look professional.'

'We know a lot about professional, don't we?' she snapped.

'Touché.'

She linked her slightly quivering fingers in an attempt to disguise her anger and nerves. 'I didn't ask for the chocolates or for some man to be bothering me, sir.'

'Do you want to talk?'

'No.' She knew he wasn't really giving her an option and she could see how it looked, her receiving and angrily binning the chocolates. She nodded, knowing it was in her interest to talk. 'Okay.' She inhaled and fanned her face with her hand. 'I had a couple of dates with someone and he keeps texting me. He sent the flowers and the chocolates. He just thinks he's in with a chance and I want him to leave me alone. The situation isn't out of hand.'

Briggs looked at her, unable to speak.

She cleared her throat and looked away.

'I see. Is he bothering you?'

She shrugged her shoulders. 'Would it matter? It's something I have to deal with, it's personal and I'm managing.'

'Are you managing? You looked like you were panicking back there, in the incident room. Don't let your team see you lose it.'

He was right. She could have looked less angered, treated it as a joke or brushed it off. 'You're right. It won't happen again.' She didn't want to tell Briggs that Rex had turned up at her house too. She didn't want him to see that she wasn't as in control as she wanted to be.

'I'm also worried that you haven't looked too well these past couple of days and the welfare of everyone here is my responsibility.'

'I think I just ate something dicky, one of my dodgy takeaways, sir. I'm okay now, I just had a bad night.' She knew her unruly hair and pale face probably made her look sicker than she had felt. She also knew that her upset stomach was just a reaction to the things Steven had said to her outside the station. She couldn't exactly tell Briggs that her abusive dead husband brought a prostitute home and forced her and the woman to do things to each other while they cried at knifepoint. Her neck began to prickle and the redness seeped up, covering her nose, chin and cheeks. Briggs also knew her intimately and at this precise moment, he could sense exactly how she was feeling. She wondered how long he would make her squirm.

He smiled. 'If that's all it is. Just don't go spreading anything over this way and let's hope it was just a takeaway and not some icky bug. As for later, I think we should meet at the location around six this evening and scope it out. Is that okay for you?'

She unlinked her fingers. 'Yes, six is fine. See you there.' She stood to leave, relieved it was over.

'I'm looking forward to staking someone out. It's been a while since I've got away from the old desk. Here's to something more exciting!' He held his cup up and took a sip of his drink.

'Well, I'll see you later then.'

'Look, if you ever need to talk, I'm always here, in a personal and professional capacity. You know that, don't you?' She knew he had a soft spot for her, he had for a long time. He would keep her on the case and he'd be there for her no matter what. She considered if the roles were reversed, if some woman was bugging him when he didn't want to hear from her, or if he looked upset. Would she be there too?

She nodded and returned his smile. She also knew that he never believed her when she said she was fine. Would he be there if ever he knew the whole truth about her past? She shivered as she closed his office door.

CHAPTER THIRTY-SEVEN

'I hate work, still wish I was in Tenerife,' Nicole said as she grabbed her keys and waved goodbye to Aimee.

'Catch you later,' she replied as she sat at the kitchen table, head in hands. Her slightly greasy hair was falling from the loose hair clip, tickling her face and nose.

Her mobile buzzed on the table. Rhys was calling. Swallowing, she felt her heartbeat speed up. She couldn't answer. She'd told him it was over and to never come back. She remembered the grip he'd had on her chin, him squeezing hard. She wouldn't answer. The buzzing stopped as her voicemail kicked in.

A few seconds passed, he called again, hung up, called again and again. She scraped the chair and stood to attention as Barney began to bark. A breeze picked up and the old shed began to creak at the bottom of the garden. A strip of asphalt fell to the floor. Another job that Rhys had promised to do. She shivered as a splash of raindrops began to tap on the window. He was out there, she knew it. The phone rang again.

Tears fell down her face as she stared at the lit up phone and slid down the wall sobbing. Shed banging, rain tapping, dog barking and the damn phone. She wanted to scream and shout for help. Nicole – she wished her friend was still here. 'Go away,' she yelled.

The phone stopped ringing. She reached out and looked at the screen. Twelve missed calls in less than five minutes. Her heart was in her mouth as it rang again. 'What?' she yelled as she answered. He knew she'd answer eventually, he was always right. Mr bloody always right.

'I'm struggling out here, babe. Please don't tell me it's over. I know I upset you—'

'You hurt me.' Tears slid down her cheeks.

'You had a knife to me. I forgive you, Aimee, I love you. None of that matters. I'll do anything. Don't listen to Nicole. She's just trying to poison what we have. She's just a jealous bitch who can't get anyone and she wants you all to herself.'

The same old story. The one that had almost made Aimee tell Nicole it would be best if she found a place of her own. She wasn't falling for it any more. It was as if a veil had been lifted. She could now see what was once so invisible to only her. Rhys was trying to distance her from everyone who meant something to her and Nicole was her oldest friend. 'Rhys, it's over! Just get over it. You think I'm going to dump my oldest friend for you? That's never going to happen.'

'And this is why you'll never be happy, Aimee. She's holding you back.'

'No. You are. You always were and I can see it now. I had that knife in the kitchen because I was petrified of you, not because I wanted to hurt you. You know the detective, she has a witness. Someone saw you with Jade and you were being rough with her, hurting her. Did it end there or did you follow her? Did you pin her to something like you do to me, not allowing her to move? Maybe she wasn't a doormat like I was. Maybe she told you to get off her and you didn't. Maybe she was about to report you or tell the others what you did to her. Like the things you did to me—' She sobbed like she'd never stop, hyperventilating. Breathe, she couldn't breathe. She gasped and coughed.

'Don't come the victim with me. You tell me you like it the way we do it and that you love me and now this. Aimee, don't make me out to be a monster. Making things up will only make you look stupid in the end.'

Shaking she held the phone to her ear. She could simply end the call to end the torture but she wouldn't. He'd be angrier if she hung up on him and she didn't need his rage coming to her doorstep. She needed him to go quietly and never bother her again. 'Please, Rhys, please just go and never call me again. Please.'

'But, I love you, babe. I. Love. You.'

She could hear a warmth in his voice confusing her even more. It was the same warmth she'd originally fallen for. 'You're slowly killing me. Please stop.'

'You're killing me. I love you and I never hurt Jade. The whole Swap Fun thing was a stupid idea and it's made me realise what I stand to lose. When this mess is over and I can prove I'm innocent, I just want to come home and be with the woman I love. We can get married, maybe have a child. Remember, we always said we'd like a little girl called Rachel after your mum or a little boy called Henry. We can have it all. I'm ready to commit to you with everything I have. I'll be the husband you deserve. I promise you. Please just give me a chance.'

The back gate slammed. Her body stiffened. He was walking down the path. 'Please don't come here. I need to think. Go back out of the gate now and think this through, Rhys.' She closed her sore eyes and blew her nose as she waited for the door to open. There was no way he'd listen to her. He wasn't the type.

'Out of the gate. I have no idea what you're talking about. Is this another silly game you're playing? Is it meant to mean something that I'll never fathom? You sometimes think you're so clever. That's your problem. Think you're better than anyone else.'

Within seconds his tone had changed. She ended the call. If it wasn't him, who was in her garden? Something was off and it wasn't just Rhys. It was ever since she'd allowed Rhys to set up her profile on that stupid Swap Fun website. The door handle rattled as she trembled on the kitchen floor. 'Just go away,' she yelled.

CHAPTER THIRTY-EIGHT

Rain pattered against the living room window. Diane pulled the fleecy blanket further up towards her chin as she shivered. *This Morning*, a television programme she normally loved filled the solitude but she couldn't concentrate on anything. After all that had happened, every hour went by slowly. Someone had broken into her house and she couldn't get it out of her mind. Every part of her home felt dirty, like it was contaminated.

Sleep hadn't come at all. Her heavy eyelids threatened to close as her breathing became heavier. A random snore brought her out of her slumber and she awoke with a start. What if he was to come back? The intruder knew things about their past, her and Samantha. Was he part of her past, is this why she had been chosen? Maybe he was punishing her for all the wrongs she'd done. Shame burned through her cheeks. Eventually the police would dig up something from her past should these incidents keep occurring. If nothing else these days, she had respect. Would the community turn on her if they knew what she'd done? She'd even changed her name to escape it. It had been so easy. Move from her town of birth to the town her brother had moved to and start again. No one had questioned it and her past had never threatened to meet her present. It had all worked out well, until now.

She tried to curl up a little on the settee. It was no good. Her legs weren't going to bend in that way. Her hip twinged and her swollen fingers lost their grip on the edge of the blanket, making it slip a little. Her eyes filled up. Being only in her fifties, she saw other women her age looking like they were still forty, out enjoying themselves with great jobs and loving families. She had nothing and there was nothing to look forward to. Her once lovely long chocolate brown hair was now mostly grey and limped in tangled clumps over her shoulders. The menopause had also treated her badly, putting her through the wars. She envied every woman who'd sailed through it. One health problem after another had plagued her since. She stared at the screen. Some of the presenters and guests were around her age. They looked so full of life and radiant.

Back then, men had swarmed around her, just like they had with Samantha. They'd loved her shiny hair, her hourglass figure and the way she could wiggle in a pair of heels. They loved the crimson lipstick and the smell of her perfume. She could have had anyone but she chose to profit from her looks. Not in the way a model profits from being the star of an advertising campaign but in more sordid ways. At seventeen she had the looks but soon her reputation made sure that most of the decent boys didn't want to know. It was a different time in the eighties. They may have had the big hair, the educational opportunities and the shoulder pads, but women were still being patted on the arse by the guys they worked for. No one judged either the women or the men for this, but they all judged her. They all wanted to shag her when they got paid and they all went home to their wives and listened to them bleat on about what a tart Diane *from-down-the-road* was.

She stared at her reflection in the murky window. 'Worthless whore,' she whispered as tears filled her eyes. That's all she was. A new name meant nothing. Deep down, she was nothing but a whore and the town she left had said it out loud. No wonder her bro had moved away, the teasing must have forced him to. No one cared if she was okay at seventeen. No one had offered to help. Maybe things would have been different today, just maybe. Maybe social services would have stepped in to help and she'd have continued studying, got a good job and had the husband and family she'd dreamed of back then.

Her home phone went. As she reached out to answer, her bones creaked. She brought the received to her ear. 'Hello.' She wiped her eyes on the corner of her blanket. The caller was silent. 'Hello?'

The call went dead. She placed the receiver down and pressed 1471 only to be told that the caller had withheld their number.

A cold shiver ran through her body. First the card, then the break-in, now a phone call from someone who'd hung up. A million thoughts flashed through her mind. Was the intruder checking to see if she was in? Maybe this time he was going to come for her, maybe hurt or kill her.

She wasn't worried about dying but the thought of someone coming to her home and hurting her more than she already hurt sent a shudder through her body. She trembled as the phone rang again.

Reaching for the receiver, she held the phone to her ear and waited. She could hear the caller breathing at the other end. 'Derek? Who is this?' she cried. A thought crossed her mind. 'Samantha, is that you? Please, just say something, anything. The silence is killing me. I miss you, Sam. Did you send me the card?' Breaking down, her sobs filled the living room. It couldn't be Samantha but for a moment it felt like she was really talking to her. All the heartache at her disappearance came flooding back as the caller hung up. 'Come back,' she yelled, her voice cracking.

It wasn't Samantha. Her closest friend would never put her through this much pain. 'Come back,' she cried.

CHAPTER THIRTY-NINE

'Aimee, what the hell?'

Nicole dropped her bag on the table and kneeled beside her friend.

The phone slipped from her hand and fell to the floor. 'I thought you were him.'

'Come here.' Nicole held Aimee close until her tears subsided. 'What happened? Did he call?'

She nodded and wiped her nose. 'I thought you were him. I did it. I finally told him to never come back.'

'We'll get through this and the old Aimee will shine back through. You'll see. You did the right thing.' Nicole grabbed some tissues and passed them to Aimee. 'Here, I'll put the kettle on. Chamomile tea?'

'Please. Why are you back home so soon?'

Nicole switched the kettle on and grabbed a couple of mugs. 'I left my phone on charge and I need it. Thought I'd dash back and grab it. I'll have to have this and run. I'm not going to be Miss Popular for being late but stuff 'em. They need me more than I need them. What's been going on, hun? There's something you're not telling me.'

Aimee ran her hands through her greasy hair. Nicole was right. Without pausing for breath, she reeled off the details of the party that Rhys had taken her too.

'Jeez. It's complicated then.'

'They think it's Rhys as he's absconded but there were others at that party. It was off, the whole night was off. I can't put my finger on it but everyone turned up to this stupid party and looked fed up when they were paired off, as if none of them really wanted to be there. I can't believe I did it. It's going to ruin all that I've worked for. I'm going to need to move and start again.'

Nicole placed the tea on the table and offered her friend a hand up. 'No you're not. You've done nothing wrong. The police will catch whoever did this. They will get Rhys eventually. With no money, he can't run for long. He can't just vanish.'

'You were right too. I'm so sorry.'

'I could see it all along. I just hoped I wouldn't lose you as a friend. Drink your tea. When I'm gone, have a shower and get to that park. The run starts soon, doesn't it?'

Aimee nodded and smiled. 'You're always right. Bestie friends, just like when we were kids?' Aimee held her hands out and they did their little clap routine, the same one that they used to do in the playground at school. They laughed as Aimee sipped the tea.

'Right, I'll grab my phone, then I really have to get to work. Looks like my lunch break has gone for today. She ran upstairs, leaving Aimee with her tea. The shed door still flapped. She placed the cup down, opened the kitchen door and began to walk down the garden. She'd wedge it shut somehow and later she'd peel the bit of roof off that was making the rest of the noise, but not in her slipper socks. She slammed the door closed and placed the small stone mushroom in front of the door. *That's better.* She almost jumped back three feet as Barney ran out of the back door and started scratching and barking at the corner of her fence. She glanced across and her heart pounded as her gaze met the eye that was staring through the small hole in her fence.

She listened as her watcher ran along the path. Was it Rhys? She couldn't be sure. She darted to the back fence and opened it, only to see the bottom of a foot turn a corner. 'Nicole, get here now.'

'What is it?' Nicole said as she left the house.

'There was someone here. I saw an eye through that gap.' She pointed at the fence. 'That's what Barney has been barking at. There was someone watching me.'

'Someone or him? He's not going to go that easily. We should call the police.' She went to call.

'No, I don't need them prying. They'll catch him eventually. If he wants to be so sad as to watch me through a gap in the fence—' She regained her breath. 'No. I just want all this to go away. I don't want my clients upset by this. Jade's murder has already hit the news and I want to keep my name out of everything. I'm going to have a shower and I'm going to work.'

'I think you're wrong about the police.'

'Well, it's my call.'

'He still has a hold on you, doesn't he?' As Aimee went to reply, Nicole stormed off, leaving the gate once again flapping back and forth in the wind.

Aimee kicked it shut, flinching as her toe hit the wood. Nicole was right. She went to call the police but stopped. 'I hate you Rhys Keegan.' She placed the phone back in her pocket and swore under her breath as she headed back inside, the dog yelping at her from the other side of the fence.

CHAPTER FORTY

It wasn't right. Gina flung off her loose black trousers which landed on the rest of her dirty laundry. As soon as she had a moment, she'd catch up on all the washing she needed to do. She had no idea when that would be. She grabbed her black jeans, they were much better for surveillance. They were comfortable and she could stretch and bend in them. They also made her look slimmer and firmer than she really was. She shook her head as she pulled them on. There was no point in trying to impress him if they couldn't be together but for some reason, she couldn't help herself. She had an hour to spruce up.

Her hair suited her when she wore it up. It was just long enough to fit into a small ponytail. She sprayed the sides. Her phone buzzed on top of the washing basket. She saw Briggs's name flash up on a text message. Her heart fluttered in the way it had in the past. She was going to be working with Briggs that evening. Just him and her in the car together as they watched what was happening at the party. Jacob, O'Connor and Wyre would be close by too but the car would contain just them.

She grabbed the little bottle of perfume and squirted the smallest amount on her wrist before reading Briggs's last message.

I'm heading back to the station. See you there. We'll go in my car.

As she went downstairs, the phone rang. 'Wyre, everything okay?'

'Yes, we're at the station. All set for later and just going over the schedule for tonight. It's all very precise, thanks, guv.'

Gina knew she'd worked out the logistics of everything with precision. There was no room for error. She pulled the tight jumper over her head. This was not a date. She removed it and replaced it with her loose jumper, the older one that was slightly bobbly. 'Great. I'm on my way in so we'll run through everything one more time before we set off. I want to know that everyone is clear on what's going to happen. Are Smith and Kapoor there?'

'Check. They seem rather excited about this little mission. The wig actually looks good on Kapoor. They both scrub up, guv. I don't think you'll recognise them.'

Gina smiled. Just the type of people Swap Fun would love to have at one of their parties. Smith – run-of-the-mill, like most of the other men that took part. Kapoor, she was younger and was definitely a match for Aimee, she would definitely draw some of the attendees her way. She also knew Kapoor had a good eye for faces and she'd been studying their witnesses and suspects all afternoon. Both she and Briggs would be watching everything. Hopefully this would be an exercise in learning more about the group. She also needed to put names to Swap Fun profiles and see if any of the attendees at the last party would be at this party.

'Just one other thing. I have managed to get an address for Derek Alton. There has been no one in all day, but I've instructed uniform to keep going back until we've reached him. And Colin Wray – we have him booked in tomorrow morning.'

'Nice work. Catch you soon.' As she ended the call another message from Briggs pinged up.

*Gina, if you'd rather go with one of the others in your car,
I can take someone else.*

It would make life easier if she wasn't with Briggs. She stroked her cat as she closed it in the kitchen, entered the alarm code into the keypad and locked up. It wasn't much but that small amount of human contact with someone she had once been so intimate with almost made her feel alive again. Nothing would happen and she needed to show him that she wasn't letting things get to her. She wasn't unhinged or affected by her past. The case would not affect how she did her job and she could accept him being senior to her even though she'd seen him naked. She had a lot to prove. Maybe he did too.

CHAPTER FORTY-ONE

Rain drizzled down the windscreen. It was seven thirty. Gina and Briggs were at their post. As per her planning, they were located down a winding road, beside a row of trees that separated the house in the distance and the river that trickled behind them. The road they parked on ran alongside SwapFunSarah's drive but would not be obstructed by their guests. There was ample room for at least eight cars outside the house.

She shivered as she thought of another victim that they had found in the very same river a couple of miles downstream at Marcliffe. That of Nicoleta Iliescu, murdered by Jeff Wall. That case had been the start of her flashbacks, her nightmares and her anxiety – a trigger, reminding her of her past and the treatment she'd endured at the hands of Terry. She shook her head slightly. That case was in the past now.

She looked into her lap as she thought of Jade Ashmore, the reason they were sitting under the dark grey skies, in a car, waiting for a party to start. She had to let go of all the things she couldn't control. The counsellor had told her that, but she hadn't told the counsellor half of it.

'Look, people are arriving,' Briggs said, breaking their half hour long silence as he stared through a gap in the tall trees.

The house was quite grand and a boat was moored up on the river at the end of their garden. The reddish stone house was lit up by designer lighting that looked like a fading strip at each side of the huge front door. The couple knocked. As the door opened,

James Brown's, 'Get up Sex Machine', escaped from the door. So apt, she thought. The couple went in, led by the woman of the house, SwapFunSarah.

The party appeared classy from the outside. She imagined the guests would be greeted with a glass of champagne. Fizzy bubbles escaping from a raspberry that sat at the bottom of the flute. The pristine host would serve hors d'oeuvres, maybe devils on horseback. That's when the classiness would end and their agenda would be addressed. Was it just a night where new members would meet up or was there going to be some action?

'I hope it is just a meeting of new people,' Gina said. 'I don't know how Smith and Kapoor will handle things if their names are placed into a glass.'

'It would certainly give us all something to laugh about back at the station.' Briggs sniggered as he kept his attention on the house.

Gina checked her watch, there was still ten minutes until the party officially started and their two undercover officers would arrive. She inhaled. 'New aftershave.'

He smiled. 'You noticed.'

She shook her head and laughed. 'I just noticed it was different, that was all.'

'You approve?'

She nodded. 'It smells good.' He smelled good. He looked good in his casual jacket and grey shirt, too good to be this close to. She really hoped more people would be turning up soon. Her stomach flipped. Steven and Dawn pulled up on the drive. Dawn teetered uncomfortably on the uneven block paving in the stiletto boots tugging down her short ill-fitting dress that clung to all the wrong places. *Why do you let him do this to you?* She knew the answer to that question without even having to ask. She knew that Steven got what Steven wanted, just like Terry. If Steven wanted her to wear those clothes, even though they were the wrong size and she looked unhappy, she would wear them. Just like Terry – it was his way or no way.

'Are you okay with this? He can't see you, understand?' The moment of light-heartedness they'd shared a moment ago had been replaced by an air of seriousness. She couldn't compromise the case in any way.

'I understand, sir.'

'Okay, Harte, they're going in. Where are we right now with Steven as a suspect?'

'Not enough to make an arrest but he could have done it. Problem is, so could some of the others. All we have is circumstantial.' She let out a slight huff.

'You want it to be him, don't you?'

She ignored his question.

'Don't go there, it's dangerous and it will kill your career. Investigate thoroughly and the culprit will be found and it will be watertight for the CPS. We can't compromise the case due to personal feelings about suspects because of our pasts. If at any point you don't think you can handle being a part of this investigation, then you can back down on this case.'

She turned and rolled her eyes. 'No way. I'm as committed to finding out who killed Jade Ashmore as you are, and I am a professional.' She just hoped her actions could convince him of that fact. He was right, he could see straight through her protective veil. He knew how much she despised Steven. She made a note of their attendance and briefly described the first couple. She knew Jacob, Wyre and O'Connor would also be observing from the other side of the house.

The rain subsided and, from afar, they could see that several people had turned up, dead on time. Cars pulled in and were manoeuvred around until suitably parked. Amongst them, she saw Smith pull in. 'Here goes, sir.'

'Indeed.' It looked like Smith and Kapoor were exchanging pleasantries with the other guests.

'They have scrubbed up well.' Smith wore smart jeans and a casual, untucked shirt. Kapoor wore the blonde wig, along with a black shift dress and little heels. Smart but sexy. Understated but high impact. It was a look Gina could only ever hope to carry off. The blonde wig was a disguise but the people attending were all about not being themselves for a night. Another couple laughed as they held ball masks to their eyes. As the man lowered his, Gina half expected to see Richard Leason but she didn't recognise the man at all. In fact, she hadn't recognised anyone apart from Steven and Dawn. 'I don't recognise anyone else so far.'

'No, maybe the rest are staying away after what happened at the last party. What do we know about the host?'

Gina turned a page in her notebook. Unable to read it in the dark, she thought back to what she'd read about SwapFunSarah. 'Sarah Norton, forty-two, and no record; family-owned business involving plant hire of which she is now the managing director. It takes all sorts. Not married but very outgoing if you look at her Facebook profile. Loves her parties.'

Gina and Briggs watched as a man in a trilby hat was dropped off at the end of the road in a taxi, his head dipped as he tried not to get his face wet. His overcoat came to his knees and she could see he was dressed smartly underneath. 'Look up, whoever you are,' she said as she waited to see his face.

He turned to face the other direction as he knocked. Gina radioed Jacob and the others. 'Did you see who that was?'

The radio hissed. 'Don't recognise him, guv. Could only see his mouth under the rim of the hat, so not much to go on. Hopefully, we'll get a look later. Maybe it's SwapFunSarah's latest.'

'Thanks. Keep watching.' She ended the communication and scrawled a note in the dark. *Man in trilby, who are you?*

'I should get a trilby. I think I have the right shaped head for a hat.'

Gina laughed and playfully patted Briggs on the arm. The door opened and the sounds of 'At Last' by Etta James now filled the air. The bay window at the front of the house oozed a warm light that extended halfway across the drive. People in party clothes walked past with champagne flutes. Gina was sure there was fruit in the bottom of the glass. She had them all worked out. Smith and Kapoor walked over to the window.

Gina leaned forward. Smith was being pulled away from Kapoor by the host. She watched as he smiled, impressed by how well Smith was playing the part. Kapoor looked out of the window. 'Hold your nerve, Kapoor,' Gina said as she watched. The young woman flinched as a hand landed on her shoulder. She turned and the rest of the man came into view – Steven the slimeball.

Kapoor's frown adjusted into a huge smile as she turned to face Steven. She bit her bottom lip and shook her head. Steven winked, then vanished from view.

'We need to get out of this car and take a closer look,' Gina said as she grabbed her trench coat off the back seat. She exited the car and pulled her hood over her head. 'We need to find out who Trilby is.'

Briggs nodded and grabbed his coat off the back seat then radioed Jacob to tell them they were leaving the car.

The back door of the house opened and four people came out and lit up cigarettes. As Gina and Briggs followed the trees, they could smell weed in the air. Trilby came out through the French doors and stared out at the river as he sucked on a spliff and sipped from a champagne flute, oblivious to the spitting rain.

'Gina, not too close,' Briggs whispered as he parted a cluster of branches and crept forward, grabbing her arm.

As he pulled her back, one of the party was alerted to their presence. 'What did you do that for?' she whispered back, knowing that he'd caused her to make a sound as he tugged her arm.

Her heart began to pound as she saw Steven walk over. He dragged on his smoke one last time, threw it to the ground and stepped on it as he wandered towards them.

'Abandon,' Briggs whispered in her ear as he held her close.

'Not now, we can't.'

Steven pulled the branches away. As he did, Briggs grabbed Gina. Their eyes met for no more than a second and she nodded. They kissed hard under their respective hoods. His firm lips pressed against hers and drew her in further.

'Oops, sorry,' Steven said. 'Didn't know you were already getting some action but, hey, have a good time.' He dropped the branches and hurried back to the French doors, before heading back inside.

'That was close,' Briggs said as his hand dropped from the back of her neck, leaving a faint tingle behind. 'Sorry about that, I didn't know what to do and—'

'Shh, it's okay. We got away with it. All is back on track.' The subsequent silence that followed made the tiny gap between them feel slightly awkward.

An hour had passed and nothing much was happening at the party. People still drank, they occasionally came outside for a smoke and the music still played. Various jazzy numbers boomed out. Steven and Dawn were still the only people they recognised. The tingle on the back of her neck, where Briggs had held her as they kissed, still tingled. Not once had Rex or any of her other lovers made her tingle.

'Trilby is walking towards us,' Briggs said as he turned the radio off. 'He's seen the car. Play it cool.'

They both got out and he held her hand, leading her to the river's edge. Trilby would walk over, see that they were just a couple out for a walk and he'd head back inside with the other partygoers. Briggs pointed at the moon's reflection in the rippling water below. She needed to see who he was. Gently, she turned as Briggs played his part so well. As soon as her eyes met his, she felt her heart blocking her throat as it boomed away. With blood pounding through her head, she wanted to faint, to throw up, to shout or scream at him.

'Fancy meeting you here, Gina.'

'Rex.'

'Anyone might think you are following me,' he said with a laugh.

'That's good coming from you. The man who turns up at my house uninvited when I've told you to leave me alone. The flowers, the chocolates, the texts, they have to stop.'

He removed his hat and shook the rainwater from it. 'You're a flipping loony. I haven't been sending you anything. Maybe it's Tinder date number whatever over here.' He pointed at Briggs.

Her cheeks burned and pricked. Now Briggs knew everything. She was sure her cover had been blown.

'What would a copper be doing here? Are you watching me? Maybe you're harassing me.'

She had no idea what she'd ever seen in Rex. Her instincts about him had been right. She was nothing more than a conquest seeing as he turned up to sex parties. Briggs gripped her hand, tightly.

'I think you should leave her alone,' Briggs said in a controlled tone.

'Do you. Good luck with that one!' He put his hat back on and walked away, back to the house.

'I am so sorry, I had no idea it was him,' Gina said, feeling choked up.

'You had no reason to know. We have to abandon this mission though. Too many people have seen us and he may well go back to the party and discuss seeing you outside.'

'He knows my real name. If he talks and Steven knows I was here, he'll put two and two together—'

'Shh, let's go now. He may not say anything but if we stand out here much longer, it's only a matter of time before people really get suspicious.' His hand unravelled from hers and she followed him back to the car. 'We'll talk about this when we get back to the station.'

As they fumbled for their seat belts, Gina switched the radio back on and spoke to Jacob. 'Abandon. Smith's now at the window, give him the wave.'

'On it, guv,' Jacob replied as they drove away, leaving the party behind. Gina glanced back and saw Steven standing outside. Maybe he had just heard what had happened and was about to leave too.

'Am I in trouble, Chris?'

He didn't answer.

CHAPTER FORTY-TWO

Gina followed Briggs through the station. Jacob, Wyre and O'Connor headed straight to the kitchen to grab some coffee, ready for debriefing. Gina followed Briggs until they reached his office. The door creaked as he pushed it open and flicked the light switch, illuminating the messy paperwork that was strewn over his desk. 'Take a seat,' he said as he pulled the window too, blocking out the traffic noise from the road outside. He fell into his chair.

'Are you angry with me?'

'I don't know is the answer.'

What didn't he know? 'I had no idea Rex was going to be there, none whatsoever. If you want to penalise me for going on a couple of dates with a friggin' idiot then go ahead.'

He stood, removing his damp coat and hanging it on a peg as he passed her. 'You are all over this case and it worries me. You know one of the suspects, Steven, you told me that – actually it goes further than that; you used to be related to him. Then it turns out you know one of the other people at the party and, not only that, you've been dating him.'

'But, sir—'

'Wait. Don't interrupt me.'

She wiped a tear from the corner of her eye as she closed her mouth and waited for him to continue. This wasn't the right time to argue back with him.

'Then, only then, it comes out that this man seems to be almost harassing you. He turns up at your place, sends messages when you've told him to stop. You said there wasn't a problem, that all was fine in your life. This doesn't sound fine.'

'Is this about him or us?' Gina knew he'd been ruffled by Rex. Rex wasn't bad looking, scrubbed up well in his smart coat and, strangely, the hat had suited him.

He slammed his open hand into the side of the filing cabinet. 'This is about me caring about you and you not being able to see when you need a friend. How long was he going to keep messaging you and harassing you until you spoke to someone, maybe me?'

'I was dealing with it fine on my own.'

'You were until tonight. Your professional life has now well and truly crossed your personal life and I don't know how much longer I can keep it to myself.'

Gina paced towards his desk then back towards the door. 'You know I need my work. You know how much it means to me.' Another tear slid down her face as she looked up at him.

He passed her and fell into his chair once again. 'Don't disappoint me again. Your chances are running out, Harte; do you hear me?'

She sniffed and gave him a little smile.

'And talk to me. What's on your mind? I heard what that Rex said. Talk to me. That is one of the conditions. I need to know that you're not losing it.'

She could understand. She wanted him to trust her but how much was she about to give him? More than she had to or just enough to keep him happy?

'You know I received chocolates at work, sir?'

His brow arched as he waited for her to continue. 'I sensed you weren't happy about them.'

'I messaged him. Telling him not to send me anything again. You heard what he said tonight. He didn't know anything about the chocolates or the flowers.'

'Okay, Gina.' A warmth flooded through her body as he said her name. 'Someone else sent you chocolates and flowers, but who?'

'I thinks it's him still. He turns up at my house, he messages when I've asked him not to.'

'You're a detective. Keep it in your own time but find out if it's bothering you. It clearly is bothering you.'

He was right. She needed to sort Rex out once and for all. Now he was embroiled in her case, things had just become even more complicated.

'And Harte?'

'Yes, sir.'

'Try to stay safe and keep me in the loop with everything. Despite what you think, I really want to keep you on this investigation, you're my best detective. Some of us care you know?'

Did that mean the team or him? She hoped it was him. Her mind flashed back to their kiss, it had conjured all sorts of feelings within her and she knew that he could see that.

CHAPTER FORTY-THREE

Saturday, 11 May 2019

Sophie folded the silly masquerade mask up and placed it in her tiny handbag. That particular purchase from Ann Summers had been her husband's idea. *Let's dress up a bit, make the most of it,* he'd said. All it had done was make people think they were weird.

It had been a long evening and it was way past midnight. She sensed that something had gone down at the party, something neither the host nor the others really wanted to talk about. The single man in the trilby had looked put out for the rest of the evening. It hadn't prevented him from propositioning her though. Any other night she may have accepted his offer, but he wasn't really her type. Between him and the slimy sexist pig going by the name of Steven, she had written this one off. If this was all Swap Fun had to offer, she was probably going to delete her profile tomorrow. The others had left her alone, mostly showering all their attention on the sexy young woman in the blonde wig.

She walked alongside the river, leaving the distant lights of Bidford-on-Avon behind. She messaged her husband again.

> *I need you to come back and pick me up. You said you'd only be an hour and I'm on my own now. Just walking by the river. Call me as soon as you read this message. Did I say hurry?*

He'd managed to get off with one of the other party attendees. They'd left in his car way over an hour ago and had probably pulled up in a lay-by. She should have felt something at that thought, but she didn't. They weren't jealous types. This was something they'd done many a time before moving to this area. She needed more, he needed more, but deep down they wanted to be together. This arrangement suited them well. Their only rule was, they were never to fall in love or have a continued affair. It was always merely physical and while it remained fun, it would always remain a part of their lives.

She checked her phone. He'd seen her WhatsApp message, there were a couple of blue tick marks at the bottom, so why wasn't he answering? It was one forty-five in the morning. Her head was a little fuzzy from the champagne and she was feeling a little frustrated at not managing to meet a suitable partner. She gasped and turned as a branch cracked a few meters behind her. It had to be one of the losers she'd turned down. She stood tall and square, letting them know there was no way she'd be intimidated by them. With only the light of the moon, she caught an outline approaching. 'Who's there?'

He wasn't wearing a hat, so maybe it wasn't Mr Trilby. Or maybe he'd left his hat at the house. She'd walked a fair way. The house was now in semi-darkness with only a couple of bedroom lamps lighting the upstairs up. The beautiful outdoor lighting had now been turned off. Most people had gone home. The outline stopped, making no attempt to speak. 'Look, don't be a dick and just come out.' She really wasn't in the mood to play games.

He came closer and just as she was about to make out some of his features, he began taking photos. The flash blinded her. She stepped back, almost stumbling on the undergrowth. He snapped again and again, just giving the flash enough time to power up between takes.

'Look, can you stop it? You're blinding me.'

Her mouth began to water as she felt her stomach turn slightly. He was relentless with the camera. In a panic, she looked towards the road and noticed headlights heading towards the house or maybe that light was just the remnants of the flash, burning into her retina. 'My husband has come to pick me up. You should go,' she gasped. Her senses weren't deceiving her. She heard the engine too. It was definitely an approaching vehicle.

She flinched as she heard a rustling sound. He was shortening the gap between them. All she could see were green blobs from the flash, clouding her vision. Which one of the party attendees could this be? 'Steven? Is that you?'

She blinked several times, trying to clear her eyes. He was almost upon her. Run, that's what she had to do. She loved a kinky encounter but there was something about this set-up that didn't feel right. There were no boundaries discussed, no safe words, nothing. This person was trying to scare her, to intimidate her. Fighting her way through the bushes she darted towards the road, dragging a dead stick along that had caught on her jacket. If she reached the road, she could run along it and back towards the house. She stumbled and half-ran, her head full with the sound of blood pumping hard and fast around her body. His footsteps were behind her. She slipped under a hanging branch and almost slid in a patch of mud. *Get up, Sophie.* 'Ralph,' she yelled. If it was her husband, he'd be at the house by now. She almost cried as she imagined what he'd be doing. He'd be sitting in the car, trying to call. Why hadn't he called? She'd have heard her phone buzzing. She had to call the police. She pulled her phone out. As she went to press the buttons, she crashed into a tree. Slightly stunned, she turned to her pursuer. 'Please don't hurt me,' she yelled as she pressed another button, unlocking the phone. The flash went again. She felt the weight of what felt like steel toecaps connecting with her hand. He wasn't going to let her make a call.

Laughing, he was laughing. One thing he hadn't banked on was her ability to keep calm in such a tense situation. *Don't show him that you are terrified. Fight back.* She slipped her shoe off as he leaned over her. Before he had a moment to react, she slammed the heavy wedge into the side of his head, or was it his neck? *As hard as you can, first time* – that's what her father always said, and he was right. She had given all she had to that blow, no warning, just a swift whack.

He groaned and shuffled beside her. Now they were even. She was stunned and so was he.

Get up, get up now! She dropped the one shoe and ran, her bare foot being stabbed by sticks, nettles and stones. That didn't matter. She'd tend to her feet when she was safe. She waved frantically from the roadside and the branch that had hitched a ride on her jumper dropped to the road. Her husband turned around and was coming back up the windy path. She continued flapping her arms. With one shoe missing and her clothes torn, she knew he'd be worried. As the car approached, she squinted. Her vision was returning. It wasn't her husband. Had someone else come to help her attacker? Why hadn't her husband called her back? She began to hobble up the road but the car was catching up with her. What if it was him? What if he had gone back for his car and was coming to finish her off. Her weak arms dropped as she hobbled ahead, but she was no match for a car.

CHAPTER FORTY-FOUR

Gina lay in bed. It was almost three in the morning and she'd failed to sleep for more than twenty minutes in a row. Not knowing who sent the flowers and chocolates to the station was the worst. Had it been Rex and was he denying sending her the gifts now that he knew she was angry? Had it been someone else? If so, who? She turned again, dragging the ill-fitting sheet from the corners of the bed. Great – she wasn't destined to get any sleep at all. Not only was she uncomfortable, her bed was a creased up mess and the bedroom was cold, much like her love life. She flung her pillow towards the wardrobe and sat on the edge of the bed rubbing her eyes.

Her mind flashed back to a previous case where an attacker had broken into her house and almost strangled her to death. She rubbed her neck. The marks were long gone but the memories were still clear. She flinched as her cat scurried up the stairs and jumped on the bed beside her. 'It's not time for breakfast yet, Ebony.'

She glanced at her phone. There were no messages and no missed calls. All the personal calls she had expected would only have caused her more trouble anyway. Trouble, however, was better than the intense aloneness of her house right now. Ebony jumped to the floor and began prancing around, tail in the air as she meowed. Gina stood and the cat ran ahead, darting down the stairs and into the kitchen. A loud crash filled the silence. Gina's heart began to pound. There was someone in her house.

She took her phone from her dressing gown pocket and pressed Briggs's number.

'Gina. Is everything okay?' he answered almost immediately. Had he been lying there awake, just like she had?

'I think there's someone in my house,' she whispered.

'Go back upstairs and shut yourself in the bedroom. I'll call for backup.'

'No, I'm nearly there.' She took the last step and listened to the rustling just a few feet away. Creeping through her lounge in the dark, she grabbed a vase from the fireplace and continued stealthily towards the kitchen. With shaking hands she kept the line open so that Briggs could hear anything that happened.

'Talk to me, Harte.'

'Shh.' She flicked on the light. With a pounding heart she held the vase up with the other hand and almost cried with relief when she saw Ebony licking a pile of cheesy puffs that were strewn over the kitchen floor. The cat had edged them over, along with a box of cereal, and the contents had crashed and spilled over the floor.

'Don't call for backup,' Gina said. 'It's just my cat playing up.'

'Are you okay now?'

'All good, sir. I can't believe I disturbed you for this.'

'Well a lot has happened and I told you to call me if anything was worrying you, and I meant it. Even though we're not a couple, I well… err, I didn't stop caring, you know. Have you checked your alarm and locks?'

'They were fine last night.'

He sighed. 'Just indulge me and check them while I'm on the phone. At least I'll be able to sleep then.'

Will you? she thought. She hurried to the front door not wanting to keep him from his slumber any longer than she had to. It was deadlocked and the alarm was still set, just as she'd left it before going to bed. The back door was all locked up too. She checked her security app on her phone, scrolling through the footage, and no one had been near her house. 'It really was just the cat. I can't believe I called. I feel like a prize idiot now.'

'Like I said, I'm always here. I want you to call me if you're worried about something, Gina. Okay?'

'Clear as a bell. Thanks, Chris. Look, I'll let you get back to sleep. There are cornflakes and crisps everywhere and my cat is gnawing on things she shouldn't be eating.' She ended the call and fed the cat.

Opening the kitchen blind, she stared out. The moon lit the garden up. She hurried to the back window and looked out. Again, there was nothing. Her mind flashed to the previous case where she was being dragged under the kitchen table by a crazed attacker. That was never happening again.

She flinched as her phone rang. It was Briggs again. Her finger hovered over the receive button. They'd just ended their call, what more could he have to say. Had he felt something while they were out watching the party house? They didn't have to kiss but they had. She hadn't stopped it. It was a good disguise and it had initially protected their cover. That was all it was. She answered. 'I'm okay, honest!'

'It's not that. There's been an incident at the house we were watching last night. Damn it! If only we hadn't packed up so soon. I need you to meet me at Cleevesford Hospital ASAP.'

CHAPTER FORTY-FIVE

As Gina entered the hospital, she passed several women in hen party sashes, plastered in make-up, pushing the bride in a wheelchair. Her swollen stitched up leg was evidence of a rowdy night out. The crowd jeered and laughed as they took selfies with the patient. She followed the signs to ward twelve. A strip light flickered as she took the stairs to the first floor.

She turned and saw Briggs pacing with his phone in his hand. 'Yes, keep me updated on what's happening over there. We're just at the hospital now.' He placed his phone in his pocket and smiled, running a hand through his messy hair. She could tell he'd been up and out of bed within minutes, as had she. No longer looking and smelling like they were on a date, they both flashed an exhausted smile.

'Morning. Fill me in.'

They began walking. 'A woman, Sophie Dobbins, forty-two, was brought in a short while ago after being attacked alongside the river. She'd left the party and was walking outside while waiting for her husband to pick her up, this was between one forty-five and two. That's all I know at the moment. I'm just hoping we'll be able to talk with her so we can get a head start on finding out who did this. They were treating her wounds when I popped my head around a few minutes ago. They should be ready to see us now.' He looked at his watch and led the way.

Gina followed him through the double doors, past the nurses' station and they waited outside the side room in which their victim was resting. Jennifer, one of the crime scene investigators, arrived behind them looking sleepy and flustered as she pushed through with her bag. 'Bernard sent me. He's currently working the scene with Keith.'

'Great, we'll just make sure we have her clothes and take some samples, nail clippings, etcetera, and get them to the lab. It's too much of a coincidence, another attack following one of these Swap Fun parties.' Gina stared through the glass, hoping the nurse attending to their victim would at least acknowledge their presence.

'If you can fast—'

Briggs was interrupted by Jennifer. 'I know. Fast track as always. I'll get them to the lab as soon as I'm finished here. I can't promise immediate results but we will be on it. It depends on how much comes back from the other scene too.' Jennifer pulled a net over her low bun. 'Don't want to contaminate anything further. I don't know how useful this is going to be.' She glared through the window. 'It looks like they've cut her clothes off. She's been in an ambulance, been wheeled through the hospital. Too many people have already messed with the potential evidence so I wouldn't hold out much hope.'

The nurse left the room. 'She said she's up to speaking with you now. We've checked her over, it's mostly superficial. No stitches but she is very bruised and shaken.'

The small room was furnished with a single blue plastic chair and a television that hung from above. A jug of water sat on the cabinet next to her. The woman looked up through her brown fringe.

'I'm DI Harte, this is DCI Briggs. We'd like to speak to you about what happened. We also have a forensics officer present. May I sit down?'

The woman nodded and Gina scraped the chair close to the bed and pulled her notebook from her bag. Briggs stood at the end of the bed, the tiny room not very accommodating of his bulky frame. Even though he was SIO, she knew he'd want her to interview the victim.

'We realise you've had an awful night and you probably just want to clean up and rest but may we take your clothes and a few samples after we've spoken? The samples won't be intrusive, just nail clippings and hair. We want to find out who attacked you and this would help us greatly.' Gina offered a slight warm smile, trying to put Sophie at ease.

'Yes, take the clothes.' With a shaky finger, she pointed at the pile of clothes that had been folded up and placed in a recess in the bedside table. Jennifer shuffled between Gina and the window with an evidence bag as Gina continued interviewing their victim.

'Okay, can you tell me what happened? Take your time.'

She nodded. Her face blotchy with tears, and dirt smudged over her chin and forehead. Her right hand was bandaged. A tall thin man, probably of a similar age to the woman, knocked on the door and entered. 'Shall I wait outside, love?' he asked.

The woman nodded. Gina could sense that there was some tension between them from the way that they looked at each other. He obligingly left.

'That's my husband. He arrived just before you. Anyway, the party was coming to an end – the party at my friend Sarah's. My husband had popped out and was meant to pick me up but I couldn't get hold of him so I went for a walk. I knew he'd call me back soon.' The woman paused. 'I'd had a few glasses of champagne and was feeling a little tipsy, not drunk though. I can easily do over a bottle of wine before I need to go to bed and the glasses of champagne were small. Everyone was leaving and I didn't want to put anyone out so I thought I'd just wait around outside.' Tears welled in her eyes. 'I was just walking along the river. A few minutes later, I felt like there was someone there, someone behind me. I thought it was just one of the partygoers leaving and playing a bit of a joke so I wasn't too worried. It was then I saw a figure approaching in the dark.' Sophie closed her eyes and began to tremble as she recalled what had happened. 'I asked who they were and there was no reply. They just kept taking photos of me. The flash, it was so bright, I couldn't see a thing after the photos were taken. I was getting worried at this point. I'd been walking for several minutes and there was nothing and no one around. I saw headlamps in the distance so thought I'd run for the road. I thought it would be my husband actually.' She opened her eyes and wiped a tear from her face.

'What happened next Mrs Dobbins?' Gina sat patiently, waiting for her to continue speaking.

The woman rubbed her head, brow furrowed as she tried to think. 'It all seemed to go so quickly. I couldn't work out who it was. He started chasing me. At one point I pushed a branch out of the way and I'm sure it flicked back on him. It would be between where I was found in the road, where the ambulance finally arrived, and the river. I followed quite a direct route. I really thought he was going to rape me or kill me. He went to grab me. I took my shoe off and hit him with it. I remember him backing off at this point. This is when I ran to the road. I dropped my wedge where it happened, I remember that much.'

'Where did you strike him?'

'I'm not sure, I couldn't really see. The side of his head maybe, his neck…'

Gina glanced at the floor and saw one wedge-style shoe placed under the bed. She nodded at Jennifer. Another thing to bag. 'You're doing really well, Mrs Dobbins. So you ran towards the road. What happened then?'

'When I got there, I thought the car that I could see was my husband's but it was just someone driving past. A man who'd just finished a night shift somewhere. I was hysterical when he pulled over, thinking my attacker had come for me again. Anyway, he let me sit in his car while he called an ambulance and that was it.'

'Where was your husband at this point?'

She looked away and began fiddling with a mucky tissue that she'd been dabbing one of her sores with. 'He'd been for a drive.'

'We know about the party you attended. We know it was a Swap Fun party. Can you tell us if you spoke to anyone in particular during the course of the evening? Or did any one give you reason to be concerned?'

Her frail shoulders dropped. 'My husband met a woman there and they hit it off. It's something we enjoy doing but I don't expect you to understand.'

Gina smiled warmly. 'We're not judging you, Mrs Dobbins. We want to find out who attacked you. The more truthful you can be, the better.'

She wiped her nose and pulled the sheet up over her shoulders. The room was warm but Gina could tell that Sophie Dobbins was trying to hide how vulnerable she felt. Her secret life now exposed to outsiders. 'I was angry with him, that's Ralph, my husband. He went and left me for ages. He said about an hour but he was longer and the party was coming to a close. I didn't really know anyone there as it was my first time in this particular group. Who did I speak to? I suppose I spoke to most people there but I spent longer speaking to a man in a hat, some sort of trilby. He took it off inside but carried the thing around like it was his baby. Then this idiot kept coming over to me. I kept trying to shake him off but he was loud, telling me he could give me the best knee trembler I'd ever had around the side of the house. I know I'm up for these things, but I do like being treated with respect. He was over suggestive, over touchy, I think I slapped his hand away at one point and told him to shove off. His girlfriend kept almost staring me out as if she hated me. Then she began flirting with Ralph.'

Gina just knew. She looked across at Briggs.

'What was his name?' Briggs asked.

'I'm sure it was Stevie Boy; that was his profile. I kept trying to get him out of my way. I actually liked the man with the bald head who had come with the woman in the blonde wig. I kept trying to shake off this letch but he wouldn't leave me alone.'

Gina glanced at Briggs again. They both knew she was talking about PCs Smith and Kapoor.

'I told him to leave me alone and he even followed me to the toilet. Creeped me out a bit. He rubbed his crotch and sort of grinned with his tongue out. Yuck. That poor woman who came with him. I thought it could be him or Trilby man to begin with, sorry I didn't catch his name.'

Gina didn't need to know. It was Rex, the man she'd met on Tinder and dated a couple of times. She also knew that he was a little strange. Obsessive? She wasn't quite sure yet. If he had sent the flowers and chocolates, maybe he was a little thoughtless. He had turned up at her house without an invite a couple of times. She made a mental note to check through the rest of her CCTV footage. It was something she'd failed to do properly on a regular basis since getting the system installed. She wanted to know if he had been at other times. 'Can you describe your attacker at all?'

The woman shook her head and lay on the crisp white pillow which rustled as she got comfortable. 'No. I only thought it may be either of them. I could tell it was a man from his shape. I can't work out whether he was tall or any features, the flashes kept messing with my vision. He crushed my hand with his foot.' She held her bandaged hand up. 'He was wearing work boots with steel toecaps, hence my two broken fingers. I felt the tip of the boot as I tried to free my hand; absolutely rock solid they were. But I didn't see anyone at the party wearing that type of footwear.'

'Did you see what else your attacker was wearing?'

She shook her head. 'As I said, at first it was dark, then I was blinded by the camera flashes. I wish I had.'

Whoever arrived by car could have kept a pair of work boots in the car. She remembered Rex turning up in a taxi. How premeditated could this attack have been? Could the boots and a bag of tools to commit the attack have been left there earlier in the day, even before they arrived to watch the house? Had he planned to attack Sophie Dobbins in particular or would anyone have done? Her mind ticked over as all potential scenarios ran through it. Sophie may not have been a definite target. No one knew that her husband would hook up and take longer than anticipated with his swap partner. They were also new to the meet and hadn't met anyone there before. The attacker also hadn't really seemed to be as in control, like he didn't know the person he'd been pursuing. Had he not been quite as bothered about Sophie? Maybe he was angry a certain other person hadn't arrived. Who? Her thoughts reeled back to Steven. He was definitely capable and was as misogynistic as his brother. Gina knew all too well how he liked to treat a woman.

'Thank you so much, Mrs Dobbins. We'll leave you in the capable hands of our CSI, Jennifer. I'll call a doctor or nurse over to be here with you both. When you are feeling better, please come down to the station to give a formal statement and call me immediately if you think of anything else.' Gina pulled a card from her bag and handed it to the woman.

'Could it be the same person who killed that woman in Cleevesford? They were all taking about it at the party. I heard people asking about her, about the couple, Jade and Noah. They were all saying how it was just bad luck and that the killer was probably someone random that had followed her around the streets that night. Some of them thought it might be the man she was paired with, someone called Rhys who no one's heard from since. This is all what I heard. That probably doesn't help you much.'

'Everything helps us to build a picture. You've been so helpful.'
Gina stood and smiled as she gestured to Jennifer. She needed all
these samples to be sent to the lab and quickly.

As Briggs left her to search for the toilets, she headed towards
the exit. She did a double take and spotted Mr Dobbins pushing
the coffee machine around. 'I don't think hitting it will help.'

'It's just swallowed up my only pound and not given me a
drink. Damn it!'

'Here.' Gina pulled a coin out of her pocket and gave it to
him. She had a minute to spare while Briggs was in the men's
room. After, they were due at Bidford to meet up with Bernard
and see where the attack had taken place. 'Mrs Dobbins has been
through a lot tonight.'

He held his palm to his head and closed his eyes. 'I can't
believe I was late. If only I'd been on time this would never have
happened.'

'Where had you gone?'

'That's the thing, I wasn't even too far away. We went to
Bidford Green alongside the river where people go with picnics
in the summer. It's just over the main bridge and to your right.
I gather my wife told you about the party.'

Gina nodded. 'Who were you with?'

'Some woman called Dawn. I thought she seemed fun and
Sophie seemed to be chatting away to the man in the hat, so I told
her I wouldn't be long. Dawn's partner seemed to be trying it on
with everyone there. I thought we'd be way less than an hour but
she kept going on and on about her partner, Stevie Boy. She ended
up crying and pouring her heart out. Nothing at all happened. I sat
there bored out of my tree while she went on and on about how
Steven never did this, never did that, made her feel like nothing.
I was well turned off by that point. She made a weird pass at me
then. It was as if she didn't want to but thought she should. It's
not the way I work. I like the woman I'm having sex with to want

it as much as me. I'm not into feeling like I'm taking advantage. She then kept trying to grope me and kiss me. I told her to stop, which she did but then she cried more. Kept saying she was ugly, too fat and that I didn't find her attractive. I just didn't know what to say. Eventually, I said I'd drop her home which is why I was longer than I thought I'd be. I drove back to Cleevesford because I felt sorry for her. That's when I saw the message from Sophie. I called her. She was in the ambulance at that point. I headed here and here I am now. Thank you for the pound.'

'You're welcome. We'll see you when your wife is feeling a little better. We'll need formal statements from both of you.'

'Of course. We want to do all we can to help.' He smiled and left in search of another coffee machine.

Gina would check his information with Dawn but, at the moment, Mr Dobbins wasn't a suspect. Their little conversation had however given her a bit more insight into Steven and Dawn. Her ex-brother-in-law was fast becoming a suspect. She remembered what Briggs had said, she'd need irrefutable evidence before any move against him could be made.

Briggs headed towards her, shaking his wet hands. 'I think the hand drier's packed up.'

'Let's get over to Bidford and I'll fill you in on the way.'

'I've just had a call from Bernard while I was in the loo. How's that for timing? They've found the spot where she was attacked and he wants to show us something.'

CHAPTER FORTY-SIX

Birds filled the air with their early morning song. Gina's feet were already damp from the morning dew. New shoes had to be a priority when she got a moment. Briggs had headed over towards where Bernard and Wyre and Jacob were speaking about the case. 'Morning.'

Jacob turned. 'Oh, hi, guv. We've spoken to everyone living close by. There aren't that many as you can see. This place is quite away from neighbours. Swap Fun Sarah said she finally said goodbye to everyone about one thirty in the morning and locked up for the night. She thought Sophie Dobbins had been picked up by her husband. We have a list of party attendees, which we'll crossmatch to the last party. As we know, the only people from the previous party that attended last night were Steven Smithson and Dawn Brown.'

Gina leaned in. 'Get this, Dawn Brown was with our victim's husband at the time the attack took place. While I'm thinking about it, O'Connor will be in soon. Call him and ask him to contact Dawn and check the events of last night. We need to see if their story matches. If they do, where was Steven during the attack? They came by car. Maybe Sarah remembers if there was a car left on her drive at the end of the night.'

Wyre flicked a page on her notebook. 'I asked that very question. There were no cars but her own on the drive when Mrs Dobbins left. Some of the guests came by taxi but she can't remember who.'

'So, Steven's car was gone too.' In her mind she imagined Steven parking up close by, waiting for his moment while Dawn was occupied with Sophie Dobbins's husband. Had he sent her off to see if Mr Dobbins was game so he could at least try to orchestrate a chance of getting Sophie alone? It was a distinct possibility but all still theory for the time being. As for Rex, had he got a taxi home? This case was feeling too close to her personal life for comfort. She wanted to be in Steven's face, pushing him, interrogating him. She wondered what he'd do to her? What if everyone at the station found out who she really was? If they knew every disgusting detail of her past life they'd never look at her in the same light again. Maybe they'd respect her more for going through what she did or maybe some of them would think she was party to what went on. Who would they believe, her or Steven? She was more credible but he shouted louder. Loud or credible? She knew *loud* was just as convincing.

'Guv, I've been shouting at you for ages. You need those ears syringing,' Bernard said as he approached her in his forensics suit and beard cover, his boots covered in muck and soaked through.

'Sorry, Bernard, I'm all ears now. We'll continue this back at the incident room, when we've all had our morning coffee,' she said to Wyre and Jacob leaving them to follow Bernard. He passed her a suit, gloves, boot covers and a hair cover. 'Briggs said you called him and you've found something,' she said as she dressed. When she was suited up, they walked towards the yellow evidence markers, squelching on the soggy ground. Bernard turned off the battery lights as morning began to shine a light on what was in front of them. In the distance, mist rolled off the river, looking as though it would spill over and contaminate the fields behind. 'Blood. See this branch here?' She nodded. 'Well, just over there we found the shoe. You can see how the foliage has been parted slightly, this is the route she took when she ran and he followed. It's either her blood or his.'

'We need to get that off for testing. See if it matches anything left at the scene of Jade Ashmore's murder or Diane Garraway's house. Here's hoping there's a definite link there.'

'We've also bagged up the shoe and taken various other samples including that of the earth. We may recover some of the perpetrator's clothing and be able to match any dirt from that to the scene. Everywhere has its own unique make-up, just like us. Oh, we have footprints too, they're all a bit messy, not as clear as I'd like as the earth is so soft. It did rain a bit before we arrived. It looks like our perp was also wearing boots with a thick tread as we do have a little bit of patter left behind. I'll get the photos over to you in a short while. We haven't got an exact size but we're looking at about a ten.' Gina thought back to what their victim had said. She had felt one of the boots and had also described them as steel toecaps.

'Great job. As always, I'll be waiting on the report. Obviously, if there's anything else you can feed across to me as you go, call me straight away.' As she milled around, she thought of what Sophie Dobbins would have gone through. She'd ran through the trees wearing only one shoe while being chased by someone who'd tried to crush her hand with his foot, breaking two of her fingers. But she'd hurt him, hitting him with her wedge shoe. Gina would tell the team to look out for anyone sporting an injury.

Her phone beeped. A reminder that she had an interview at nine in the morning. This one she had to attend, but not before she rushed home for a quick shower and freshen up. Time was against her, as it always was. There was also something else she needed to investigate, something on a personal level.

She waved Briggs over. 'We really need Rex in for interview and I can't instigate that one. He was here last night. He's weird, I can verify that myself. He had opportunity and at the very least needs to be eliminated from our enquiries.'

He nodded. 'Leave it with me.'

CHAPTER FORTY-SEVEN

One thing Gina was sure of was that Swap Fun clearly linked Jade Ashmore's murder and Sophie Dobbin's attack. The culprit either attended both parties or saw both invites on the Swap Fun website which made her question whether interviewing Colin was necessary. She soon dismissed that thought. He was one of the last people to see Jade alive on the night of the fifth of May and he had opportunity and no alibi. There were also a lot of disguised profiles on Swap Fun that they still hadn't matched to real-life identities. He could be one of those hidden profiles and therefore have known exactly when and where they were all meeting.

She checked her watch. She'd have to wrap this interview up swiftly as Briggs had booked Rex in for interview in just over an hour. She needed to be there behind that glass, observing his reactions, before starting her own personal investigation.

'Wyre, are you ready?'

'Sure am, guv. He's already been seen to interview room two. It's just unfortunate that he's stinking the room out.' She grabbed gloves and a swab pack. 'Got these. You wanted a swab taken, didn't you?'

'Yes. Blood was found at the scene of last night's attack and we have other samples in evidence. I want his sample crossmatched against everything.'

Gina took a deep breath before entering the tiny square room. Wyre was right, it smelled like the back of a bin lorry. She was grateful that he had his shoes and socks on this time as watching him pick might have sent her over the edge.

'Colin Wray, thank you so much for coming in. This interview is voluntary and will be recorded. Do you need a drink before we start?'

'Nah, I wouldn't mind a puff. Is it okay to smoke?' He pulled a roll-up from a worn looking tobacco tin.

'I'm afraid not. This interview shouldn't last too long. You'll be able to go outside and smoke then.' He threw the roll-up back into the tin and clicked the lid on, then took a mint from his pocket and began to roll it around his gummy mouth, making sucking noises that were already making the hairs on the back of Gina's neck stand to attention.

Wyre started the recording device.

'Interview with Colin Wray, aged seventy years old. DI Harte and DC Wyre present. Date is Saturday the eleventh of May, 2019,' Wyre confirmed.

Gina continued with the taped introduction then leaned forward to question Colin. 'Please tell me again, in your own words, what happened in the early hours of Monday the sixth of May, the bank holiday Monday.'

'Not again. I already told you what I know when you came to my house. I don't know any more.'

'Please, we need it recorded formally. Jade Ashmore was murdered that night and as her neighbour, we're sure you want to cooperate and help us find the perpetrator too.'

He sighed and scratched his head. Bits of thin grey hair parted to reveal crepe-like skin. Gina cast her eye over his scalp and forehead. Sophie Dobbins had hit her attacker with a shoe. Surely, if Colin Wray had been her attacker, there would have been some sort of mark left behind. Colin's hair was too thin and light to disguise injuries. Maybe her counter-attack hadn't been as hard as she had thought, or the attack mark was below his neckline. As Colin relayed the exact same details as before, Gina half-listened and half tuned out, trying to figure out what was behind Colin's persona. His records showed that he was a soldier in his younger years and a fitness coach later in life; that would explain why he still looked fit. He still had the strength to be considered a suspect.

Fitness coach? Aimee was a personal trainer and he had made some comments about her that hadn't sat well with Gina during their last conversation. Her mind ran through his previous record. One of his charges included that of sexual assault. He'd been convicted as CCTV evidence showed him rubbing against a seventeen-year-old girl on a train. He had strength and he also had a warped sense of entitlement when it came to women. But why could he possibly have wanted to kill Jade? Maybe he'd seen her with Rhys and was jealous. Gina knew jealousy to be a powerful emotion. If he'd been spying on Jade's husband, Noah, while he was kissing their babysitter in the garden, what was to say that he hadn't been watching Jade for a long time? He could easily have taken a bag with his chosen murder weapon and followed her as she went looking for her husband. With his military background, he'd be well versed in surveillance techniques. They needed his DNA. A test of the blood on the branch may give them all they needed to get a search warrant and make an arrest.

Colin coughed as he smiled. 'And there you have it. That's me done. I'm off for a smoke now.' His gaze landed on Wyre's lips and Gina could see him licking his own.

'Mr Wray?'

'What?'

'We will need to eliminate you from our enquiries. To do this we will need to take a swab.'

'But I 'aven't done anything.' He slammed both hands, palms down on the table.

Gina remained silent and stared at him. He slumped back in the creaky chair. 'We could be looking to make an arrest and caution you. You can see how this looks, Mr Wray. If you didn't do anything, this test will show that.'

His beady eyes met hers. Who would blink first, him or her? He did. She smiled. His shoulders dropped as he leaned forward and opened his mouth wide. White fur covered his tongue and a sulphuric odour escaped from his mouth. Gina took small shallow breaths.

Wyre put on a pair of latex gloves. 'I'm just going to pop this in your mouth and wipe it against your cheek. It won't hurt.' His gaze turned to Wyre as she continued. 'All done.'

'Thank you, Mr Wray. You've been very helpful. We'll show you out.' Gina opened the door and the man couldn't hurry out fast enough. 'Get those straight to Bernard and Keith for analysis. Oh, and I want Dawn and Steven in. I know we checked Dawn's story earlier but I want it on record. They are the common denominator at the moment.'

'Will do, guv.'

Gina left the room and caught up with Colin Wray. He shakily took the roll-up from his tin and slipped it between his lips. As she led him to reception, she passed PC Smith in the corridor. 'Can I speak to you in my office?' she called.

He nodded and continued. She smelled the sleeve of her jacket. Colin Wray's scent was now embedded into her for the day. Going home for a quick shower before interviewing him had been a pointless exercise.

As she approached her office door, noting that she had less than ten minutes until the interview with Rex, she spotted PC Smith waiting for her to arrive.

Rex who? She didn't know anything about the man she'd met up with, slept with, let into her home.

'I have a call-out so I need to be out of this station in five,' he said as he followed her in. They both sat.

'That's okay, it won't take long.'

'I've updated the system with everything that happened last night. I thought we might get more but we mostly got hit on – well Kapoor mostly got hit on – and I remember the victim Sophie, she kept looking my way. Just before you called us out, the man in the hat came in and said one of his old girlfriend's had been lurking around outside spying on him. Everyone had a bit of a laugh about it and carried on. Then we left. I've been thinking about that all night. Who was his ex-girlfriend?'

Gina felt her face warming up. He was referring to her. How could she throw Smith off the scent? 'We've eliminated her, she isn't a worry.'

'I haven't seen anything on the system. Haven't you updated it yet?'

There was no avoiding telling him. Smith wasn't a fool and before she knew it, he'd soon be discussing it with others in the team. 'Smith, I dated him. He saw Briggs and me together as we watched the house. I met up with him twice. I don't know the man. Can I trust you?'

He nodded and closed her office door. 'Of course, guv. But I can't hide anything from Briggs that might affect the case just like I wouldn't hide anything from you.'

'And I wouldn't expect anything less. Briggs already knows as we've spoken about this but if you need to speak to him about it, go ahead. There's something else, someone is sending me flowers and chocolates as you know and I think it might be him. I'm asking unofficially, did you see who pulled up when either were delivered?'

'You say unofficially?'

'I'm looking into this myself in my own time. I want to know who sent me these things. I've been through a lot so maybe you can appreciate that I'm worried.'

He nodded. 'I was there when they were delivered. I noticed that it was a local business. The flower shop on Cleevesford High

Street, I remember the logo but not the name of the shop. I've used them a few times to send flowers to my wife.'

'At least she was happy to receive the flowers, unlike me. She's a lucky lady.'

'Tell her that! Anyway, I'm running behind. Let me know when you've finished interviewing the people at the party. Kapoor and I will keep out of the way for now.'

She smiled. 'One of the attendees is due to arrive any second. I'd go out the back if I were you. Thanks, Smith.'

Her phone beeped. Rex.

Why am I sitting here, waiting to be interviewed? I heard about what happened to that woman, Sophie, last night. It was nothing to do with me. You're just trying to pin this on me because I dumped you.

So that's how he was going to play this one. There was no way he'd get an answer from her. When would he get the message that she didn't want to hear from him again, ever? He'd tell them all that he dumped her and now she's harassing him. Idiot, she had the texts to prove it was the other way around but if he wanted to play that game, he was certainly going to lose.

She almost trembled as she thought of Steven. The weight of what they both might say may be her downfall. Downfall, she was thinking like a person that had done something wrong. She hadn't chosen to have Steven as a brother-in-law and all she'd done was go on a couple of dates with Rex. If that was all she'd done wrong, exactly how bad could it get? She checked her watch and hurried – she didn't want to miss Rex's interview.

CHAPTER FORTY-EIGHT

Gina hurried along the corridor and slipped into the viewing room. The interview had already begun and Rex was speaking. Wyre and Jacob sat opposite him, Jacob leading the interview. The night before, Rex had looked so polished at the party. In the cold light of day, he seemed so ordinary. Light jumper, jeans, hair slightly kinked where he'd rolled out of bed, stubble.

'I didn't see her after eleven. I went home in a taxi and I've already given you the name of the firm, you can check. I'm also here voluntarily so can we hurry this up? I need to get to work.'

'What is it you do?' Wyre asked.

'I work in a phone shop in Evesham. I sell phone contracts.'

Gina blushed as Briggs looked over. She knew so little about the man behind the glass.

'You have my address too. That's where I went. I went home and I went to bed.'

Jacob took a sip of water. 'Is there anyone who can verify that?'

'Am I under arrest or something? I live alone. The taxi dropped me off and I went home to bed.' Gina made a note that in an hour and forty-five minutes he could have easily changed and then gone back to the party. He could have driven back, knowing that he had an opportunity to attack some poor unsuspecting partygoer.

'You're not under arrest, Mr Satterthwaite, but a serious crime was committed that night and we need to know what happened. Do you regularly attend these kind of parties?'

He smirked as he folded his arms. 'I love these parties and go to as many as possible. I'm a single, highly-sexed man and they allow me to attend. Some people like three in a bed and I guess I can always be someone's number three. Why would I not go?'

'Did you speak to Sophie Dobbins over the course of the evening?'

He shrugged, holding both of his hands up. 'Yes, and so did all the others. I thought she was a bit of all right but she didn't seem too interested so I left her alone. I'm not the type of person that goes around harassing women.' He stared at the mirror.

Gina knew he wondered if he was being watched.

He glanced at his phone and smiled before continuing. 'But, as I said, I didn't pull that night so I went straight home. I had to be up early for work and didn't feel there was anyone there for me that was worth pursuing. Although I normally have a lot of luck, I am still quite choosy, believe it or not.'

'What name do you go under when you use the Swap Fun forum?' Wyre asked.

'Hot Rod.' Gina made a note to check all interactions between everyone on the site and Hot Rod.

'Something bizarre did happen last night though.'

'Go on.'

Gina placed her elbow on the desk and leaned on her hand, knowing what would come next. Briggs gave her a friendly pat on the shoulder. She knew she should have updated the system as soon as she'd got home last night but she hadn't managed it. Her mind had been everywhere. 'Oh no, I haven't told them.'

Briggs's shoulders dropped. 'Damn it, Gina. You must have known that would come out. You're normally so hot on the updates. The fact that he recognised you wouldn't have mattered but they should have known that before going in to this interview.'

She'd stuffed up, she knew she had. 'I'm so sorry, sir. I didn't expect an attack to occur last night and when it had, I was all-consumed with finding out what had gone on. I hardly slept and was then called out soon after going to bed. I've been up all night, been to the hospital, attended a crime scene, already conducted an interview and I haven't even had breakfast. I'm running on nothing here.'

'I'm sorry. I know we all are, but you can't let things stop you doing your job and jeopardising the rest of us. Stay on the ball or you're off the case, I mean it.'

She felt a tear force its way out of her eye. He was right. She had let important information slip through the net and now Wyre and Jacob were about to find out.

Rex leaned forward and smiled. 'I saw one of my exes alongside the river with a new man. Maybe they did it, you should look them up. She was probably jealous that I was getting on with my life. Maybe she thought I'd hooked up with this Sophie.'

'Who did you see alongside the river?'

'DI Gina Harte.' He leaned back in his chair and grinned.

'Interview terminated at eleven sixteen.' Jacob pressed the button on the recorder.

Tears fell down Gina's cheeks.

'Harte, you have to control this. You had no idea that he'd be there. He has ended up embroiled in our investigation. There was no way you could have known he was the one masquerading under the name Hot Rod on Swap Fun. I have to question your taste in men though. We'll deal with this but you will remain at a distance from him and Steven, do you comprehend?'

She wiped her face and nodded. 'Totally. I best apologise to Wyre and Jacob. I owe them an explanation and I need to update the system straight away. I am so sorry.'

Jacob entered. 'Guv, I could've done with knowing that you knew him. Do you know how stupid we looked in there?'

She knew exactly how they felt and for that she was totally ashamed. Another tear slipped down her cheek.

'Steven Smithson and Dawn Brown are here now too. No time to rest on this one. Can we catch up later?' Jacob said as he glanced at his phone.

'Of course,' Gina replied and Jacob left.

She leaned on Briggs and he folded a firm arm around her and sighed.

'Gina. I need you to go to the kitchen, have a coffee and get your notes up to date. Do it now.'

'But, sir, I need to be here to see Steven being interviewed. Don't shut me out of the case.'

He let out a frustrated groan and pulled away from her. 'I'm not shutting you out. I'll be here. It's being recorded and I'll fill you in straight away. You're getting too involved. Go and have a coffee and something to eat. That is an order. You messed up and you need to go and put things right.'

She almost knocked the chair over as she stood and slammed the door. She'd totally blown it.

CHAPTER FORTY-NINE

Gina leaned against the worktop, nervously tapping what remained of her fingernails on the chipped empty mug of coffee that she'd finished drinking ten minutes ago. She'd tried to eat a biscuit but had found herself gagging on it. She felt far from hungry even though her rumbling stomach was clearly protesting against that thought. She flinched as the incident room door pushed open, then her shoulders dropped as the cleaner wheeled a vacuum through, quickly leaving through the far door. What was taking them all so long? She wanted and needed to know what Steven was saying. Maybe he was talking about her, telling them of things he thought he knew that weren't true. If so, that may deem the end of her presence on this case. She'd be holed up in her office sifting through CCTV while the others took a meatier role in the investigation. Her fingers began to tremble and her head throbbed with the pressure of built up tears.

'Gina?' She dropped the mug and it shattered all over the tiled floor. Briggs bent down to pick up the pieces. 'Too much caffeine?'

He could tell she was jittery. 'No. I just, I don't know. I'm being sidelined here.'

'It's for your own good. I said I'd fill you in and as your superior, as one who cares I could see you needed a break. Whether you like it or not, you are now, at the very least, emotionally involved in this case. I can't have that fact clouding your judgement. Look at me.'

She did. There was no malice in his actions, she could tell that much.

'You're a good detective. I need it to stay that way. I need you to be focused, don't let your heart cloud your sense of logic. Sometimes, a little time out is needed. You know you could take some holiday—'

'I don't want a holiday, sir. I want to catch the bastard who killed Jade Ashmore. I want to find Samantha and I want to find out who attacked Sophie Dobbins. This isn't about me, I see that. I also see how it looks. It's not my fault Steven Smithson has been embroiled in the case. It's also not my fault that someone I met up with a couple of times just happened to be at a house we were staking out last night. All these things were beyond my control. As for the job, I will never give it any less than my all and you know it. I slipped up last night, and I know that may seem unforgivable and for that I'm sorry. But, I'm on this case, I need to be.' She wanted him to see how determined she was and she was sure he could. The thought of being at home, twiddling her thumbs in front of daytime television, alone, was enough to ensure she fought to remain at work. Holiday? That was the last thing she needed. CCTV duties, no way. She bent down and picked up the other half of the mug and threw it into the bin. 'There, mess cleared up.'

'If only all messes could be cleared up that easily. Apologise to Wyre and Jacob. Did you update the system?'

'About half an hour ago. All done.'

He bowed his head. 'I have and I always will have full faith in your abilities to solve a crime, Harte. Don't you dare let me down or we'll both be for the chop.'

She knew that he'd have pulled anyone else off the case had it been them. She swallowed and coughed back her emotions. 'I would never let you down, sir.' She paused. 'I need to know what happened in the interview.' She had to bring their conversation back to the case, back to what Steven may have said about her. 'Was I mentioned?'

'I sat in with Wyre. Dawn claims that she was dropped home by Ralph Dobbins and Steven was already there and didn't look ruffled at all. We couldn't see any visible cuts or bruises on his head or neck so going on what our victim said about hitting her attacker with a shoe, it's not looking like it could be him. Saying that, he could be hiding a wound. She was in a distressed state and wasn't totally sure of where she'd hit her attacker. As it stands right now, we don't have enough to charge him. He's voluntarily given his DNA which is ready for sending to the lab. To arrest him prematurely could really ruin the case, especially as you know him. At the end of the interview, once the tape was switched off, he was babbling on about how much you had it in for him. We have to watch that this doesn't escalate. I tell you something, if your ex-husband was anything like that smarmy bastard, you have my sympathies.'

'You can't begin to imagine how bad Terry was.' Steven really was determined to ruin her and save himself in the process. She wouldn't let that happen, hoping that his little sound off in the interview room wasn't the start of something bigger to come.

'Go to your office, listen to the interviews and do some investigating. See what you can fathom from both interviews. I'd appreciate your thoughts as soon as possible. We have to get on top of all the evidence we have. It's all chaos at the moment, evidence and investigation strands coming in from everywhere. I want order.'

'I'll do that and I'll call forensics, see if any results are available to us. We need something soon. Why does it all take so long?'

'I know. Not enough resources to go around, but we'll get there and you will. I know you will. Get to it.' He straightened his tie and smiled as he left.

Gina's phone pinged with a message.

It would be awful if the press got hold of the fact that we were lovers and you got me arrested. Why are you following me about, Gina?

More to the point, why was Rex still texting her after she'd asked him not to? Her head began to pound as even more pressure built up. She slammed her hand onto the worktop. Her finger hovered over reply. No, she would never reply again. What would be, would be. Replying would look even worse. Another message followed.

> *Were you watching me? Fancied a bit of what we were up to? I know you like to be in control, a bit kinky. You like messing me around. Is this why you pulled me in? This time I get to mess you around. See how you like it. The press want to interview me, saw me coming out of the station. Should I oblige?*

The last thing she needed was the press linking such a high profile case to her personally. That would be her end. She knew from the emails that had been sent that the press were hassling them for more information and they weren't about to stop. Now they were hanging around in the car park, fishing for witnesses who were prepared to give them a story.

How was everything going so wrong? She kicked a filing cabinet and gasped for breath, anger welling from her core. Pacing up and down, she struggled to see how things could improve. She had to make headway on the case before she was well and truly kicked off it or worse, suspended. She re-tied her messy hair, took a deep breath and entered the interview room, calmly smiling. She would start with her apologies. Time was ticking.

CHAPTER FIFTY

Almost out of breath, I approach the back of Aimee's house. Coming here is risky, especially after all that's happened, but I need to see you. My lovely girl – I missed you, but hey, a man has needs and you're not fulfilling any of mine as yet. My head aches a touch and it's a bit chilly this morning. I should have gone home to change but here I am instead. I grin. I won't tell you what I've been up to, a man has his secrets.

I feel my stomach. I'm quite fit, you know, Aimee. I've been following your programme on YouTube. It's just the job. Soon you will feel the results for yourself. I run my hand across my firm stomach, not quite a six pack but it's under there. A few more pounds off and a bit more work on toning and fitness and I'll be someone you'll be proud of. I don't know how long I can wait though. If I close my eyes, I can smell you, taste you and feel your curls running through my fingers. I love how your hair curls.

I feel a stir in my jeans. You do this to me. You're doing this to me. I close my eyes and think of you. I need you. I've waited too long already. Flinching, I let go of my crotch. What was that?

Damn it! What's she doing here? I thought she was at work. She normally works Saturdays. I scarper along the path and head towards the main road, waiting until she's gone. Bag flung over shoulder, earphones plugged in, she almost walks to the beat as closely as her bulky frame will allow. That's the housemate out the way and I'm ready to go in.

The stupid friend doesn't notice a thing and carries on down the road. Let's have some alone time, just you and me.

CHAPTER FIFTY-ONE

Aimee plunged her hands into the washing-up bowl and began scrubbing the breakfast bowls. So much had happened in the last few days. The local news had reported yet another incident the previous night. She glanced at the back door. The key was still on the kitchen table, where she'd left it after locking the door.

There was a knock at the front door. She wasn't expecting anyone. It could be Rhys, the police, post. She abandoned the washing-up and stared down the dark hall at the front door, contemplating her next move. It was as if she was standing in treacle, her body slowly turning to stone.

Another knock. A faint silhouette filled the small narrow window at the side of the door. It looked like the caller was holding a parcel. Had she ordered something? No, not a thing except a replacement gym mat for the one that had a tear in it. That was a couple of weeks ago and she'd been in battle with the company over a replacement. She exhaled and shook her hands, feeling her senses return to normal. The caller was about to leave. She darted to the door and opened it. 'Sorry about that, I was just elbow deep in the washing-up.' The caller wasn't holding a parcel, it was a bag.

Slamming through the door, he knocked Aimee halfway across the hallway. She grappled with the bannister, cold with shock as she pulled herself up and ran into the kitchen, pushing the door. If only she could close it, she could wedge it with a chair. Gasping, she reached for the chair. As she did, he slammed his way through.

He wiped his arm over his sweat-lined forehead. The faint red mark on his neck was revealed as he reached out towards her, his T-shirt shifting slightly. 'Please, please don't hurt me. I know you don't want to hurt me.' He grinned as he pulled a mallet from his bag.

'Oh, but I want to. You make me want to, but first, I have to teach you a lesson.'

Her legs buckled as he brought the mallet down. She dodged out of the way making him hit the table. She could see he was seething now. She ran for the door, she'd locked it. The key. It was on the table. She'd locked the back door to keep herself safe, now she felt anything but. 'Please, don't hurt me.'

'You just can't see what you've done, can you?'

'See what, tell me.' Maybe she could keep him talking.

'What you do. The way you are! You're just like her.' He brought the mallet down. She guarded her head with her hands, feeling the strength in his blow as it made impact with her wrist and forearm.

The neighbour's dog began to bark as it ran down the garden. It knew she was in trouble. Barney had been trying to warn her and she hadn't listened. She knew someone was watching her and she'd been right. 'Barney,' she called, hoping that the dog would continue to cause a nuisance and attract her neighbour's attention.

'Shut up, bitch.'

'Barney.'

She went to stand. Knocking on the window would cause more noise. As she did, he struck her head with the mallet until her flecked vision faded. She could hear the dog but she could no longer shout. Dribble ran down her chin and her ear began to ring.

'The other one died on me, she deserved it too – it was a bit too soon but it was always going to happen. You're not going to die, not yet. Stand.' He pulled her by the arm.

She tried to stand but her legs gave way. Collapsing back onto the floor, the room spun. Her vision – it was like she was looking through a tunnel, a long tunnel with a fuzzy wall. The ringing was louder, then it became constant and piercing. The tugging on her arm, more violent. She was sure she was walking, either that or the hallway was moving, like she was on an escalator. Daylight, rain, wet. Her hair, rain, or was it blood? The car on her drive. She'd parked on the road, so she thought. Barney, he was still barking. His owner was shouting out the back door, she could hear it over the house. Sobbing, she knew that meant he wasn't looking out of his front window. Bushes, that's all there were at the side of her house. Her large lean-to shimmered ahead. Was it shimmering?

She felt her teeth rub on the blanket that lined the back seat of the car. A prick to her neck was the last thing she felt before he covered her up with another blanket. 'Where are you taking me—'

Sleep, so tired, so sore, nightmares, Jade, blood, he was chasing her. The river, she was falling and falling. Choking. No, she was in her bedroom, Rhys stared at her with bloodshot eyes, grinning as he blocked off the bedroom and then there was Sally, her client. Sally was after her too. They all wanted to hurt her. They were all in it together.

Rumbling sounds, maybe she was still in a car. Was she in a car? Relaxed muscles. Deeper and deeper she fell into the abyss of her mind. Breathe – she couldn't. The smell, diesel and air freshener. Deeper and deeper. The rumbling of the engine, so relaxing. She wanted to fall. Count. One, two, thre—

Pain, gravel piercing skin. Daylight, now darkness. She closed her eyes, wanting to sleep. A sliding door, clanking.

His robotic voice echoed through the room. 'And of course there was Jade. After all those years I never thought I'd see her again. You, young lady, you are part of that same problem. It was meant to be you but when I saw her there, I just knew I had to take care of business. I couldn't let it go and I can't let you go.'

Uncontrollable sobs filled her lungs. Her brain wasn't working, it kept drawing her back to the dark abyss. She couldn't fight it.

'And all I wanted was a normal life and from the beginning it was never going to be. She brought those men into our lives. When that happens, people get hurt. I had to stop you before you became that person. Pretty little Aimee will always be Pretty little Aimee. Don't be sad, I'm helping you. I can't let you ever become like her.'

She listened as his sobs sounded in time with hers. Hypnotically, they lured her back where she wanted to be. Her sobs softened to the rhythm of his, until silence took over. The abyss was waiting.

CHAPTER FIFTY-TWO

As the interview with Steven came to an end on replay, Gina's face burned with embarrassment. Just as the tape was switched off, her name was mentioned and she knew what had come after, Briggs had told her. Her phone call to forensics hadn't given her anything new to go on as yet. Their mystery attacker was still preserving his anonymity.

Briggs had messaged a few minutes ago and prepared a brief press release, appealing for witnesses to Sophie Dobbin's attack. Another reason for the press to hang around for a scoop.

She flicked open her notepad. There was something that had been bothering her, something she needed to investigate. If Rex had sent her the flowers and the chocolates, she needed to know. She had the name of the flower shop. Smith had seen their van pull in and she knew the only florist that worked on Cleevesford High Street was Blossom's Bouquets. She'd called them, giving them the time and date of the delivery. An email on her personal account pinged up on her phone.

> Hi Gina,
>
> Just following up on your call earlier. I've had a look at our order book and can confirm that the sender of your gifts was a man called Trevor and he paid in cash. I don't have a surname unfortunately or any further contact details. Hope that helps.
>
> Hayley – Blossom's Bouquets.

Her mind whirled with everything that was happening. The flowers, a man called Trevor. She didn't know anyone called Trevor so why would anyone of that name send her flowers and chocolates? Paid cash – it was obvious that Trevor was not Trevor, but who was he? Was he Rex? If so, she had no idea why Rex would just not send them using his own name. The concealment felt more like harassment. The thought of someone playing with her made her skin crawl. She had to tell someone, she should tell Briggs. CCTV, maybe the shop could show her exactly who this person was. Her investigation wasn't official. She had no right to demand it, she'd have to rely on the goodwill of the florist when it came to giving it to her. She replied.

Hi Hayley,

Thank you so much for getting back to me – much appreciated. I don't know of anyone called Trevor and I'm a little concerned for my safety. I know this is a lot to ask but do you have CCTV? Is there any way I can get hold of a screen grab of the sender. I would be hugely grateful if you could assist me in getting to the bottom of this.

Many thanks,

Gina.

Before hitting send, she was tempted to finish the reply off with DI Gina Harte but this was a personal investigation at present and she'd done enough damage for one week. She wouldn't use her DI status to get what she wanted. She'd only just smoothed things over with Jacob and Wyre, the last thing she wanted to do was upset anyone else on the team.

The name Trevor ran through her mind. The harder she thought, the less she came up with. She stared at her email hoping that the florist would hurry with her reply. Another message pinged up.

Mum, I thought you were going to come and visit soon. I haven't
heard from you for a couple of weeks and Gracie keeps asking
about you. Please don't let her down. Hannah.

She buried her head in her hands, she'd forgotten completely.
She had promised to call the previous weekend but with all that
was happening, it had slipped her mind. Again, she'd failed in
her motherly duties. Since Hannah had moved, she'd missed her
granddaughter more than she ever thought she would. As soon
as the case was over, she was going to visit. She quickly replied,
telling her daughter she'd call her soon.

An email pinged up.

Hi Gina,

It's not something we like doing but I don't like the thought
that someone has used my service to harass you. I like that
flowers and chocolate make people happy, not cause them
anguish. I took the liberty of taking a screenshot when I looked
for their details. I was curious myself, curious to know if my
CCTV system was up to standard. I've attached a photo of
Trevor for you. Be warned, it's not clear at all. It's grainy and
a little blurred but if you know this person anyway, that might
not matter.

Hayley – Blossom's Bouquets.

Her finger trembled as she clicked on the file. How dare he?
Through the grain and blur, there was no mistaking who was
sending her these gifts. She grabbed her half-eaten sandwich and
threw it across the room, lettuce escaping everywhere. She called
Briggs. 'I know who sent me the flowers and chocolates.'

CHAPTER FIFTY-THREE

The abyss – Aimee was climbing and clawing her way up and out. But where was she going? She squinted but however hard she tried to focus, all she could see was black. As she turned, her shoulder wedged into a cold wall. Dampness seeped through her top, she shivered. Cold, so cold. Through chattering teeth she let out a small squeak. Why couldn't she say what she wanted to say? She wanted to call out for help.

Nothing to grab onto, nowhere to go, nothing to see. Breathing laboured and shallow. She reached out, grabbing for anything but there was nothing to grab. Was she still asleep?

A memory filled her thoughts. 'Hello,' Aimee called. 'Rhys? What happened?' She was at home. Nicole, had she left for work? Her house, there was someone outside. The dog was barking but then she remembered someone knocking at the door.

Her pounding head, arid mouth and growling stomach sickened her. It felt like she'd been drinking. But she didn't really drink, it wasn't a part of her clean eating routine. She fought to lift her hand to her sore head. Wet and stinging. She flinched. Senses returning, she tried to grab, hit. It was as if she was in a box, a tiny stone box. She shuffled slightly and punched the wall behind her, nothing except her own cracked knuckle. Above her – when she tapped, the sound was different, like wood. Hyperventilating, she began to scream and yell. 'Get me out.' Breathe, she couldn't breathe. Buried, she was in a hole, in a wall, in a grave. Oxygen, no oxygen. Fighting with everything she had, in all directions was fruitless.

Breathe, breathe. Her head was awhirl with no sense of space or time, nothing to see. Cold but hot. Clammy but parched. Nothing, the abyss, her grave—

She closed her eyes, focusing on the patterns forming in her confused mind. She slipped down, like a feather floating from a bird perched in a tree, swaying from side to side and upside down through tempestuous wind pockets, finding freedom in the night skies. No stars and no moon, just floating in empty space. 'I can't breathe—' she spluttered. That's when the loud, rhythmic clunking monster began to take chase. Clunk, clunk, clunk. Don't look back. Never look back. She closed her eyes.

CHAPTER FIFTY-FOUR

Diane lay on the settee as she stared at the paracetamol next to the toast she'd made several hours ago. Water glistened in the glass as a ray of sun emerged through the cloud, shining through the dirt on the lounge window. She listened to the children as they laughed and played on their bikes outside her house.

She'd stared at the phone all day but still the caller hadn't tried to make contact again. There was no way Samantha would ever remain out of her life for this long if she were alive. So many years had gone by and she'd lived in hope that one day, the woman she thought of as her daughter would walk through the door. A tear slipped down her cheek, landing on the arm of the settee.

The back door rattled and was followed by a loud knock. She forced her head off the damp patch, almost screaming out as she un-wrangled her stiff body. She snatched the painkillers and threw them in her magazine rack, hiding them out of the way. No one could know of her plan, they'd have her committed and that would spell the end of her, or worse, they'd try to stop her.

Hobbling through the house, she spotted her brother staring through the window, raising his eyebrows and pointing to his watch. Always in a hurry, nothing had changed there.

As she turned the key, she caught sight of herself in the window. That bedraggled image was soon replaced with her brother's angry face. On unlocking the door, he shoved his way in with a small bag of groceries.

'God it stinks in here. I don't know how you can live like this. No wonder you're always miserable and depressed.'

She sighed and fell into a chair at the kitchen table. She was depressed because of the pain, because of Samantha. A few dirty dishes and a pile of clutter were the least of her problems. 'If you're going to go on at me, bro, you may as well just walk back out that door now. I'm not in the mood.'

He ignored her and placed a casserole dish on the side. 'Stew, not your favourite I know, but it's what we had for dinner last night and I don't expect you to be grateful anyway.'

'I don't ask you for this. I don't ask you to come here, make me feel like shit and leave food I don't like. You make me miserable. You! I'm sick of it.'

'Why don't you just hurry up and die, for heaven's sake. You're such a moaning cow. After all that I do for you. How would you live if you didn't have me? Think about that one. I'm the only person who visits you, the only one who helps you and this is how you speak to me. Do you think I want to be here all the time, coming back and forth? I should be enjoying my life now but no, I'm stuck looking after you all the time.' The veins on his neck protruded through his tight skin. How could he be so cruel? She remembered the sweet little brother he'd once been.

'You know something, you ungrateful sod, I should have been enjoying my teen years but no, I was bringing you up after Mum died.' Had she just said that to him? Her bottom lip quivered as she waited for his comeback.

He sucked in a deep breath and fixed his wide-eyed stare on her as he sat on the chair next to her. 'Is that what you call it? Bringing me up. Whoring around is what I call it. Just like your friend Samantha, you were both a pair of whores. I can spot people like you a mile off now, that I thank you for, but the rest…'

Tears filled Diane's eyes. 'I had no choice. I did it all for you. We needed to eat and all the jobs I had, they weren't enough. I made sure you had shoes for school, days out with your friends—'

'And I had to listen to how you earned all that money through our thin bedroom walls, every single night. Those men – to them you were nothing more than a piece of meat. You get what you ask for and that's what you deserved.'

She brought back her swollen wrist, revealing her old scar and slapped him across the face. Her breathing quickened and her eyes welled up. 'How dare you!'

He dropped to his knees in front of her and grabbed her hair. 'You know something, Samantha was just like you were back then. I know, she practically flung herself at me. I didn't want to but I thought why not? Let's get to know her better, work out why she was the way she was. You know something, I sort of hate myself for getting close to her. She used me, you know. Just wanted to make that stupid married man jealous. I wasn't the only man she used either.'

'If you've hurt her, I'll—'

'What? Stupid, frail, little Diane. What makes you think I hurt her?'

Her mind flashed back to the phone call. 'Did you leave the card and break into my house? Did… did… you call me yesterday?'

A grin spread across his face. 'Someone's been calling you. Who knows? Maybe I did, maybe I didn't. Maybe I'm screwing with you, after all, you screwed me over all those years ago. Maybe I'm not screwing with you and it was one of your old clients hoping for one last shag before you fall apart.' He laughed, his glassy-eyed gaze fixing on hers.

'It can't be.' No one knew who she was any more. She remembered a particular client who became more violent than the others, the one who burned a circle in her brother's buttock with his cigarette, the one who dragged him out of the house in just his underpants and left him crying in the snow, humiliating him and holding her hostage for three hours. Her heart broke as she thought about what they'd been through but they'd needed the money. Her heartbeat sped up another notch as she realised she could have at least tried to prevent all the bad things that they had both gone through.

Her past was finally catching up with her through her brother's anger. He'd always kept his distance but now he was letting it all out. They were just kids at the time and she acted in the only way she knew how following the death of their mother. 'What are you trying to tell me? I can't work you out. That call wasn't to do with the past. It was to do with Samantha, I know it.'

'You're assuming it was me! Always going against me like you always did. How do you know it wasn't to do with the past? We're in a different age now, we have Facebook, Twitter and Instagram. Anyone can find anyone now. You're there for all to see. It's impossible to hide and you know what, if your past comes back for you, it takes me with it. Whose fault is that? Or maybe, just maybe, the past needs to come out.'

Head in hands, tears dripped into her lap, soaking her dressing gown. 'I'm sorry I let you down. I wasn't much more than a child and we were both grieving for Mum.'

'All those bad things happened to me and it was all because of you. That arsehole who used to make you cry like a baby for a lousy few quid, he didn't stop at you. I bet you didn't know that, did you? When you were out, he'd come over and threaten to tell everyone about you and I had no choice. I wish it was only his cigarette that had damaged me. You were too busy thinking about yourself though. Did you wonder why I was so quiet and shy, no friends, always on the outside of everything? Did you ever wonder why I used to scratch until I bled? No, it was always about you and how you suffered to make me happy. When we lost Mum, I needed you to be there but you went off the rails with your drinking and whoring. Look at you now, pathetic. We reap what we sow and look at what you're reaping now. When I look at you, all I see is the past. You allowed them to hurt me and you need to pay.'

He was right. She'd done everything wrong. He'd never opened up like this. Resentment spilled from his mouth. She had no idea things were so bad for him or that he'd suffered so much. She sobbed and yelled as she thought about what her little kid brother had been through. 'I'm so sorry, please forgive me. I need you to forgive me.'

'I. Will. Never. Forgive. You.'

'I need to know, did you hurt Samantha? Did you call yesterday? Was it you?'

He leaned forward, his nose touching hers. A faint smell of weed on his clothes. This was a smell she'd never detected on him before. He was mad, paranoid. 'You're asking the wrong questions. That's your problem. She wasn't family, I'm your family. I've just told you how hurt I was and all you do is ask about her. If only you'd cared about me as much as you did her. I was just a child! I was nothing to you. I've given you chance after chance to make it up but all you do is suck the lifeblood out of me with all your problems. All I wanted was for you to love me and care about me, the way you cared about Samantha.'

She exhaled as he pulled back from her, stood and kicked the kitchen cupboard. He paced back and forth as he wiped his nose and gasped. She knew he wanted to cry, she'd seen him act up like this as a little boy, only now his behaviour all made sense. He wouldn't cry though, he'd always get angry and destroy something in the house. She remembered that little mousy-haired boy, a bit scruffy, always getting beaten up after school. He'd loved their mother so much, more than anything. She should have thought more about him and his feelings as their mother was dying before his very eyes. Instead she'd gone off the rails and expected him to fend for himself. That was her way of coping but she didn't expect him to understand that. What happened next, that had been about survival in order to stay in their house and not lose her brother to the care system. She had promised her mother she'd never let him go, just before the heavy doses of morphine finally lured her into her final sleep.

'I was never as good as Samantha. You're a class act, aren't you? Look at you now, pathetic, and it's all your doing.'

'Did you hurt her? Just tell me.'

He grinned as he grabbed the door handle and thrust it open. She watched it bouncing on its hinges as he hurried down the path. He was right. She was nothing. If her past came back and her community knew who she really was, who knows how they would react. The woman who slept with strangers for money while her little brother was in the next room. The woman who let her little brother suffer at the hands of those men. Her little brother who was no longer the kid she knew and loved before their lovely mother died. Tears poured into her lap. She'd done everything wrong. Her mother would have been so disappointed.

She shuffled out of the chair, back into the living room, slumping on the settee. Thoughts of him being hurt by that man, the one she'd allowed into their home, thoughts of Samantha and her past, and the fact that all this was connected, filled her mind. It should have seemed clearer now but all that she had were muddied thoughts. Her past was already back, her brother was making sure of it.

She reached for DI Gina Harte's card. She should tell her about the phone call, even tell her that Samantha could have been having a relationship with her brother. Dropping the card, she realised she couldn't. He'd be arrested and he'd hate her more. She couldn't do that to him after all he'd been through. It would be the last straw. She'd already done enough damage by ruining his life.

Screaming, she reached into the magazine rack and pulled out the paracetamol, emptying them out on to the little table, one by one with her clumsy fingers. She didn't want to struggle any more. She didn't want to be in pain every day and she didn't want to think about her unthinkable past, carrying such a heavy burden. She couldn't tell anyone what she thought her brother had done. It was all her fault and she had to pay the price. Maybe then he would finally forgive her.

A memory flashed through her mind of her brother, pre growth spurt. The signs had been there but she'd been so wrapped up in her own misery – the bedwetting, the anxiety, the inability to mix easily with his peers. She was guilty of not only ruining her life, but his. It was all her fault, her brother's pain and Samantha's disappearance. *Hurry up and die* – his words were loud and clear. She stared at the tablets through teary eyes. If only she was brave enough to take them.

CHAPTER FIFTY-FIVE

Gina tapped her fingers on the desk as she watched Jacob and Wyre re-interviewing Dawn. The woman suddenly seemed keen to talk, claiming that she'd failed to mention something in her previous interview.

Steven had long gone, leaving Dawn alone in the station. She glanced at Briggs. He was never going to leave her alone during this case, always with her like she needed to be constantly monitored. She silently ground her teeth as she thought back to the photo that Hayley of Blossom Bouquets had sent to her. He wasn't going to get away with continuing where his brother had left off. She'd told Briggs that Steven was playing with her and they agreed to keep what they knew separate from the case. He spoke to the team, telling them of her position in the case, making her feel like an open book, something she hadn't really felt during her career to date.

'Dawn, just go over what you said about the evening,' Wyre said.

She wiped her nose with the crumpled tissue. 'He was disappointed that nothing had happened for him that night; that he hadn't slept with anyone. I knew from looking at the invite online that it wasn't going to be a swapping party, it was more about meet and greet, getting to know new people in the area that had these same interests.' She ruffled the tissue and pieces of it broke away and fell to the floor. 'He kept poking me in the ribs saying he was still going to bag a shag as he called it and that I had to try, that it would turn him on. That's when Sophie's husband smiled at me. I'm not sure if it was the wine or if I really liked him but before I knew it, I was in his car and we'd left Steven talking to his wife.'

'And?' Wyre leaned forward, head slightly tilted as she tried to put Dawn at ease.

Gina shook her head. 'Dawn wasn't at the party when this happened. She can't tell us anything.'

'I know but we need to know what she was lying about,' Briggs replied.

'I know, I know. Sorry, sir. Thank you for letting me be here.' *Thank you for letting me be here.* It was like some sort of a joke, as if she were the one being investigated.

Dawn continued and Gina's attention moved from her own frustration to what was happening in the interview room. 'We drove to a grassy area over in Bidford, right by the river and we just talked. I tried to please Steven, I showed this man, Ralph, that I was game but he could tell I wasn't. I don't know what came over me then, I poured my heart out to this stranger in a car and he was such a gentleman, everything I'd love in a man that Steven wasn't. After a while I realised I liked him but he pushed me away. I think I scared him off with my ridiculously overemotional state. I couldn't face Steven after that. I didn't want to go back and see that he was with Sophie or any other woman at the party. Anyway, Ralph drove me home to Cleevesford. When we arrived, he saw that he had messages and missed calls from his wife so he rushed off, said he needed to hurry back to pick her up.'

'Do you know what time this was?' Jacob asked.

She shook her head. 'I have no idea. It was way after midnight. I went to bed and lay there hoping that Steven would be in a good mood when he arrived back.'

'So now we can establish that Steven wasn't home when you arrived?' Wyre glanced at Jacob.

'Yes. I'm sorry I said he was already there when I arrived home but he came back not long after I got in. I just got confused with what had happened and times. I heard him unlock the door and swear as he kicked my shoes in the hallway. He didn't even come up the stairs. I spent all night awake and upset, wondering if he was angry with me.'

'Why would he be angry with you?' Wyre asked.

The woman shrugged her shoulders. 'I don't know. Maybe he was fed up I'd not gone back to Sarah's house. Maybe he'd not managed to get off with Sophie, he hates rejection and I think he had his eye on her.'

'Can you remember when you left Sarah's house?' Wyre moved her black fringe from her eyes and tucked it behind her ears.

'No. Now I know what happened to Sophie, I wish I knew when I left the party with Ralph. I wish I'd looked at the time when Steven came home. I was too busy lying there with a nervous stomach wondering if he'd come up the stairs and start a row. Thankfully he didn't.'

'Did he drive home?'

'His car was on the drive when I woke up in the morning and I did hear him pull up, so yes. He was parked just outside the grounds of the house. He doesn't like getting the car blocked in.'

Gina watched the woman intently through the glass, bouncing her leg under the desk as she waited for Dawn to say more.

'Harte, I can't hear a thing with you making a racket,' Briggs said. 'You know when you tell O'Connor about being annoying?'

It pained her to think she was as annoying as O'Connor. 'Sorry, sir. It was him, I know it.'

'It's not looking good for him, I must say, but with him knowing you, we need more than usual. You know what Wyre is going to ask next?'

Gina nodded and hoped that Dawn would agree to what they would ask.

Wyre let out a small cough. 'Dawn, may we have permission to search your house? We know Steven has his own flat but from previous notes, we know he lives with you most of the time. It would really help us to eliminate him from our enquiries.'

'Are you saying he could have done this? That he could have hurt Sophie or killed Jade? Am I living with a killer?'

'I'm not saying any of that. We would simply like to eliminate you both from our enquiries.'

Dawn began to weep. 'I just want this to all be over. I've been stupid thinking it could work between Steven and me. My friends, my family, they all hate him, say he's been bad for me but I didn't listen. I'm listening now. Yes, go ahead. I want to know who hurt these two women and I'm not prepared to get into any trouble with you lot for Steven.'

'Yes,' Gina said as she punched the air. 'Did we take Steven's DNA while he was here?'

'Yes, but no results for that test as yet. I'm hoping we find something at Dawn's house to hurry the process along.'

'I'll go and get ready and we'll head over there immediately. We can't give him time to find out we're going in. He'll be straight over to destroy any evidence.'

'You're not going, Gina.'

'What?' She waited for his reply. Open-mouthed. She needed to be there, to see everything unfold in real time. She wanted to be the one to arrest Steven. 'I need to be there.'

'I said no and you know why.'

'Please, can I at least wait in the car? Please, sir, I need to be involved.'

'You can wait in my car at the other end of the street and I'll keep you updated at all times. I will be there to supervise the search. I want everything done by the book. You interfere and I will suspend you. Got it?'

She smiled. 'Thank you, thank you, thank you!' She flung her arms around his neck then quickly released him. He straightened his collar up and smiled back.

'Just tell me, Harte, is there anything else you're not telling me?'

She thought back to Steven's threats to expose her with his lies. 'Only that he'll say or do anything to discredit me. It won't be true but he hated me when I was with Terry. He stood by, enjoying it when he was cruel to me. I don't know what I ever did to him and I'll never know why he is the way he is. I wish he'd just leave me alone.'

'What's he likely to say?'

'I can't predict that one, sir.' She could, but she wasn't going to tell him.

'You know I'd do anything for you, Gina. If you ever need my help, just say.' His look almost pierced her thoughts. She could never let Briggs risk himself for her. She'd never take advantage of his feelings like that. No, she'd find her own way out of this one.

CHAPTER FIFTY-SIX

Gina watched from the other end of the street. It was no good, Dawn Brown's caravan was blocking her view of the search. Briggs stepped in front of the car and was talking to Wyre. A couple of officers came out of the house, carrying evidence bags. She sat bolt upright, rocking the car. They'd found something. Grabbing her phone, she texted Briggs. She needed to know what was in those bags. They'd been rooting through the house for over an hour and only now they were bringing things out. Another officer had his head buried in the boot of Dawn's car and was feeling around the crevices. Neighbours peered through their windows. Gina wondered if Dawn knew any of them, or if indeed any of them were her friends. She suspected that Steven chose her friends for her.

She checked her phone, no answer. Tapping on the door handle, it crossed her mind to get out of the car and storm over, demanding to know what they'd found. She was still a part of the investigation team and Briggs telling her to keep back was making things worse. She let go of the handle, she wasn't risking suspension for Steven.

Steven wasn't even there. Briggs had suspected that Steven would have mentioned something to Dawn about being Gina's ex-brother-in-law. If he had told Dawn, she hadn't let on during her interview at the station. She had come across as defeated, as needing to end the relationship and the police's interest in her. She suspected their relationship would be well and truly over when Steven found out that she voluntarily let the police search her house.

Wyre came out with another evidence bag and filed it in the van.

A car passed her. Heart in mouth, she turned away. It was Steven. She didn't catch his expression but she knew immediately that he'd seen what was happening and, at this moment, he'd be seething. Briggs's fringe blew up as a gust of wind caught it. He looked over as Steven pulled up behind the caravan, parking across the pavement blocking the evidence van in. Leaving his car door open, he stormed over to Briggs. Gina opened the window a touch, trying to listen to what he was saying, but it was no use. She was too far back. The sound of traffic whizzing around the ring road that backed the new estate filled her head.

Exhaling, she flopped back in the seat. Being there was a total waste of time. She wasn't involved. Briggs still hadn't replied and she was clueless as to where the investigation was going. She pulled a pear drop from the centre console and popped it in her mouth.

Something wasn't right. Briggs had led Steven back towards his car and was whispering in his ear. It looked like they were having hushed but stern words. He passed something to Steven with gloved hands. Steven's face reddened and he clenched his fists as Briggs snatched the tiny object back. Her foot tapped in the footwell as Steven stood speechless before storming into the house. Briggs began walking over.

She opened the door and stood on the pavement, willing him to walk faster. He had something to tell her, she knew it. 'What was all that about, sir? I saw you pass something to him.'

'Nothing. That was a private chat between Stevie Boy and me.'

He was holding something back from her. How dare he do that after all she'd been through. More than anything, she needed to know what was happening with Steven. 'What have you found?'

'That I will answer. We found a large stash of weed in the spare room, along with a few wraps of what appear to be cocaine. It was stored in a locked cabinet and apportioned into little bags. At the very least, we are pulling him in for dealing. Of course, he might deny it and try to say it belonged to Dawn but we had to bust the cabinet open as she didn't have a key. And why would she give us full permission to go through her house if she knew that the drugs were there? She didn't even ask for a solicitor.'

Gina's mind flashed back to what Diane had said about Samantha. After seeing her mystery lover, she turned up at Diane's smelling of marijuana. 'But—'

'Yes, great minds think alike. His prints will be all over the packets, not hers. They're off to the lab.' Briggs stepped into the driver's side of the car, Gina followed.

'That's not all you found, is it?'

He shook his head. 'We have seized magazines, some of them pornographic. We know Diane was sent a card and it contained a message spelled out in pieces of magazine. There's a lot of material to go through in the search for a few missing letters. We also found some receipts in the upstairs waste bin next to the drug cabinet. There were two from Blossom's Bouquets for the flowers and chocolates. We have now confirmed that he's been sending you the unwanted gifts. What we don't know is why.'

Gina knew why. He was playing with her mind, hoping she'd crack. He'd seen her at breaking point when Terry had played mind games with her. Terry used to send her flowers and chocolates after he'd given her a beating, as if that would ever make up for all he'd done to her. At first, she'd lapped up his apologies, blaming herself for being a bad wife. She had soon realised there was no pleasing him.

After he'd forced Gina and the prostitute to perform at knifepoint with tears sliding down their faces, he'd sent her those very gifts the following morning. The poor prostitute had left in shock, holding her forty pounds in cash.

'Harte, are you okay?'

'Sorry, yes, sir. You know about Terry and me, what went on. After he'd been violent, the next day he'd always send me flowers and chocolates. I know it's a familiar story but yes, that was me, a walking cliché. He's trying to mentally stuff me up because he feels threatened. It's not going to work, I can tell you that much. I'm not that Gina any more.'

'Good, glad to hear it. That Gina belongs in the past and new Gina is who we all know and love.' He paused.

'What else?'

'We also found a pair of black gloves in his locked up cabinet. He's also a smoker, just like our perp.'

'Yes, the cigarette packet we found by Diane's had Jade Ashmore's fingerprints on it. He's been playing with us. I don't want him to win.' Gina felt her body tensing. She knew full well that the evidence was nowhere near complete to have him on a murder charge or link him to Samantha. Everything was circumstantial and there was no sign of the murder weapon. Close, but not quite. Forensic evidence would seal the case though. However, the drug possession and possible dealing were tangible and he'd be brought in. He had to crack. She felt a shiver reach her neck and she shrugged her shoulders a few times to eradicate the feeling. If he felt penned in, would he start attacking her character like he'd promised? He was dangerous.

'You're worried about what he might say, aren't you? That the rest of the team will get to know about your past and what happened to you. Don't be.'

She let out a huff sound. He had the potential to affect her career. Between Rex threatening to speak to the press and Steven threatening to twist her past into something that might turn her colleagues against her, how could she not be worried? She felt her chest tighten. Panic rose. Heart hammering, salivating mouth, sweat prickling her armpits, boiling hot. She began loosening her coat and shirt, fanning her face with a notebook. Breathe, Briggs couldn't latch onto what was happening.

He pulled a paper bag from the storage in the side of his door and passed it to her. Grabbing it, she placed it over her mouth and breathed into it until she'd calmed down a little. Sweat began to run down her forehead but she was cold and shivery. 'Thank you.' She passed him the bag.

He blocked her hand. 'You keep it.'

'I'm sorry. I'm so sorry.'

He shuffled in the car seat. 'Look at me, Harte.'

She turned to face him.

'You can get through this. It's just another case. Step back and look at everything objectively. It's not about you. Yes, you got caught up with the wrong people in life but this is all about a murdered woman and a woman who's been missing for years. It's about them and we need to focus on that. Do you understand?'

She nodded as she wiped a tear from her face.

'He's not going to bring you down, you have to trust me on this one.'

One further look into his eyes left her unable to speak. What had he done? She felt tears welling up in her eyes, tears she'd save for later, when she was alone.

The sound of a door slamming caught their attention. Gina stared at Dawn's house as O'Connor brought Steven out in cuffs and bundled him into the back of a police car. They'd arrested him and now it was all going to kick off. The worse thing about it all was that she wouldn't know exactly what he'd said until the interview was over.

CHAPTER FIFTY-SEVEN

The clunking had continued for what seemed like forever but suddenly, quietness enveloped her small space. All Aimee wanted to see was the sky, she didn't mind if it was raining or dark. She wanted to see the moon, street lamps; cars driving with headlamps on, pubs lit up at night, anything but this dark void she was shoehorned in.

As the drug wore off, the clunking monster had turned into machinery. Was she near a factory unit or on the industrial estate? Had he buried her in the grounds or was she stuffed into the wall, where forever she'd stay until she finally let out her last breath? Maybe she'd lie there rotting until one day, someone would come along and find her bones. Gasping for air, she began to weep as she thought about her kidnapper.

She'd only met him the once. Thoughts flashed through her mind. She jogged around the area on many occasions. Maybe he'd seen her then. They both lived in Cleevesford. Maybe he'd seen her in one of the shops or at the pub. Rhys, he still hadn't made further contact. Maybe he'd been angry and they'd plotted this together. He hated her enough and he'd never let anything lie if anyone dared to upset him.

Rhys would often move things in her garden, leave her gate open in the night to make her think she was going crazy or being watched. He was a game player and maybe this was one of his games. He'd told her these stories with a certain level of humour in his voice when she'd caught him out. She'd even laughed at one point, especially when she'd forgiven him after catching him in the act. What had seemed like a practical joke back then now seemed sinister. She should have seen it. It was now her turn. How he'd teamed up with her kidnapper, she had no idea. All she knew was that if he had any involvement, he'd be around watching and laughing, sitting in the darkness waiting to say it was all some kind of joke.

'Rhys, if you're there, please let me out now.' Something dropped to the floor. She could hear behind the thick walls. She wasn't in a grave. Whoever was out there was sitting at the same level as her.

They weren't going to answer. She had to be wrong about Rhys. Would he really conspire to kidnap her and confine her to this hole to make his point? Her mind was all over the place. She recognised her captor, she knew he'd got on with Rhys at the party. They'd even shared a spliff together at one point. She thought he'd seemed nice enough, but not now. Not now he'd invaded her home, hurt her, kidnapped and imprisoned her. Not now. She began to shiver. 'Please, I know you're there. We can talk about this. You can't leave me here forever. I need the toilet.'

She flinched as he cleared his throat. A second later, a door slammed. 'Come back!' Once again, she was alone in the dark. It was worse now, she was fully aware of what was happening to her. Sobbing, she curled her arms around her cramping legs and rocked back and forth in the tiny space.

CHAPTER FIFTY-EIGHT

What to do, what to do? Aimee has made things difficult for me. I stare out of my windscreen and watch Gina's house. I know about her alarm and CCTV system so I stay back, observing. Maybe I could leave a note.

'Argh!' I pummel the dashboard until my knuckles are red raw. How had I let this happen? I wanted Aimee to like me, meet me at the right moment and now I'd lost that chance forever.

I stare at the fields and all I see is darkness. There are no street lamps around here. Don't know what to do. Hitting the side of my head as I ponder that thought, I watch as the DI pulls up and greets her cat before she disables her alarm.

Write a note now – I could post it quickly and drive off. I have a hooded jacket, she won't see me and my car is too far away from the camera. No, I won't write a note. Maybe I won't say anything. I got it all wrong.

Now I see it. Aimee was wrong for me. She'd never willingly go for a man like me. Just because I've researched her and know her well, it doesn't mean she knows me. She knows nothing about me apart from what's on my Swap Fun profile, even then, she doesn't know it's me.

Gina closes her curtains. Now I can't see a thing. What did I expect? She's not dippy like Aimee. Gina is a real woman, experienced and tough. I like that. Sorry Aimee, I don't think I can help you out here. Gina, I may help you if you stop being a bitch to me.

How can I get closer to you, see what you're doing. I want to watch as you get changed into your casuals or your nightclothes. I want to see you in the comfort of your home, stroking your cat, eating your dinner – normal everyday things. I gently close the car door and place my dark hooded jacket on. What the hell. I'm going for a look. Maybe after, I'll know if I want to help you or not.

CHAPTER FIFTY-NINE

Gina lay in bed, laptop in front of her. All the evidence had been updated. Bernard had called confirming that the blood they'd found at the crime scene where Sophie Dobbins had been chased and attacked did not match that taken from Steven's sample. It didn't belong to Sophie either. Their perpetrator didn't have a record as nothing on the database was a match. Her fingers twitched as she fought the urge to slam down the lid on her laptop.

Steven's interview was probably still in progress. Every minute seemed like an hour as she waited for a phone call. Would it be Briggs or one of the team? Her face and neck began to burn up. Maybe they were all sitting in the incident room, drinking coffee and discussing her personal life.

She jolted up as her back gate slammed. It was locked from the inside, it always was. The new gate was secure. She launched out of bed in her nightshirt and ran into the back bedroom, staring out into the darkness of the back of her garden and beyond. She gasped for air as she watched the wide open gate creaking back and forth in time with the heavy breeze that had picked up over the course of the evening.

A car sped along the road past the front of the house. She darted back to her bedroom and parted the curtains. The vehicle was no longer anywhere to be seen. She logged into her security app and began scrolling through the images that the CCTV had captured. A mottled figure slid alongside the house. She flicked to the other camera. The same dark figure climbed over her gate with ease. A few moments is all the intruder stayed for until he slid the locks on the back gate and left the garden. She flicked back to the front camera, car headlights filled the screen. Useless. The image was so grainy, she could only make out that the car was a hatchback. The registration plates were totally unreadable and the image of the intruder was blurred.

With trembling hands she grabbed her mobile. As she went to call Briggs, an incoming call from Jacob flashed up on the screen.

'Jacob, how's it all going?' She didn't know whether she first needed to know what Steven had said or report the intruder that had been in her garden. One thing she knew for sure was that it hadn't been Steven. Steven hadn't chased and attacked Sophie either. So much of her wanted it to be him so that he'd finally be locked away, but people like him never quite pay for all the bad they do in life. He'd probably be let out on bail with a charge of possession. He'd wheedle out of a dealing charge, she knew he'd manage that.

'Hope I didn't wake you, guv, but I thought you'd want to know who we've just pulled in. You might want to get here as soon as possible.'

Without hesitation, she grabbed the trousers that were on top of her clothes heap and pulled them on. For now, her intruder had to wait.

As she hurried into the incident room, Wyre and O'Connor turned to look at her. Smith walked past with a cup of coffee and Briggs was at the front of the room adding notes with Jacob to the incident board. She pulled her hair back and tied it up, wondering if someone would say something about the interview with Steven. She had to ask, be the first person to mention it. Maybe they were too embarrassed to bring it up with her. It would have to come out sooner or later and at this precise moment, she'd mentally prepared for it. 'How did the interview with Steven go?'

O'Connor tapped his pen on the desk. 'Well, he admitted to using the drugs that we found. It was borderline on quantity as to whether he could be dealing so that's all we have on him at the moment. We've cautioned him and let him go. Given the results that came back from forensics, that's all we could do. He's not our attacker. At least that's what all the forensics results are telling us. He's not a shoe size ten either like our perp, he has pretty small feet. He's a seven.'

She wondered if O'Connor was hiding something about Steven. She glanced across at Wyre knowing she'd be able to tell if they were holding something back. 'Anything else?'

'Apart from him being a disrespectful shit in general, no, guv.' O'Connor threw his pen to the table. She could tell he was tired. It had been a long day and her usually chirpy colleague was getting a little tetchy.

She caught Briggs's eye and he shook his head a little. She then knew her secret was still safe. Steven hadn't said a word about her. Almost falling into her chair, she inhaled and smiled.

'I hate that man,' Wyre said.

Gina shared that sentiment. At least everyone at the station had got to know exactly what Steven was like should he reappear in the case again.

'Good news, I hear.' Gina leaned in, waiting for one of the team to fill her in. 'Tell me all about it then. I got the mini version over the phone.'

Briggs stood next to the board, biting the end of his pen as Jacob took a seat at the head of the table. Another one of her colleagues who looked like he hadn't slept for days. 'It's Rhys Keegan. As you know we've brought him in.'

Gina slipped her coat off. 'Where was he found?'

'We received a call from Paul Brent who owns the land. He's a farmer. He was just passing Crump Lane and in the distance he noticed a car blocking his access. The car had come off the road, travelled a little way down the rubbly pathway and was parked in the shrubs. He originally thought that there had been a crash but there was no damage to the car when he had a look. He then saw Rhys sleeping in the back of his car so knocked on the window and told him that he had to leave. Rhys got out and was drunk and abusive so he called us. He also pulled a hammer from his boot and struck the farmer's four-wheel drive several times. Uniform arrived on the scene, recognised Rhys and the car. They then called us and brought him in. We've placed him in a cell to sober up. You'll get no sense out of him tonight, he's paralytic.'

'Great work. We finally have our main suspect. Possibly the last person to see Jade Ashmore alive. Well done everyone. As soon as he knows what day it is, we'll have him in the interview room.' She smiled. Briggs smiled back, allowing his gaze to linger just a while longer. Steven was now gone from the case leaving her able to be more hands on. She hoped he'd allow her to interview Rhys Keegan.

As the incident room filled with chatter about the case, she walked over to Briggs. 'I have something else to report.' She wasn't about to sit on any information that may be relevant to the case. An intruder in her garden probably had nothing to do with the case whatsoever, but failure to say anything immediately would land her back in trouble, even if that trouble only extended to Briggs.

CHAPTER SIXTY

Sunday, 12 May 2019

Rhys Keegan's bloodshot eyes and overgrown facial hair were evidence that he'd been lying low for days. The smell of stale beer, sweat and whisky filled the room. His long brown hair had tangled into unruly lugs. Gina and Jacob had been questioning him for fifteen minutes and, so far, he'd given them very few words in response. She didn't know if he was purposely not speaking or if his hangover was just kicking in. The forty-seven-year-old man looked older than his years in his sickly-looking state. Gina wondered what Aimee had ever seen in him.

The duty solicitor looked like she was picking the nail varnish from her nails. Her bobbed grey hair bouncing every time she moved.

'Mr Keegan, can you tell us what happened on the night of Sunday the fifth of May and the early hours of Monday the sixth of May, the morning Jade Ashmore was murdered.'

He shook his head, forcing his hair to cover half of his face, entwining itself amongst the inch of beard that sprouted from his chin. 'Jade knew exactly what we were doing. We were all at the party for the same thing.'

'What was that?'

'Okay, it was a wife-swapping party. We all linked up on Swap Fun and Dawn, the host, invited us to her party. Me and Aimee

wanted to go so we went. We like things a bit adventurous in
the bedroom. We all had a few drinks, got to know each other
and randomly picked our partners from some sort of pot and I
got Jade.'

'How did you feel about that?'

Shrugging his shoulders, he cleared his throat and coughed
into his hand. Gina pushed a box of tissues across the table. 'Well,
looking at the rest of the talent, I was pleased. When you've been
used to someone of Aimee's quality, you get picky, if you get me.
I really didn't want Maggie and I wasn't keen on the thought of
ending up with Dawn. So, when I picked Jade out, I was happy.'
He slouched back in the plastic chair and began rolling bits of
tissue up and dropping them on the floor.

Gina glanced down at her notes. 'What happened then?'

'Really?'

Gina frowned and paused.

'Okay! We went to Jade's summerhouse. To be fair, I was
pleased we didn't end up in the woods. It was a bit chilly and,
yes, I wanted to enjoy it.' He paused and leaned his head to the
side and stared up at the ceiling. 'God, my head hurts.'

'And?'

'Well, you know what we did.'

'I know a version of what happened. There was a witness.'

He wiped the sleeve of his checked shirt across his nose. 'It
was the old perv from next door, wasn't it? Dirty bastard. Okay,
nothing much happened. We had a glass of wine and then got
straight down to it. I took her against the window, told her it
would be more fun if there was a chance of being seen. I saw the
perv looking out of the window so thought I'd give him a show.
She was happy to do that. She didn't complain anyway.'

Gina flicked back a couple of pages in her book and glanced
at what Colin had said. 'The witness described you being rough
with her.'

'And you believe the old perv? It was a little vigorous, that's all. She wanted it like that. I wasn't rough, it was role playing. She liked being dominated, I'll tell you that for free. Can I get some painkillers and water? If not I'm going to chuck up. My head feels like there's a train running through it.'

'As soon as we finish the interv—'

The solicitor uncrossed her legs and dragged her chair away from the table. 'With all due respect, Detective Inspector, my client isn't very well and needs a short break.'

Gina slammed her notebook shut. Ten minutes, that's all they were getting.

They'd all taken their seats once again and the recorder was rolling. 'What happened when you and Jade had finished in the summerhouse?'

'She looked upset, said she regretted what we did and started blarting. She threw her clothes on and said she was going to look for her husband. I think his name was Noah. Lucky git got my Aimee. We knew they were in the woods somewhere. I supposed she was heading that way.'

'Could it be that she was upset that you were rough with her, forceful even? Maybe she was about to find her husband and tell him. I'm thinking you tried to follow her, stop her talking.'

He pushed his hair behind his ears with his grubby fingers. 'No. You're making things up. I didn't follow her. I grabbed my things and left.'

'But you didn't go home. You knew you'd been seen treating Jade roughly. Did you follow her after that? Did you kill her? Is that why you went into hiding? Is that why you ran, Mr Keegan?'

He leaned over and whispered in his solicitor's ear. The woman looked as though she might heave from his sweaty scent. 'My client will not be saying any more except that he did not hurt or murder Jade Ashmore.'

Jacob threw his pen onto the table. 'Interview terminated at seven sixteen.'

Gina stood. 'Another officer will be here in a moment to interview you about the criminal damage to the four-wheel drive you attacked with a hammer last night.'

The man shrugged his shoulders. 'Whatever. Can I have a smoke now?'

Gina left the room. She was still in the dark about where he went after the summerhouse. The onus was now on them to prove that he followed Jade and attacked her before running home to get his car. She checked her watch. Keith in forensics had been taking samples and filing the contents of his car for a few hours. He had to be able to tell her something. Maybe he had found their elusive mallet, the one that had swiped away half of Jade's face.

CHAPTER SIXTY-ONE

Gina slammed her office door. Rhys Keegan had refused to say where he had been. If Creepy Colin had been telling the truth, maybe Jade was upset about how he treated her. Maybe she told him exactly what she thought and threatened to find her husband, Noah Ashmore, and tell him. Scared of the repercussions, Rhys could have followed her and attacked her. Where would he have got the mallet from? Unless he had planned the attack, he was unlikely to have anything like that on him. His car, it could have been close by – he lived close by and he knew which direction she was heading in. Every party guest knew where the locations were. Jade was upset, definitely a little tipsy. It may have taken her longer than normal to walk back to where all the action was taking place. It was doable, Rhys could easily have gone to his car and got the murder weapon.

An email from Keith pinged through. No evidence that could be linked to Jade Ashmore's murder had been found in Rhys's car. He'd ended the message requesting that she return his call.

She pressed his number and waited for him to answer. 'Thanks for getting back to me so fast, Keith.'

'Sorry, it probably wasn't what you wanted to hear,' he replied, his voice slightly breaking. She heard him drinking, before he cleared his throat and began again. 'I'm glad you called, I was just going to try you again. We have finished processing all of the evidence from Dawn Brown's house. Nothing came back on Steven Smithson's magazines, no cuttings out, etcetera. Nothing we found links him to Jade Ashmore or the break-in at Diane

Garraway's house. There was nothing in his car either. No prints, no bodily secretions, no hair, not a jot.'

She kicked her desk leg and leaned against the window ledge. Her job had just been made harder. 'Thanks for updating me.' Keith said his goodbyes and ended the call.

Names ran through her head, Maggie and Richard Leason. Creepy Colin Wray, the babysitter, Tiffany Gall. Had Tiffany been so into Noah Ashmore after their kiss that she'd watched what was going on, left the child alone in bed and followed her? Her father said that after Noah's return, she'd gone home. She shook her head. No, she was missing something more obvious.

She called Wyre. 'Have you seen Noah Ashmore recently? I know you've been updating him.'

'Yes, guv. I've just got back. Jade Ashmore's parents were with him and his own father turned up with some groceries.'

'Anything look out of place?'

Wyre paused. 'No, guv. He's turned down all our help and the family seem to be grieving. They want to know who killed Jade, obviously. He's angry, upset, exactly as we'd expect.'

'Was Tiffany Gall anywhere to be seen?'

'No.'

'Thanks, Wyre.' She ended the call and began twiddling her pen around in circles on her fingertips, as a random collection of thoughts battled in her mind.

Her office phone began to ring. She grabbed the receiver. 'DI Harte.'

'We have a woman called Nicole on the phone. She's asked for you specifically. It's about Aimee Prowse.'

'Thank you. Put her through.' Nicole, the name wasn't familiar to her but the mention of Aimee's name set her heart racing.

'Hello, DI Harte. How can I help you?'

There was a slight pause. 'I'm concerned that my friend Aimee didn't come home last night. It looks like there is a bit of damage in the kitchen. I tried to call her all night, then I found her phone in the living room with no charge. I'm worried something has happened to her. I've called her family, clients and friends, no one has seen her.'

'We'll send someone over right away.'

On hearing the news, the adrenaline coursing through her body was soon replaced by an undertone of nausea. Aimee had been missing all night.

CHAPTER SIXTY-TWO

'Wake up, bitch!'

Aimee woke with a start as the bucket of freezing cold water sloshed over her face. His voice faded as the sound of her thumping heartbeat filled her head. Dark, it was still dark. How could he see? Slowly, her vision focused on a dim industrial light in the corner of what looked like a workshop. 'Let me go,' she yelled as she failed to stand. He laughed as she fell back into place. All those years of core strengthening hadn't prepared her for a situation such as this. The cold, the shaking fingers, the tremble in her legs and trunk. The weakness she felt from not eating sickened her. As she rocked back and forth in her crumpled up position within the wall, she knew this might be her only opportunity to get out. Placing one hand in front of her, she tried to grip something, anything. Crawl, she had to move, keep warm.

'Going somewhere?' A heavy boot crunched the fingers of her left hand. The cold didn't do a good job of protecting her from the sheer agony of a couple of broken fingers.

Whimpering, she tried to look him in the eye, plead with him. 'Why are you doing this to me?'

Laughter erupted from her captor's mouth, first a cackle, then huge hysterics that filled the air. 'You really want to know. I thought Jade was different, then she turned up at that party. It had been a long time but I'd recognise her anywhere.' He pulled a tiny piece of paper from his pocket and stared at it. 'See, that was her back then. Can you believe I spent all these years feeling sorry for her, only to see her turn up for a cheap shag? When you've put someone on a pedestal and they let you down—'

'What has any of this got to do with me?' Tears cascaded down her cheeks. She swallowed and the walls of her throat almost stuck, causing her to gasp. She needed water.

'It's got everything to do with you. The wholesome lifestyle you portray to the outside world – a lie. Clean living when you sleep with all these people. Nothing but a cheap liar. I admired you, you know. Your dedication to purity and cleanliness that you portray on YouTube, but you're dirty, just like the others.' He held the photo closer to her eyes, then pulled out another photo.

She squinted in the low light. It was definitely a younger Jade. As she cast her eyes on the other photo, she gasped for breath. Her throat was sticking, closing. He'd been watching her. He'd killed Jade and now it was her turn. She kneeled up and thrust her upper body forward, pushing as hard as she could. His laughter filled the air as her stiff bones managed a few shuffles along the concrete floor. Bits of wood pierced her leggings and stabbed her knees. Flashes filled the room, blinding her as he took photos of her misery. He was enjoying every moment, torturing her with a small chance of freedom.

He gripped her curls in his tightly clenched fist and dragged her along the floor, back into the tiny upright grave.

'No, don't shut me in there. Please, I won't try to escape, just let me stay out here.' Her sodden teary face gathered bits of wood shaving as he let go of her hair and began dragging her by her feet. She tried to reach out and grab the leg of the workbench. Pain flashed through her cracked fingers, up her arm. 'I want to go home.'

'She wants to go home,' he mimicked, trying to imitate her voice as he slammed the heavy wooden door shut. The lock came across and she heard him scraping something across the floor. He was pulling furniture across the secret door, she knew it.

Once again, crunched up in the tiny crevice, the cold dampness penetrated her clothing, clawing under her skin. With chattering teeth, she tried to yell and cry out but nothing was happening. With her strength diminishing rapidly, she knew her time would be up soon. She recognised the symptoms of hypothermia. Soon she'd seize up and drift off into her death sleep. She heard a distant slam followed by the pulling down of a roller shutter. He was gone and he'd left her there to die.

She tried to pull at her vest top, crying as her broken fingers became tangled in her spaghetti strap. Strip off, she needed to lose the cold clothing. It was too cramped. Her fingers were stuck. She was stuck. She exhaled, blowing the sawdust from her mouth.

The life she was leading flashed before her. Nicole, her lodger and best friend, would be missing her. She only hoped she'd called the police and they were looking for her. Hopelessness set in as she wondered how on earth they would ever find her here. So much of their focus had been on finding Rhys and this man was right under their noses all the time, existing without suspicion.

The other photo he'd showed her pushed to the front of her mind. He'd taken that picture while she'd been out running, bending over tying up her laces. She tried to think back and couldn't pinpoint the exact time when it might have been taken. That was one of her usual routes. He could have been watching her for ages. Her heart rate slowed down as her limbs numbed. She was losing it, slowly slipping into unconsciousness.

She was jogging through the estate, looking for him. She'd only seen him for the first time at the party but that photo had to be taken long before that. She slipped over a step into an open drain and was falling. *Not the abyss, please, not the dark abyss.* 'Don't close your eyes,' she said through chattering teeth. 'Stay with it.' It was no good. She had lost control as she hurtled into the darkness, wondering if she'd ever wake up again.

CHAPTER SIXTY-THREE

Gina followed Jacob through to Aimee's lounge and sat close to Nicole. Keith shuffled behind them, huffing and puffing as he carried his toolkit to the kitchen. She heard him mutter something about his aching back under his breath but his muttering soon faded.

'I still haven't heard from her. She never goes anywhere without her phone, which is why I'm worried.'

'I know and we'll do everything we can to find out where she is.' Gina knew full well that wasn't going to put Nicole's mind at ease.

The young woman pulled her oversized cardigan around her middle and folded her arms in front of it. Sitting forward, her back looked slightly hunched.

'What time did you get home from work yesterday?'

She shrugged her shoulders. 'I don't know the exact time, I think it was about seven. I normally finish at five but I did a little overtime.'

Jacob made a note.

'Tell me what you saw.'

'The back gate was flapping away in the wind which was unusual in itself. That would have done Aimee's head in. As I walked through, I closed it. I went in through the back door as I always do. When I came in, something didn't feel right. The kitchen table had been shunted away from the wall and there's a chip in it.'

'Did you touch these?'

She exhaled and nodded. 'I pushed the table back in its place and put the chair under the table. I also wiped it with a cloth. I remember calling for Aimee. There was no answer. My first thought was that she'd met up with that idiot, Rhys, and gone out with him. You wouldn't believe how disappointed in her I was. Anyway, I warmed some food up in the microwave, sat in front of the telly and thought no more of it. I tried to call again before going to bed about midnight but she still wasn't answering. I only noticed the next morning, when I started to tidy up a bit. Aimee and I have different standards when it comes to cleaning. While I was on holiday, the place had turned into the pits so I cleared the rubbish from the lounge. As I plumped the sofa, I noticed Aimee's phone. She'd never go anywhere without her phone.' Nicole rubbed her eyes.

'We will need the phone; maybe that will give us some clue as to what happened.'

She pointed to the corner of the room at the phone which was plugged into a charger. Gina passed Jacob an evidence bag. 'Did Aimee say anything to you, something that may have been worrying her?'

Nicole leaned back slightly, revealing her pale round face in full. 'I was always worried about her. It was Rhys. Since he moved in, she seemed different. It was all about him and what he wanted. Of course, she kept telling me there was nothing wrong but I heard the rows. I rent the bedroom next to the one they slept in. I'd often hear her yelling out, like he was hurting her. I did mention it to her once and she just said that sometimes he was a bit rough in the bedroom but she told me she didn't mind. I knew she did though. He also knew I didn't like him. When she was around he would be all nice, offer to make me drinks, full of false concern when I wasn't well or something – things like that. I had a flu virus a couple of months ago and he was all over me when Aimee was around, offering to fetch me blankets, go to the chemist, make me soup. As soon as she was out of the way, he'd ignore me when I spoke to him. He even jabbed me in the ribs a couple of times, *by accident*, of course. She couldn't see it. He's a nasty piece of work, always getting his own way. I don't know what she saw in him but I don't know what she saw in any of her boyfriends. Most of them were at least double her age. It was her thing. I just always knew I'd be there for her, whatever happened.'

Gina watched as Jacob caught up with his notes.

'How do you know Aimee?'

'We've been best friends since school. She's my best friend, always has been. I know she was infatuated with Rhys but he was bad for her.'

Gina glanced around the room. It didn't look the same as the other day when she'd interviewed the highly-defensive Aimee. The woman who was so worried that her reputation would be ruined from any scandal that may come out of everything. All the dusty glasses of water were cleared away and the room had been cleaned. A ray of May sun emerged through the window and the wind chimes clanged together as the breeze through the open window aired the musty room.

First Samantha went missing all those years ago, then Jade Ashmore was killed and now Aimee was missing. At the back of her mind was Sophie Dobbins and her attack. Her heart almost skipped a beat. She inhaled swiftly as her attention turned back to Nicole.

'What happens next?'

'We need to get her phone back to the station, see if we can get anything from it. A forensics officer is working the kitchen, looking for prints, taking swabs and looking for points of entry. You say the back door was unlocked and the gate was open?'

Nicole nodded. 'It was, but something else was strange. The runner in the hallway was all rumpled up and the end of the rug was trapped in the front door.'

An image flashed through Gina's mind. Aimee in the kitchen and an intruder. Did he come in through the back or knock at the front door? A scuffle occurred in the kitchen, shunting the table away from the wall. Maybe he dragged her out onto the drive. Had the perpetrator parked out the front? If Aimee had been hurt or kidnapped, he wouldn't have wanted to walk her too far at the risk of someone seeing. He had to be parked by the house.

'There is something else.' Nicole hugged her cardigan closer.

'Okay.'

'The neighbour's dog has been a right pain recently, always barking. It's not like him, Barney is normally a good dog. I wonder if he was trying to warn us, picking up on someone out there, watching. It sends shivers down my spine.'

Gina and Jacob exchanged a look. 'We'll order a door to door, see if any of your neighbours have noticed anything unusual. If there's anything else you can think of in the meantime, call me straight away. Here's my card. My direct number is on it.'

Nicole took the card and placed it straight in her pocket. 'Thank you. Am I safe to stay in the house?'

'Just make sure the doors and windows are locked. If you hear or see anything suspicious, just call the emergency number immediately. If you're worried or scared, you can also call me.'

'Thank you.'

Keith pulled his face mask down and called her out into the lean-to, then spoke in a hushed voice. Nicole continued to convey her worries to Jacob.

'I've found a smear of blood on the floor and I can see that there was an attempt to wipe it away. It's going straight to the lab now. There is also evidence of a struggle, a few items were strewn under the table and the back of the chair was damaged. Again, I found a trace of blood and hair. I've called for more assistance and the kitchen and hallway are now a no-go zone. I just wish the housemate hadn't tampered with everything. It's going to make our job harder.'

'Check the drive too.'

He nodded. 'I'll cordon it off now.'

Gina popped her head around the lounge door. 'Nicole, is there anyone you can stay with for a few days?'

She nodded. 'I'll go to my mum's. I don't want to stay here alone.'

'I think you'd feel better there,' Jacob replied as he stood.

Gina had no guarantees that the attacker wouldn't come back. Something bad had happened to Aimee, she knew it. Her heart rate quickened. She only hoped that another body wouldn't turn up or worse – vanish; just like Samantha had.

Something was missing. Their perpetrator had been clever up to now. She only hoped something had been left behind this time. She shuddered as she thought of her own intruder the previous night. Shaking her head, she pushed it out of her mind. It couldn't be related. Steven had now been cleared and for some reason he had backed off completely. Or could it be related? Samantha, the party animal, the fun young woman who'd been having a relationship with more than one man. Jade Ashmore, attended a partner-swapping party. The photo turning up showing both Jade and Samantha at the same party all those years ago. She couldn't see where Aimee fitted in to all this, let alone herself if there was some link.

Perceived sexual deviance flashed through her mind and she felt the colour drain from her face. No one else knew about her past and that night, no one. Or had Terry shared that information adding his own twist to the truth. This person saw Aimee as some sort of sexual deviant and, as her theory went, he was punishing her. Why the photos? He likes to keep a record.

Jacob brought her back into the moment. 'We have to go, guv. Diane Garraway has just called in a hysterical state. She was waffling on about Samantha, then she hung up.'

'Let's go and check on her.'

CHAPTER SIXTY-FOUR

Gina hammered on the door for the second time but Diane still didn't answer. 'Do you think she's in?' Jacob asked. Children ran around screaming as they chased a football on the small patch of grass in front of the houses.

'She looked like she could barely walk last time we saw her.' Gina stepped over the patch of muddied earth in front of the living room window and peered through the smeared glass. Diane lay on the sofa, vomit glistening down the side of the settee where she lay. 'Call an ambulance.'

She darted around the side of the building and ran through the open back gate, hoping that the back door would be open and it was. Charging through, she entered the chilly lounge, grabbed Diane's wrist and began searching for a pulse.

She could hear Jacob relaying the address over the phone.

'Overdose, looks like paracetamol. She's vomited but we need an ambulance pronto.' She counted the missing tablets. 'I'd say fifteen paracetamol but I can't be sure.'

'They're on their way, guv.'

'Diane.' Gina gave her a little shake. 'Diane.'

The woman murmured and half-opened an eye. Gina grabbed a tissue and wiped the side of her face. 'An ambulance is on its way.'

'I caused all this pain. I did bad things,' she half-whispered. 'My brother, he said—' Her eyelid began to droop as her body juddered. 'Samantha—'

'It's DI Harte. You called and we're here. Help is on its way. You're going to be okay.'

'My brother.' She began to half-sob and cough before spraying Gina's shirt with a stream of vomit. The woman gagged and choked. She was already on her side.

'Let it all out, Diane.' She stared down at her shirt and almost gagged herself. She felt the woman's clammy head and Jacob entered with some kitchen towel. She heard sirens approaching as she mopped herself and Diane with the tissues. 'Help is here, hang on, Diane.'

The woman no longer responded and her pulse was faint.

'Diane. Stay with me. The paramedics are here.'

Jacob opened the front door and two paramedics entered, pushing Gina aside as they began treating the woman.

Gina went into the kitchen and wet some kitchen roll before wiping herself down. As she inhaled, she gagged again. The overpowering smell was turning her stomach. The thought of Diane being in so much emotional pain that she had tried to take her own life filled her with sadness. She guessed that Diane had taken the overdose then called the station asking for Gina. If she and Jacob had decided to grab a coffee on the way, or get some petrol, or even quickly check in at the station, Diane may not at least be in with a chance. It was no good. She couldn't wear her shirt. She began to peel it away and Jacob barged in.

'They're taking her to the hospital now. Shall I get someone to head over there? Sorry, guv.' He turned to face the hallway while she continued to clean herself.

'Yes, give Wyre a call. We need to know what Diane wanted to tell us. She kept mentioning a brother. Ask O'Connor to look into this. I want to know who he is as I don't have any details of her family on file. I thought she had no family.' She slipped her jacket back on and did the buttons up. 'And tell them to grab me a shirt from lost property.' Gina rolled her shirt up, ready to dispose of it. She wandered back into the living room, thinking about why Diane had tried to take her own life. Diane was all alone, no friends, in severe pain and poverty. Diane had no one.

She swallowed hard and almost wept as she saw what she thought might be her own future flashing in front of her. How many friends did she have? None that she'd let into her life. Family? A daughter who had moved, more than likely to get away from her. The only thing she did have was her health, but that wasn't guaranteed. She thought back to her own mother, taken suddenly by cancer. Her father, a good man who had missed her mother so much that he'd turned to drink. She understood why Diane had felt like she had nothing. Like Diane, she had done things that were bad. Her mind was awhirl with what bad things Diane thought she'd done. She wiped her eyes. That wasn't the future she wanted but old habits die hard.

'Guv? Should we get back to the station?' Jacob stood in the door entrance. She could tell he was on the verge of gagging.

'Yes, but first I need to make sure I lock Diane's house up and take her key with me. She's already had enough happen with the card and the break-in.'

'Are you okay with that while I wait in the car and call the station?'

'Go on, get out of here.' He didn't need telling twice.

She grabbed some more tissues and a wet soapy cloth and wiped the sofa down. Only a small gesture but one she was sure Diane would appreciate on her return. She couldn't leave the mess to dry up and smell. She reached down the side of the sofa with the damp flannel and flinched as her fingernail caught on something hard down the side of the settee. An address book, a tatty brown leatherette pocket-sized book. She gently pulled it out and opened it. None of the few pages left were fixed in. The short list of addresses were all the people that Diane had in the world. Most were crossed out, maybe friends that had moved, passed away or she no longer kept in touch with them. She scanned the names, not recognising any of them. The yellow musty pages suggested that she hadn't used this book for years. She found Samantha listed, her address written in spidery writing under her name. A few more pages fell to the floor, again, most of the addresses were crossed out. Gina flicked another page and her jaw dropped as she read the text.

This address book belongs to …

Underneath the text, Diane had written her full name and it wasn't what Gina had expected. She'd changed her name. Gina knew she'd never been married. She grabbed her phone, heart pounding as she waited for Wyre to answer. She knew exactly who Diane's brother was and she wasn't going to waste a single minute. As she relayed what she'd discovered, she grabbed Diane's keys and locked up. 'Meet me there, and bring me a new top while you're at it.' She slammed the front door closed and threw her soiled shirt into the wheelie bin.

A text pinged up.

Gina, I have to talk to you. It was me at your house last night. Don't be angry, just call me. There's something you need to know.

Her hands began to shake as she thought about Rex climbing into her garden, watching her. It could be a trap, maybe he was in talks with the press and all this was to entrap her into saying something she might regret. Then again, she now had a text that showed him to be stalking her. She called up his number as she headed back towards the car, still unsure whether to ring him or not.

CHAPTER SIXTY-FIVE

I've had it now. She'll call me, I know she will and I'll have to tell her everything. Gina saw me last night, I know she did and now she's going to hate me even more. I pull the reporter's card from my pocket and place it on the side. Gina won't believe that I've always told her the truth. I told her I didn't send her any flowers or chocolates but she chose not to believe me.

The reporter keeps ringing. I wish she'd go away and leave me alone. If she were to latch on to my sordid little secrets, who knows what she'd make of them. I had to message Gina, I'm in too deep and I don't know what to do. I can picture her annoyance. It's not as if I really know her and I suppose I hoped she'd take my mind of Aimee. *Come on, Gina, call me, please.*

My heart won't stop humming away and my mouth tastes of the whisky I had earlier to calm my nerves. What have I done to you, my darling Aimee? What have I done? Will you ever forgive me? Will you be there in that café one day, trying to escape the pouring rain where we'll meet? That was how it was meant to happen. I was waiting for the right time. I saw the way Rhys treated you. I would have been so much better. I worshipped the ground you walked on, my love. But you've gone now and it's all my fault.

I grab the bottle and pour another shot. The cheap whisky burns my throat as I think of you, Aimee. I also think of Gina. I let her down too. What my future holds, who knows. It won't be long before I'm exposed.

I screw the reporter's card up and drop it to the floor, stamping on it several times as spittle flies through the gaps in my teeth. I stamp and stamp until I'm exhausted. I just want it all to go away. Staring at my phone, I wonder if she'll call. She has to call. Aimee's life depends on Gina calling. 'Come on!' I shout as I break down.

CHAPTER SIXTY-SIX

Hurrying through the streets of Cleevesford, Jacob swung the car into Lavender Lane, almost throwing Gina's phone from her hand as he pulled up behind Wyre's car.

Gina gripped her phone. 'Are you okay going in first and explaining why we're here? There's an urgent call I need to make and it may help the case.'

'Sure, guv.' He stepped out of the car and walked over to Wyre and O'Connor.

She pressed Rex's number as she sat in the car. 'This best be good and don't you dare come to my house again or I swear, I'll throw you in a cell myself. What right did you think you had, climbing over my gate?'

'Gina, please. I wanted to tell you something. I've been pacing all night wondering what to do. I can't believe I… I'm in such big trouble.'

'What is it?' Her patience with the man was running thin. She watched through the windscreen as their prime suspect's wife's head dropped and she burst into tears. Had she lied to them about him coming home on the night of Jade Ashmore's murder in order to protect her husband? Gina knew that now. Jacob and Wyre followed her in and closed the door as O'Connor waited outside. She needed to be there, with them. Aimee's life was at stake. She heard Rex take a couple of deep breaths. 'For heaven's sake, spill it out. I haven't got time for this.'

'Okay. I've been watching Aimee. I know I was wrong to do that and you can do what you like to me after. I confess, I've been stalking Aimee. I saw her on the Swap Fun website and there was something about her. I saw her out and about a few times, just at the shops or out jogging and, I suppose, I became infatuated. She wore her name on her shirt, giving away all her social media links. I soon found her, followed her…'

She slammed her palm onto the dashboard. This was all she needed. She began to tremble. He'd been watching Aimee, following her, checking her out online. He'd just confessed to all that. 'Do you know what you're saying? What have you done with her?' She stared at Richard and Maggie's home, their little old house in a corner plot. 'Rex, tell me now. Tell me!'

'That's the thing, I haven't done anything with her. I like to watch, I hoped we'd meet and yet I wanted her to fall in love with me. I wanted you too but that's another story. You wouldn't believe how hard I try and how poorly my efforts are rewarded. I thought Aimee would be different. She liked guys my age. You were pushing me away.' He took a deep breath. 'I saw the person who took her.'

'Why the hell didn't you come straight to the police?'

He took several deep breaths. She imagined him pacing, grimacing as he wiped sweat from his forehead. 'I shouldn't have been there. I knew I'd be in trouble—'

'So you failed to report a kidnapping.'

'I wanted to say something earlier. I really did—'

'I haven't got time for this right now. Just give me a description of who you saw and what you saw. After that, go straight to Cleevesford Police Station and make a formal statement.'

Silence hung between them. 'I'm so sorry, Gina. I'm sorry for everything. I'm sorry I came to your house when you didn't want me to. I've stuffed up.'

She checked her watch. 'Description, Rex. You still have time to do the right thing. Tell me who you saw. What did he look like? It's not too late.'

'He barged through her front door. I was watching her from the back garden through a small hole in the fence.' He sniffed before continuing. 'He dragged her around and tried to attack her with something. I couldn't see what. I failed to go in, I failed to help her. I could have stopped what was happening.'

'What did he look like?'

'Stocky, crew cut, I think. Almost bald, slightly chubby. I don't know who he is. I recognised him from the Swap Fun events. I saw him at a meetup once but I didn't remember his name. I spent all night looking through Swap Fun but nearly all the members use fake names.'

She gripped the door handle, her knuckles white. The description was just what she needed and finding Aimee was her priority. 'Go straight to the station, Rex. Ask for DCI Briggs and make a statement. Do it now and don't hold anything back.' She ended the call and hurried out of the car.

An old rusty sign leaned against the window of the little front garden. C.L Furniture Restoration and Carpentry. Her stomach almost flipped as she thought of the mallet. He'd have a mallet. The L stood for Leason and Diane was a Leason before she changed her name.

'O'Connor, can you get Jacob? Tell him we need to leave now. Wyre can stay and interview Mrs Leason and we'll head straight over to Cleevesford Industrial Estate. We're going to C.L. Furniture.'

'Yes, guv.' He handed a shirt to her. 'Wyre said you wanted this.'

She smiled and grabbed her phone and called for all units to be present, requesting that they stay back until it was safe to approach. Aimee's captor was dangerous and she knew just what he was prepared to do. A call flashed up from Briggs.

'I know where she is, sir.'

Jacob darted out. There was no more time to waste.

CHAPTER SIXTY-SEVEN

Jacob pulled into the industrial estate and Gina and O'Connor searched for C.L Furniture and Carpentry. 'Stop,' Gina called as she slammed the dashboard, causing Jacob to do an emergency stop. 'We just passed the road but we'll get out here and sneak around. I don't want to alarm him, not if Aimee might be at risk.' The row of large industrial units were all closed, shutters down, just as she'd expect on a Sunday. Only one shutter was up. That was where they were heading. Gina hurried out of the car and put her stab vest on as she gently jogged alongside the building. They were going in.

Her heart began to race as she thought of Jade Ashmore, Samantha Felton, Sophie Dobbins and Aimee. She now knew from what Rex had said that it was highly likely that Aimee was in that workshop.

The grey oppressive breeze blocks with barred windows looked uninviting, but that's how he wanted it. Keeping everyone away was his aim. She poked her finger between the bars and rubbed a layer of dust from the glass. Peering in, she spotted a huge workbench at the far end of the large grey room. It's ceiling reaching the height of a house but having only one level, gave the room an even darker feel with only one window providing light. Machinery chugged away in a factory down the road, clunking over and over again.

Glancing around, her attention was grabbed by the many wooden structures that littered the floor and walls. Large shelves housed different sized pieces of wood. To her right sat a small stage in which some of his more intricate work was displayed. She scanned the surfaces, looking for the mallet but she couldn't see it. The morning sun bounced off something square and shiny as she shifted her weight from one foot to the other. Shining like a prism, it caused her to squint as she focused. A camera with a flash attached to the top. 'He's got a camera,' she whispered to Jacob who had crept up close and was awaiting her further instructions.

He walked away, just far enough to hear the caller on his phone. 'Backup is in place, guv.'

O'Connor passed him and hurried over to Gina, still adjusting his stab vest. 'Are we going in?'

'We're going in.'

CHAPTER SIXTY-EIGHT

Dark, so dark. The shivering, the pain from shivering. *Stop it, stop it!* She couldn't stop it, the shivering was out of her control. Squashed, suffocating. Aimee tried to move her arm but it was heavy, like stone. Maybe she was turning to stone. At the bottom of the abyss, there was nothing, no trees, no buildings, no people, no sense of direction. With a swimming head, she tried to turn her neck. Pain forced it back into the one position she could keep it in.

'Hello,' she tried to whisper but the sound emerged as gobble-degook. The rag in her mouth tightened and a large hand gripped her nose. She tried to thrash but he had her pinned. Her heart boomed in her chest, each reverberation rattling in her throat, filling it, blocking it. *Open your eyes.* Her body wasn't responding. Cold, so cold. The concrete floor was hard, her body was numb. Cramped into positions she normally wouldn't stay in for this long. At least yoga had made her supple. As she clenched her toes over and over again, a small amount of feeling emerged through the pins and needles. Pain; her broken fingers were in agony.

'Keep still or I'll put this through your head.' The monster in the darkness had spoken. What was he going to put through her head? Using her throbbing hand, she felt the object he was holding against her. Square with a handle. Her mind wandered to a square block on the sea front. She wanted to sit on it and watch the tide coming in. When the sun came up, that's what she'd do. She'd drive down to the beach and watch the sea. A smile washed over her.

'When does the sun come up?' she whispered through the rag.

Crash. She felt a sickening crunch followed by wetness creeping down her face. The tide had come in and she'd missed it. It was now coming to wash her away. Choking, it washed over her. Freezing cold, shivering – she had reached her end. The sun would never come up and reveal a beautiful beach. Even the darkness was running away from her, fast, then nothing.

CHAPTER SIXTY-NINE

As Gina crashed through the workshop door, she flashed her torch in all the corners, back and forth. If he was here, she wasn't going to allow him to take her by surprise. O'Connor followed her closely, then Jacob rushed in behind him. Backup was ready and waiting. As soon as she had Richard Leason in her custody, she'd call them in. She needed to be sure that Aimee was safe.

'Mr Leason, please come out. This is DI Harte, DS Driscoll and DC O'Connor.' She had to assume he was in the building, hiding somewhere, in one of his nooks and crannies, behind some furniture. 'Aimee, if you can hear me, call out.' She remained in silence for a few moments and heard nothing. His wife, Maggie, was sure this was where he'd be and Gina knew that he was not at his sister's. She'd not long left Diane's house and secured it. He hadn't been there. 'Mr Leason?' She nodded back at Jacob.

He reached for the light switch but nothing happened as he flicked the switch. The only light in the room was the shaft of sun that came through the small barred window and the door. She motioned for the two detectives to follow her. To her left was a collection of tools hanging on the concrete wall. Bags and tool boxes were strewn underneath. One bag thrown on top of another. Tools spilling out. Random screwdrivers, saws, drill bits and screws were mingled together. The smell of varnish filled the air and there was another smell that caught the back of Gina's throat. Human waste.

Her gaze fixed on the door in the corner of the room. As she reached for the handle straight ahead, a tremble ran through her body, finally resting on her fingers. The jittery shadow cast from Jacob's torch exposed her fear. 'I'm opening it,' she whispered.

O'Connor and Jacob poised themselves for what could happen next. As Gina's hand rested on the door handle, she glanced back and saw sweat beginning to drip down O'Connor's face. 'Now.' She burst through the door, torch leading the way, only to face a small concrete room with a filthy toilet leaning against the back wall, next to a cracked hand basin. She slammed the door and took a step back.

'Aimee,' she called. 'They're not here.' She began walking around the room, passing the workbench, staring at all his half-finished furniture restoration projects.

She exhaled, regaining her composure. In the right-hand corner of the room was a small recess about two feet deep where a mop and a broom were propped up. She walked over, examining the wall. The mop was tangled with cobwebs and looked as though it hadn't been used for years. Wood chippings and sawdust had been swept into this corner. She gazed at the floor and noticed a sawdust-free spot. Walking into the shaft of sunlight, she stared at the wall before refocusing on the dust motes dancing in front of her eyes. She tapped it and listened. 'The wall. It goes back further.' An old dustsheet hung from a curtain rail along the top of the wall. She pulled it away, exposing what looked like a concrete back wall. Gina's breath quickened. She went to touch the tiny handle and as the cubbyhole burst open, she fell back into the workbench as the door slammed into her.

'Come any closer and I swear I will put this through her neck. No one will be able to save her then.' He held a shard of pointed wood to the young woman's throat.

'Richard, please put it down and we can talk.' She was staring at a wide-eyed, desperate man who had nothing to lose. Aimee looked like a little doll as he held her in front of him, eyes closed, body flopped over. He was strong, she could tell. He had all her weight under one arm.

'I'm going to carry her out of the building and get into my car with her. You're not going to follow me. Once I'm far away, I'll leave her somewhere safe, but I'm not going with you. You're not locking me up.'

Gina held her hands up and backed off. She watched as Jacob carefully stepped out of the unit. She knew he'd be getting a message to backup, telling them that they were in a hostage situation. She couldn't risk anyone storming in and putting Aimee in any further danger. She glanced at the woman, unconscious and blue. She couldn't see her chest rising and falling. The bloody gash on her forehead had lifted a bit of skin. Glancing behind the man, she spotted the weapon, the mallet they'd been looking for, adorned with fresh blood.

Richard Leason dragged Aimee towards the toilet. 'Get in the cubbyhole, all three of you.' The tip of the wood pierced Aimee's neck. She knew he was serious. The man looked deranged. Veins bulged from his neck as he stared directly into her eyes.

'Please don't hurt her, Mr Leason. She hasn't done anything wrong.' She held her hands up and stepped back towards his little secret compartment. The closer she got, the denser the smell of ammonia was. It was the smell of a confined person, a smell she'd come across before. An overwhelming sadness took over as she thought of an earlier case, that of kidnapped Deborah Jenkins, confined to a little room in a barn. The stench was the same but this was a completely different situation.

'You by the door, get here too,' he called as he stared at Jacob, then O'Connor. 'Get over there with her.' A thin trickle of blood seeped from a small prick to Aimee's neck. The young woman began to murmur in his arms. She was alive, but it was far too early to celebrate. Now she needed to keep her alive and she didn't look to be in a good state. Jacob and O'Connor joined

Gina at the back of the workshop. 'I'm going to lock you all in the workshop and you'll hear from me soon.'

'Just let her go. Lock her in with us, then go,' Gina pleaded.

'I know your game. There will be more of you. You'll be on the estate, on the highway, everywhere. You must think I'm stupid. Without her, you win. Until I am safely out of the way, she stays with me.'

'You don't have to do this. You won't be able to run forever.'

'Wanna bet? I have my rainy day sorted. I've rebuilt myself once, left a bad past behind and started again. Yes, it will be harder but I'll do it.' Gina stepped forward, hoping that their conversation had lulled him into feeling a little less threatened, just enough to let his guard down. 'I see what you're doing, one more step, she dies.'

'Why Aimee?'

Sweat beads fell into his eyes. His large nostrils widened as he exhaled. 'She was just like the others. I thought she was different, then again, I thought Jade was different.'

'Richard Leason, did you kill Jade?'

He grinned and let out a laugh. 'Enough of the talking.'

'Did you know your sister, Diane, has been rushed to hospital this morning?'

'Do I look like I care?' He began to fumble in his pocket for his keys, momentarily bringing the hand that held the wood down by his side. Had Gina been closer to him, she'd have dived at him, brought him down, but by the time she'd have managed to move towards him, he'd have guessed what she was up to.

It was too late. They were all at the back of the building and he was right next to the door. 'Don't chase me and she gets to live.' As he slammed the door, Gina ran towards it and was stopped by a loud crash against the door. She heard a scream she recognised, it was PC Smith. Then a car engine revved up and wheels spun before whizzing off. Smith pushed the door open and yelped as the piece of jagged wood stuck out from his neck. 'Ambulance now,' she yelled into her phone. 'Two victims, one is PC Smith. Stab wound to the neck. Another, young woman, unconscious, wound to the head.' She sat on the road, next to Smith as Jacob and O'Connor tended to Aimee.

'Sorry, guv. I messed up,' Smith gargled, little specs of blood hitting her own neck.

'Shh, help is on its way. You saved her.'

He let out a little smile. 'I poked him in the eyes as we were fighting,' he mumbled as he drifted out of consciousness.

'She's alive, guv.' Jacob removed his jacket, rolling it up and placing it under Aimee's head. Aimee began to thrash as she incoherently rambled.

Smith lay in Gina's arms, bleeding out. He'd obviously been lurking outside as they were talking, listening to everything, and he'd taken it upon himself to tackle Richard. He'd saved Aimee though. She felt tears welling up in her eyes as she gripped her colleague. 'Smith, stay with me.' She gave him a little slap but the blood from his neck continued to pump out, covering her wrists and her lap. Sirens filled the air and an ambulance sped up to her. She moved out of the way, allowing the paramedics to take over as she sobbed against a wall, kicking it over and over again. Richard had escaped.

'Guv.' PC Kapoor ran across the car park, her hair flapping out of her ponytail. 'We need to get to Cleevesford High Street now. He's already taken the bus stop out.' Kapoor took a few deep breaths before staring as the paramedics attended to Smith. 'Smith, Smith,' she cried.

'Stay with him,' Gina yelled as she wiped her bloody hands on her trousers. She and Jacob ran for the car, leaving their bleeding colleague in the hands of the ambulance service. O'Connor almost fell into the back of the car as they pulled away. She was going after Richard.

CHAPTER SEVENTY

Jacob sped through the industrial estate, heading towards the High Street with the sirens on. Cars parted. They reached a small traffic jam. Driving along the pavement for a few meters, they were soon back on the road. Gina spotted the bus stop. One side had been caved in and a huddle of people stood around, watching. There appeared to be no injuries. Uniform were already tracking Richard Leason in their marked police car. She needed to be the one on the scene to make the arrest. He was hers.

'He's racing up King Street in his car.'

'Turn left, we can block him off at the end of the road.'

They almost tipped in the car as Jacob took the sharp turn.

'There, pull up in the middle of the road.' She grabbed the radio. 'We're at the far end of King Street, blocking the road. Get out.' She yelled. O'Connor fled out of the back door, followed by Jacob. Just as Gina stumbled out of the passenger side, Richard rounded the bend and crashed into the side of their car. His car spun and skidded along the road, finally stopping up a grassy bank.

Gina stumbled across the road, snatching his keys out of the ignition as she wrestled Richard out of his car. His strength still astounded her. 'Richard Leason, I'm arresting you for the murder of Jade Ashmore, the kidnapping and assault of Aimee Prowse, assault of Sophie Dobbins and the attempted murder of a police officer.' The attempted murder charge was one she really hoped wouldn't be changed to murder and Samantha was at the back of her mind. That one could wait until she'd had the chance to interview him. She swallowed as an image of Smith's bleeding neck filled her mind.

'You're hurting my arm,' he yelled. Jacob stood above her, offering the man no sympathy. O'Connor was on the other side of the road still, coordinating the other officers and leading the ambulance through.

'Mr Leason, you do not have to say anything, but it may harm your defence if you do not mention when questioned, something you later rely on in court. Anything you do say may be given in evidence.' She cuffed and passed him to the uniformed officer, shaking her head. All the hurt Richard Leason had caused, and he hadn't sustained a single injury. As for Gina, after a bit of wrestling and running, she felt like she'd been mown down by a bulldozer. Life certainly wasn't fair. 'Get him to the station.'

The charges weren't all she wanted to prove. There was the matter of their missing woman, Samantha Felton; the twenty-six-year-old friend of Diane Garraway who hadn't been seen since the year 2012. Gina needed to speak to Maggie Leason before she spoke to Richard. He could stew in a cell for an hour. She grabbed her phone and called Wyre. 'Bring Maggie Leason into the station. We've arrested her husband and we need to speak to her. Also, arrange a search warrant for their house. Have you heard anything from the hospital? Smith was taken in—'

'I heard, guv. We're all a bit tense here. I just called. He went straight into surgery. His wife has been informed and she's there too. One of our own, guv. It really brings it home?' Didn't she know it? Too many times members of her team had suffered abuse and attacks and things were getting worse with every funding cut. Murder – that had never happened to one of her team before. Her legs weakened, almost buckling. She leaned on Richard's battered car as she regained her composure. She hadn't called or messaged her daughter back. She'd do it later but she'd never tell her what had happened today. When she moved away the loneliness that Gina had felt was raw even though they hadn't been close, but now, she was glad that Hannah wasn't around to hear what had happened.

Forensics would now be going through Richard's workshop. Her mind flashed back to the camera. Sophie reported that her attacker had taken photos of her as he chased her down. A photo of Jade and Samantha had been sent to Diane. Gina suspected that the more recent photos on his camera would be of Aimee.

Where are you, Samantha?

CHAPTER SEVENTY-ONE

Maggie hunched over the table in the interview room. Gina twisted her stiff ankles as she waited for the woman to compose herself. She'd just spoken to Keith who was at their house working the potential scene after the search warrant had been granted. She needed to find out exactly what Maggie knew.

She had been crying continually, wiping her nose and eyes for about the tenth time. As she went to grab another tissue, Jacob noticed that there were no tissues left. 'It can't be true.' She ran her tear-sodden fingers through her short blonde hair. Her usual olive skin took on a paler tone emphasising the dark circles under her eyes.

'He held a woman hostage in front of us, Mrs Leason, and he stabbed one of our police officers, PC Smith. He is currently receiving emergency surgery and might not make it.' The whole room began to fill with the smell of smoke from Maggie Leason's jumper.

She began to gasp and hyperventilate. 'He told me it was nothing to do with him and I believed him.'

Gina quickly turned the page to the bullet points of the interview with Maggie previously. 'You told us that your husband, Richard Leason, had come straight home soon after you did, around midnight to twelve twenty.'

The woman stared at the wall behind Gina and tears began to run down her face. 'I believed him when he said he had nothing to do with it. He told me they'd suspect him and that I knew he'd never do anything like that—'

'So you lied to us.' Gina slammed her notebook closed and pulled out a photo.

'He promised me he didn't do it, he promised.'

'We found photos in the workshop and in your house amongst Richard's belongings. Do you recognise these?' Gina had printed out the small collection that Bernard and Keith had sent her from the workshop and the house. 'For the benefit of the tape, I am showing Mrs Leason four photos. One of Jade Ashmore lying dead where her body was found, one of Samantha Felton and Jade Ashmore at a party a few years ago, one of Aimee Prowse being held in his workshop and one of Sophia Dobbins in the woods on the night of her attack.'

'I recognise Jade and Aimee from the party.' Maggie scrunched her eyes as she stared at the photos.

'If you'd told us the truth to begin with,' Gina pointed at the photos in turn, 'Sophie would never have been attacked, Aimee would never have been kidnapped and PC Smith wouldn't be undergoing surgery from which he might never wake up.'

The woman broke down. Gina needed her to break before she pushed her further on Samantha Felton. 'I'm so sorry.' She wiped her nose with her arm. Gina pulled a packet of tissues from her pocket and slid them across the table. 'Thank you.'

'This woman here, Samantha Felton, do you recognise her?'

Maggie picked up the photo and scrutinised it. She nodded as she blew her nose. 'Yes. It was a long time ago. We were at a disco at the social club in Cleevesford. Richard was taking photos, it was his thing. He wanted to practice so that he could become a professional but he wasn't good. I told him that and we argued. I didn't mean to have a go but it was annoying me how he seemed to focus so much attention on her, Samantha. In many ways she reminds me of Aimee, centre of attention and highly admired by the opposite sex. I got angry and left him. I remember hearing a few days later that Samantha had vanished but thought nothing of it.' The woman stared at the back wall again and her eyes widened. 'No, no, it can't be.'

'What is it, Mrs Leason?'

'No,' she yelled as she began punching the table.

'Mrs Leason, calm down and tell me what happened. Samantha has people who care about her. We need to know where she is. If you know something, now is the time to share that information. Your sister-in-law, Diane, is not only recovering in hospital, she's worried sick about Samantha.'

'Sister-in-law?'

'Diane Garraway.'

She stood, the chair toppling over behind her. Placing her head against the back wall, she began to hit. 'How could he lie to me like that?'

'Please sit, Mrs Leason. What are you trying to say?'

She grabbed the chair, positioned it back in front of the table and sat. After a few deep breaths, she continued. 'I didn't know I had a sister-in-law. He told me his parents were dead and he never mentioned a sister, ever. Our whole life has been a lie.'

'I know this is hard for you, but it's really important. Go back to Samantha. Do you remember anything after the disco at the club?'

She slowly nodded as the colour drained from her face.

'Are you okay? Do you need some air or a short break?' Gina was sure the woman might faint or throw up.

She turned the chair and placed her head between her legs and held a hand up. 'I'm okay. It's just the shock of it all.' After a moment, she slowly sat back up and rubbed her eyes. 'He sent me away the next day. I went to my mother's. He wanted to surprise me and said I'd spoil things if I didn't leave him to finish the garden. He'd been all apologetic about our argument and I believed him. When I arrived home two days later, he'd slabbed the garden and built a beautiful shed and a pagoda at the back of the garden. I was so happy. If he has anything to do with it, Samantha might be—' The woman darted out of the room. Gina heard her heaving in the distance.

'Interview ended at sixteen thirty-seven. To be resumed later.' Jacob pressed the stop button.

'Take five and let Bernard know what we've just found out. I want that garden turned upside down. It's going to be a long night. We also need to find out if Aimee or Diane are in a position to speak to us yet.'

CHAPTER SEVENTY-TWO

Richard had been sitting in silence for fifteen minutes as Gina had explained what the interview with his wife had produced. She glanced at her phone. It was far too soon for Bernard to have arranged for the shed and slabs to be dug up, but she still hoped that news would arrive swiftly.

'Richard, do you understand the charges against you?'

He nodded. His solicitor whispered in his ear. It was clear that he had no defence. Along with his capture, finding the murder weapon, then there were all the witnesses that had seen him in action earlier that day. His collection of photos had sealed his fate.

'Why Mr Leason? Richard.'

Richard whispered to his solicitor. 'He said it's Mr Leason to you.'

Jacob shook his head and sighed.

It was going to be one of those interviews. 'Mr Leason, we have secured the mallet that you attacked Aimee with. This weapon has blood on it. We are expecting the results to come through any minute. If one of those blood samples is proven to be that of Jade Ashmore, we have our evidence. You're now wishing you cleaned it better, am I correct?'

His large face reddened and his brow crumpled. He was trying too hard to hold back his reactions and they were all betraying him. His solicitor whispered and Richard Leason's shoulders dropped.

'Am I correct?'

He slammed his fist on the table, shaking it slightly. 'I didn't mean to kill her.'

'Like you didn't mean to kill Samantha Felton. We are digging up your garden as we speak, but I've already told you that. It's time to come clean, tell us what you know.'

The solicitor whispered in Richard's ear once again and Richard whispered back and sunk in the chair. 'I wanted to get them back to my workshop, give them time to think about what they were doing. They fought back. If they'd have just calmed the hell down, they'd all still be alive. I didn't want them to make the same mistakes in life as Diane.' His voice trailed off and he withdrew into his own world.

Gina almost wanted to jump up and down with glee. They had everything they needed, except motive. She'd start at the beginning. 'Why Samantha?'

He flinched as her voice brought him back to the moment. 'Her and my bitch sister were good friends and I suppose I wanted to show her that she didn't need Samantha, she only needed me. It didn't take long to drag Samantha from her. I suppose I had a small fling with the woman. She reminded me of my sister when she was younger, giving it to any man around. Soon, she began to sicken me.' A grin spread across his face.

'What then?'

'She needed to understand that the things she did were wrong and had consequences. Innocent people would get hurt, they always do. Sleeping around would not only hurt her, it would hurt those around her – innocents. She didn't once think about Derek's children when she was screwing him. She wouldn't listen, she just kept screaming and screaming. I only wanted to shut her up.'

Why was he angry with Jade? 'You left the photo and card for your sister to find. Why did you want her to see the photo of Jade and Samantha together all those years ago?'

'Don't look too hard into that. I was just screwing with her.' He shook his head slowly and let out a little laugh. 'The stupid cow never stopped going on about Samantha, all the bloody time – on and on. I thought I'd make her pay. If she was going to go on all the time, I was going to give her something to go on about.' He scrunched his brow as his grin faded. 'When I saw Jade at the Swap Fun party at Dawn's house, it hit me hard. All those years ago, I thought Jade was different. She was like me, on the periphery of all the action, the one being hurt. Back then, she sat there in the social club watching Noah sticking his tongue in Samantha's ear.'

Gina glanced at the photo of Samantha and Jade at the social club. 'Go on.'

'I'd spent years feeling sorry for her after feeling a connection when I saw her. We'd been kindred spirits, so I thought. Then there she was at Dawn's house, giving it all up at this party. I knew she was just like the rest. She let me down. I lost my faith in people all over again.' He paused and wiped the sweat from his forehead. 'I didn't realise it would be that easy though. I thought I'd have to plan her rehabilitation for a while but then I found her walking around the streets, half cut. I finished up quickly with Dawn in that stupid caravan and went searching around the locations. It was so easy. I was prepared of course because I knew Aimee would be at the party, it was all for Aimee originally. Then Jade turned up and I can't tell you how let-down I was. I wanted to find her, help her see that what she was doing was wrong. She had a child. I had to stop her before anyone was hurt.'

Gina swallowed. Reliving that night she saw Jade's caved in face, using the cold pavement as a pillow. She'd love nothing more than to grab this sicko by the ear and slam his head into the table. 'Rehabilitation? You killed her.'

'I didn't mean to. I didn't think she was dead. I just wanted to stun her so that I could get her back to the workshop. I wanted to tell her how disappointed I was in her, make her realise that her child would get hurt. I guess I hit her too hard.' He shrugged his shoulder and leaned back. A smile crept into the corners of his mouth.

The lack of emotion in Richard's face was unnerving. A shiver ran down her spine and her hair began to uncomfortably tingle. He was enjoying telling his story and she'd let him continue. 'We have a blood sample, left behind from the person who chased Sophie Dobbins before attacking her. I suspect it will match yours. Did she hurt you when she hit you with her shoe?'

'Not really,' he said as he sniggered. 'Look, barely a scratch.' He leaned forward, showing the tiniest of marks on the back of his ear. Sophie can't have hit him as hard as she'd thought. 'I used a bit of Maggie's make-up to cover it up. Anything else you want to know? I'm all talk today.' His solicitor shook his head and coughed before whispering to the man again.

Richard was becoming animated in his replies. Shoulders shrugging and fingers pointing. He was not only losing it, he was enjoying losing it, and Gina was glad. She knew this was the one moment in his life where he was being heard. There was more to come from Richard.

'Why Aimee?'

'Again, the error of her ways. Sleeping with that older man, her constant flirting and she wanted it with Noah so badly, I could tell. I knew what Noah was like from the past. Back then at the party, the way he treated Jade when he was dancing with Samantha, and now there was another attractive young woman acting like a stupid whore. I wasn't going to kill her.'

'Just like you weren't going to kill the others.'

'They were an accident!' He stood and punched the wall, the skin on his large knuckles splitting and dotting blood over the wall. 'I just wanted her to see…' He paused and let out a forced laugh.

'What did you want her to see?'

Sweat ran down his face and he stared at her with his mouth open. 'Actions have consequences. Before she could hurt someone with her loose ways, I had to intervene.'

'Someone saw you when you kidnapped her, didn't they, Mr Leason?'

'The other man. See, that's one of the reasons I had to take her. Look what she was doing to everyone, to all the men. They all watched her, wanted her. It would lead to bad things. Someone would eventually get hurt.'

'In what way?'

'I just don't know! With the others I saw it happening, people and children were getting hurt. With Samantha, I was getting hurt; that stupid married man Derek was getting hurt and his children would have suffered if I hadn't have stepped in. With Jade, she'd changed. The demure woman at the party with her dignity intact had lost it. She had a child. She should have been at home looking after her. One thing leads to another – that poor little girl would have felt it at some point. I had to help her child.' She saw a distant look in his eyes as he went silent. There was something about the children that had caused his grin to drop.

'Why do you care about her daughter?'

'Because children are innocent,' he spat. His bottom lip began to tremble. 'If she carried on like that, the child would have got hurt. Noah would have gone and that little one would have been in danger.'

'Danger?'

'Other men in their lives. Mother's bring men home and those men hurt children.'

She was getting somewhere. 'How?'

His veins were almost popping out of his neck and his face was almost beetroot-red. 'These men abuse them, they rape them; they humiliate them. I saved her child.'

'You killed the child's mother.'

He shook his head rapidly and began to tremble. 'No, no, I saved the kid. I saved her. It couldn't happen again to someone else. I just want these women to see. I told Diane to stop but she wouldn't.'

'Is this to do with Diane?'

'The men paid her. They'd come over when she wasn't there.'

'When you were a child?'

He yelled and began hitting himself on the side of the head. 'I can never tell. I can never tell. I can never tell.' He scarpered to the floor like a scared animal and shuffled on his bottom into the corner of the room. 'Don't let them hurt me.' Tears streamed down his face. 'Stop talking.' He clamped his hands over his ears.

'Mr Leason?' Gina shouted as she stood and walked over to him. The solicitor remained in his chair and stared at his phone.

'Ouch, keep them away. I need you to protect me,' he said in a childlike voice. He leaned forward and began bashing his head against the back wall, again and again. 'Don't let them hurt me. Don't let them hurt me. Please, don't hurt me.'

They'd lost him. Jacob ran across the room towards her. This man had put PC Smith's life in danger. A part of her wanted to leave him to continue bashing his head against the wall until his own brains were spilling out. A part of her also wanted to understand him more. He'd been hurt and he'd never had the chance to process everything that happened to him as a child, and, right at this moment, he had reverted back to being that petrified child. She wrapped her arms around his head and held him with all her strength, trying to stop him from bashing his head into the wall again. 'Call an ambulance.' That's all she needed, three people in hospital. 'And make sure uniform go with him. I want the room under twenty-four-hour guard.' She now had plenty to charge him with but on looking at him, she wondered if he'd put in a defence of insanity or diminished responsibility. He looked to be genuinely affected but when she was interviewing him, she was sure she was speaking directly to a psychopath. She might never know if his breakdown was genuine or real. If he was playing them or had genuinely regressed back into his childhood trauma. A psych evaluation would tell her more.

Jacob grabbed his phone and called for help. His phone beeped. 'It's an email from forensics. They have some news about the Leasons' garden. And there's news on Smith.' He stared at the phone open-mouthed.

CHAPTER SEVENTY-THREE

Gina ran along the hospital corridor, straight to the recovery ward and saw Smith lying on a bed with monitors beeping all around him. The wound on his neck had been packed with dressings. 'I'm thirsty,' he mumbled as he tried to open an eye. His wife smiled and wiped a tear away.

'Mrs Smith,' Gina said. The woman held his hand as she looked up.

'The dog is in the bins eating candyfloss. Shall we see Mick Jagger before we have a wash?' Smith closed his eyes, forgetting about his thirst for a short while.

Mrs Smith gently placed his hand on the top of the crisp white sheet and crept over to Gina.

'How is he? We heard he'd come out of surgery.'

'It was a success. He's going to be fine. They missed the major artery but he still lost a lot of blood. I didn't fully understand what they told me but he's going to be fine.' She turned away and began to sob. Gina placed an arm around the woman.

'If there's anything you need just call me or call the station. Anything? I'm going to head over to see someone else in the hospital, but I'll be back in a while. I'll bring a drink and something to eat.'

The woman wiped her long brown hair from the side of her mouth. 'I'm not hungry. How can I eat when he's like that?'

Gina pulled away and placed her hands on the woman's shoulders. 'Because you need your strength. When he comes home, he's going to need a lot of help for a while.'

'Why is the cake in the shed?' Smith called out, his eyes still shut.

'You're right.' Mrs Smith smiled and sat in the chair next to her husband's bed and held his hand again. Another couple walked towards the bed, an ashen-looking round woman and a tall man; both looked to be in their late sixties. Smith's parents. Gina slowly crept away. She had other visits to make and Jacob would have arrived at the hospital by now.

CHAPTER SEVENTY-FOUR

'He's one screwed up man, guv,' Jacob said as they walked along the corridor heading to the ward at the far end.

'I know. All those lives wasted. I don't envy Wyre having to speak to Noah Ashmore.' She shuddered at the thought of the conversation they'd be having now. She'd seen it before, families torn apart by violence and murder. He'd have to manage alone with his daughter, attend to her grief and heartache. She knew he'd been playing around and their relationship had been far from perfect, but the loss wouldn't be any less because of that. Samantha Felton's family would also have to be told about the remains in the Leasons' garden and Richard Leason's workshop. The bottom half of a young female body had been found under the pagoda and the top half buried in his cubbyhole in the workshop. Her stomach almost turned as she imagined the poor woman on his workbench being sawn apart. She thought he'd probably been trying to chop the body into smaller pieces but had given up. Bernard had reported saw marks on some of the other bones. Richard had obviously given up and buried her in two halves. Gina knew she had to be the one to speak to Diane.

Gina's phone vibrated in her pocket. 'DI Harte.'

'Guv, the officer who went in with Aimee just called. She's been assessed and has asked for you.'

Gina made a mental note of the ward number and headed up the stairs. 'This way. Aimee Prowse has come around and wants to speak to us. I could seriously do with a clone.'

Hurrying along the corridor, past a row of coffee machines, Gina took a right and pressed the buzzer outside the double doors. A nurse looked up. Gina and Jacob held their identification up to the little window and the nurse released the doors. 'That was quick.'

'We were already here.'

'Oh yes, I heard about your colleague, I'm sorry. Follow me.' The woman's loose bun bounced as she walked.

'How is she?'

The nurse slowed down while Jacob and Gina caught up. A uniformed officer was sitting outside a room. Gina knew that's where Aimee was recovering. 'She has two broken fingers, mild concussion and is severely dehydrated, but she's taking fluids. I will warn you, she's on some heavy duty painkillers, at her request. With that and her concussion, she may not make as much sense as you'd maybe hope, but she's going to be fine.'

'Thank you.'

The nurse held her hand out, gesturing towards the room. 'If there's anything else I can help you with, just head back to the nurses' station.' She smiled and left.

Nodding to the officer, Gina smiled and opened the door. The young woman was lying under a white sheet, her pale skin almost matching its tone. 'Aimee, it's DI Harte. How are you feeling?'

She stirred and opened her eyes. 'I wanted to tell you… he took me.' Aimee went to sit slightly but soon returned her head to the pillow. 'Woah, not good.' She felt around the bedside table. 'Water.'

Gina grabbed the glass of water and held it under Aimee's chin as she sipped from the glass.

'Thank you. That man, Richard, took me. I was in my house and—' Aimee lay on her back and stared at the ceiling. 'It was him, he locked me in a coffin wall.' The woman coughed and sobbed. 'I thought I was going to die.'

'You're safe now. We've arrested Richard Leason.'

Aimee glanced in her direction. 'You have him?'

'We do. You just concentrate on getting better and you can tell us everything then.'

Someone knocked on the door. Aimee's friend Nicole entered followed by the nurse. Aimee rolled over in bed, yelping as she turned. 'It may be best if you come back a little later. The doctor is on his way to examine her further and she really needs to rest.' The nurse's instructions were firm.

'Oh my goodness, look at you!' Nicole ran over to her friend and placed a loving hand on her shoulder. 'Your mum is on her way and Rhys came over, asking about you. I told that idiot where to go.'

Aimee gripped her friend's hand and smiled. 'Love you, Nicole.'

Gina nodded, knowing that Aimee was now in safe hands. 'Take care, Aimee, I'll speak to you soon with regards to making a formal statement.'

Aimee ignored her and began crying for more pain relief. That's all they were getting from Aimee for now.

Gina had caught Richard with Aimee at his workshop, she had all the evidence she needed. As soon as she'd told Rex that he needed to go to the station and report what he'd seen, he'd done it. Wyre and Briggs had taken his statement and had charged him with stalking Aimee. Gina had given him no choice in the matter. Either he tell them all he'd seen and explain why or she'd hand her CCTV into the station and get him charged with harassing her. She hoped that being arrested would give him the jolt he needed to see the error of his ways. Ultimately his evidence would help them with the case against Richard Leason.

As they left the ward, Jacob checked his watch. 'What a day!'

'It certainly has been a day we'll never forget.' Gina stared at the coffee machine as she thought about what would happen next. Placing a few coins in and selecting a latte, she waited for the coffee to spurt out. 'Can you grab a sandwich from the shop and take that and this coffee to Smith's wife? I said I'd be back with food but there's something I need to do.'

CHAPTER SEVENTY-FIVE

'Hello, Diane,' Gina whispered. Diane turned and half-smiled.

'Detective? I'm sorry you found me the way you did.' She sipped a cup of tea and heaved slightly. 'I didn't want to live, I don't want to live. My brother was right. I'm a bad person, I've done bad things. I hurt him—' Tears slipped down her face. 'Why didn't you just let me die?'

'Diane—'

'I deserved to die.'

Gina was out of her depth, Diane needed counselling. How on earth was she going to deliver the news of her brother's arrest and breakdown?

'I've had enough of living with secrets.'

Diane paused and had another drink. Gina knew how she felt. Is this what her future looked like? Would her secrets begin to weigh her down so badly she'd crush herself to end the agony? She went to speak but Diane interrupted.

'I need to tell someone. Can I tell you?' Diane slowly turned and stared directly at Gina, her wet eyes glistening. There was another person in the small ward, sleeping to the sounds of the television. Gina pulled the curtain halfway to give Diane a little privacy. 'Years ago, when I was in my late teens, our mother died. We watched her slowly get sicker until one day; that was it. We were expecting it, but knowing didn't make it any easier.' Diane paused and stared at her lap. Tears soaked into the hospital blanket as she slowly relayed her story. 'I didn't want to lose Richard to the care system, he was a few years younger than me. We had no money so I did things to make money, things I shouldn't have been doing. Men were my way to money and very soon I had my regulars.' She shook her head back and forth, words refusing to escape as she let out an almost silent pained squeal.

Gina placed her hand on Diane's shoulder, waiting for her to find her next sentence.

'I didn't know they were abusing him. I let them into our home. How can I ever live with the fact that I let these brutes abuse my baby brother? He hates me and you know what, I hate me. I hate me so much, I want to slash at my wrists, I want to drink poison, I want to ram my head into a wall over and over again. I want to get in a car and drive it straight into a wall or over a cliff. I wanted it all to be over and you made me live – now go away.' Diane turned away.

Gina almost missed a breath and felt her body raring up as if she was suddenly awash with fever. This is what secrets do to a person and one day, she might be just like Diane. Her daughter would always resent her, she knew they would never be close. She thought of a young Diane selling her teen body to any man around, while all the time, thinking she was doing it to protect her brother.

'Do you hate me?' Diane turned back to her. 'Now you know the type of person I am, do you think I'm dirty, disgusting? I didn't want Richard to go into care so I had to provide for him. It's all my fault.'

Gina undid a couple of buttons on her shirt and took a few controlled breaths. 'Of course I don't hate you, Diane. You were just a girl. I'm sad that things were so hard for you and you didn't get the help you deserved after your mother died. I'm also glad I found you and that you're here now. You don't realise how much you have to give. Look at the relationship you had with Samantha, she needed you and you were a wonderful friend to her. You have so much to give but you have to let go of the guilt that is weighing you down as it's holding you back. Forgive yourself – you were a girl, a desperate girl who felt she was doing the best she could. I'm so sorry the system let you down or you felt that you couldn't trust it.'

Diane burst into tears and gripped Gina, leaning her head against her chest. Gina placed an arm around her, allowing her to weep until she eventually calmed down. After a few minutes, she loosened her grip and shuffled back. 'Have you heard from Richard? Does he know I'm here?'

'Diane, I'm really sorry to tell you that we've arrested him for the murder of Jade Ashmore and the abduction of Aimee Prowse.' Gina's foot tapped on the floor as she waited for Diane to respond.

'And Samantha?' Diane was joining up the dots.

'We have found a body under your brother's pagoda in the garden.' She didn't have the heart to tell Diane that only half of the body was there.

'My beautiful friend,' she cried as she lay down and hugged her pillow. Gina sat beside her. Diane had no one. Gina had nothing to hurry home for. She wouldn't leave, not for a while.

EPILOGUE

A Month Later

Half an hour to go. Gina had arrived at the coffee shop far too early for her meetup. She scrolled down Facebook and smiled at the photos of Gracie that Hannah had posted. She was growing up so quickly. Whatever happened, she wasn't going to break their date next weekend – she was going to have lunch with her daughter and take her granddaughter out for a couple of hours. She closed Facebook and stared at the Tinder app. Thoughts of Rex ran through her mind and she shivered. He'd been a prize weirdo. He also knew better than to come near Gina again. She pressed on the Tinder logo and deleted the app.

There was only one person she'd ever care enough about and she couldn't allow herself to get caught up with him. His relationships never really lasted and hers had been laughable since their affair. Both of them trying to show the other that they were fine and getting on with things. How did she know? Her phone buzzed. This is how she knew, he called her often and she didn't tell him not to. 'Briggs?'

'It's my day off,' he replied.

'Okay, Chris.'

There was a slight pause. She could hear some music in the background, something jazzy and light. 'I just thought I'd give you a call. I haven't heard from you for a few days.'

'Well I've had a few days off. I'll be back in next week. You miss me, don't you?'

'You know I do, Gina.'

'Chris, if I ask you something, promise you won't answer with a lie?' She gripped her steaming hot coffee and took a sip while she waited for him to answer.

'That depends on what you want to ask. I think I know where this is going.'

The café was busy. Several people laughed as they talked about the latest sitcom that they were watching. She grabbed her drink and headed outside, sitting while watching the world go by. 'That's better, I can hear now. I'm going to get straight to the point. Steven never bothered me again after the search of Dawn's house. Steven doesn't go away that easily. I want to know what you said to him.' She shivered even though the June sun was almost burning her arms.

'What makes you think I said something to him?'

She remained silent.

'Okay, okay. That day outside Dawn's house. I passed him a make-up compact. It was so easy, he just took it. After he passed it back to me, I told him it was prime evidence in an unsolved murder case from twenty years ago. I said if he didn't leave you alone, the case would be reopened and his prints would match the prints on the compact. I said as long as he leaves you alone, the compact would remain hidden forever and would never see the light of day. You're right about him being stupid, he lapped it all up, called me a bastard and stormed off.'

Gina's pulse was heavy, each beat of her heart seeming to take forever. He'd risked everything to help her and in many ways he had also been stupid.

'Gina, say something.'

'Why would you do this?' Not only had she ruined her own life with secrets, she'd now left Briggs with a huge burden to carry

'You know why. There's not much I wouldn't do for you. I'd draw the line at eating kale.'

'You shouldn't have. You know, sir. You're the only man in my life who's treated me with any respect and I'm thanking you for that.'

He paused and exhaled. 'Yet I'm the only one you seem to be pushing away. Do you see a pattern?'

A tear crept down her cheek. Memories of Terry, Steven, Rex and the unfulfilling Tinder dates ran through her thoughts.

'I'm sorry,' she said with a sniffle as she ended the call. Gina knew he'd be upset. In another time and place, she'd run to him and kiss him, tell him that she loved him and stay with him. It was all way more complicated than he was suggesting but still, his words had hit her like she'd been slapped across the face.

Clip, clip, clip. The noise stopped beside her. She placed her phone in her pocket and looked up. 'Diane, I'm so glad you could come for a drink. How are you feeling?'

'Taking one step at a time.'

Gina smiled. Diane had combed her hair and even put on a little make-up. The loose jeans and corduroy jacket she wore looked dated but she looked smart and clean. Diane was a woman who had very little but she'd certainly made that little amount go a long way in readiness for their coffee date.

'It's so lovely to have someone to meet up with for a drink. I haven't been out socially in years. Thank you, Detective.'

'Call me Gina. What can I get you?'

A LETTER FROM CARLA

Dear Reader,

I'd like to thank you for choosing to read *The Liar's House*, the fourth book in the DI Gina Harte series. Did I say fourth? I can't believe how fast this past couple of years have gone.

I can't express how much I enjoyed writing this book so I truly hope you enjoyed reading it too. If you did, I'd be grateful if you would leave me a review on Amazon, iBooks, Kobo or Google. Being a writer, I find reviews invaluable and I'm always appreciative when a reader has taken the time to leave one.

If you'd like to be kept up-to-date with my news and new releases, sign up to the following link. Your email address will never be shared and you can unsubscribe at any time.

www.bookouture.com/carla-kovach

Lastly, I love chatting on social media and can mostly be found on my Facebook page and on Instagram. Please do pop by!

Once again, here's a massive thank you for reading *The Liar's House*!

Carla Kovach

 CKovachAuthor

 CarlaKovachAuthor

 carla_kovach

ACKNOWLEDGEMENTS

I love writing the acknowledgments. It's always at this point I realise how many people have helped me in my writing quest.

My editor, Helen Jenner, is the best; always giving me fantastic edit notes. Without her, my work wouldn't shine half as much. As always, I'm appreciative of everything she does and I can't wait to work with her again on the next book.

The Bookouture publicity team are amazing. Noelle Holton and Kim Nash are always there to cheer our books on. From *author live* interviews to constantly working away on Twitter, you deserve your reputation as the dream team. I can't thank you both enough.

The next huge thank you has to go out to bloggers and my Bookouture buddies. Book bloggers are amazing and work so hard for the love of books. I know their time is precious and I'm always extremely grateful when they have given some of it to me. As for my Bookouture buddies, I'm so honoured to be a part of this amazing family. The support and love given almost makes me want to weep with joy. Through ups and downs, the Bookouture family is the best.

As this book was dedicated to friends, I have to move on to a special set of friends of whom I think the world. Thank you to the lovelies who beta read my work. That's Brooke Venables, Vanessa Morgan, Derek Coleman, Lynne Ward and Su Biela. I'm thrilled to have you all in my life and long may our friendships continue, as well as our love of books.

Finding a happy place, somewhere where the words flow, can sometimes be a challenge, which is why I want to extend my gratitude to Redditch Library. I think I wrote most of *The Liar's House* in one of their quiet corners. Oh, and thank you to my writing buddy, Mark Wallace. It's great to have someone spurring you on

Finally I'd like to thank my husband, Nigel Buckley. He's always there, picks me up when I'm down and celebrates with me when I'm up. He truly is my rock!

Printed in Great Britain
by Amazon